FOUR AUNTIES AND A WEDDING

Berkley titles by Jesse Q. Sutanto

DIAL A FOR AUNTIES

FOUR AUNTIES AND A WEDDING

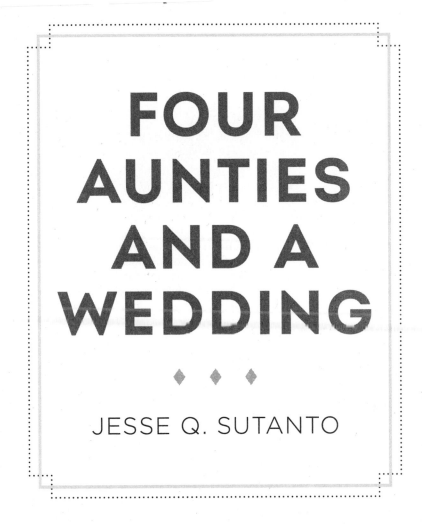

FOUR AUNTIES AND A WEDDING

♦ ♦ ♦

JESSE Q. SUTANTO

BERKLEY
New York

BERKLEY
An imprint of Penguin Random House LLC
penguinrandomhouse.com

Copyright © 2022 by Jesse Q. Sutanto

Library of Congress Cataloging-in-Publication Data

Names: Sutanto, Jesse Q., author.
Title: Four aunties and a wedding / Jesse Q. Sutanto.
Description: New York, NY: Berkley, [2022]
Identifiers: LCCN 2021034758 (print) | LCCN 2021034759 (ebook) |
ISBN 9780593440766 (hardcover) | ISBN 9780593333068 (ebook)
Classification: LCC PR9500.9.S88 F68 2022 (print) |
LCC PR9500.9.S88 (ebook) | DDC 823/.92—dc23
LC record available at https://lccn.loc.gov/2021034758
LC ebook record available at https://lccn.loc.gov/2021034759

Printed in the United States of America
1st Printing

Book design by Tiffany Estreicher

*To my readers, thank you for loving
the aunties as much as I do.*

Dear Reader,

Thank you so much for picking up *Four Aunties and a Wedding*. When I wrote the first book in the series, *Dial A for Aunties*, I wanted first and foremost to share a slice of my amazing family and culture with the world. I feel so lucky to be able to do that again with *Four Aunties and a Wedding*. In *Dial A for Aunties*, I was concerned about straddling the line between authenticity and stereotype, wanting to show the kind of broken English that my family speaks without turning it into a source of ridicule. I've been so grateful and touched by the warm reception *Dial A for Aunties* has received. With the sequel, I wanted to tackle the subject of the Asian diaspora.

Like Nathan, my husband is half Asian and half English. My mother-in-law is Chinese-Singaporean, and when I first met my husband, I was so excited because I'd been very homesick in Oxford. I grew up in Singapore and Singlish is the language I'm most comfortable speaking, so to meet another Singaporean in a foreign country was such a breath of fresh air.

I excitedly asked my husband what his favorite Singaporean food is (mine: roti prata), where he went to school in Singapore, and can we please speak Singlish to each other, lah? Every single question was met with a blank stare. As it turned out, my husband may be half Singaporean, but he left the country way too young to remember much about it aside from "It's hot."

Later on, after we had dated for a while, I was excited to meet his parents. I thought his mom would retain more of Singapore, but as it turned out, she too spoke flawless British English, and aside from cooking the most delicious Chinese food, she had integrated seamlessly into English culture. She even asked me to call her by her first name rather than the Asian way of calling her "Auntie."

The first time my parents met my husband's parents, the meeting was a very awkward one. Both sides were clearly baffled by each other. I'd hoped that they would find similarities since both my parents and my mother-in-law are technically immigrants, but instead, the meeting only highlighted their differences. Fortunately, both sets of parents made efforts to bridge the gap and we all get along beautifully now, but it took some work to get here.

The experience really hammered home how different every Asian diaspora experience is. A lot of the time, we tend to get lumped into one single category: Asian. An umbrella term that ignores the huge differences that arise based on not just where we're from, but when we left and where we settled down. In *Four Aunties and a Wedding*, I hope to show how varied the Asian diaspora experience can be, and how there is no right or wrong way of "being Asian."

Jesse

FOUR
AUNTIES
AND A
WEDDING

PART ONE

◆

PLANNING THE PERFECT WEDDING

(It's all about the dress, really.)

1

I try not to breathe as the last corset hook is yanked into place. "Ow, that's digging into my rib cage."

Yenyen huffs a breath through his teeth and gives one last vicious tug, which forces a squeak out of me. "In the past, brides would break their ribs to fit into their wedding dresses," he says, and it strikes me that he's not saying it in a horrified tone, but rather a wistful one, which is somewhat worrying. "How do you feel?"

I risk breathing again, and to my surprise, despite the torturous time I had getting stuffed into the dress, once I'm in, it's actually—dare I say it—comfortable. What sort of black magic is this? I could've sworn I would hardly be able to take even the tiniest sip of air. I blink at him in surprise. "I can breathe in it."

I can't quite see his eyes behind the round, purple-tinted sunglasses, but I'm pretty sure I hear them roll.

"Aduuuh, of course you can breathe in it, silly. Yenyen's creations aren't just beautiful, they're also built for maximum comfort."

I can't help but smile at him. Yenyen has a tendency to refer to himself in third person, which should sound mildly deranged but actually comes off as somewhat endearing. His real name is Yenzhen, but nobody is allowed to call him that. Within the Chinese tradition, it's common to have phonetically repeated names as a pet name, and as Yenyen says, he's everybody's best friend, so we must call him Yenyen.

"Now, are you ready to see it?" he says.

Am I? My heart rate rises. My cheeks grow warm. This will be the forty-millionth dress I've tried on. I swear I've tried on every wedding dress L.A. has to offer, and each time, there's been something that Ma or my aunts didn't like. Over the last few months, as we exhausted every bridal boutique in greater Los Angeles, their comments have seared themselves onto my brain.

"Sequin not shiny enough."

"The lace look itchy, is making me itchy, is making you itchy?"

"Body too slutty." (Second Aunt meant bodice. I think.)

And so on and so forth, until Nathan announced that he'd arranged for Indonesia's premiere wedding dress designer to come to L.A. with custom-made dresses. Including—and this is the pièce de résistance—dresses for the mother and aunts of the bride.

I swallow and nod at Yenyen. "I'm ready."

"Okay, keep your eyes closed, though!" He gathers the skirt behind me as I turn slowly to face the floor-length mirror. After a minute of rustling and fussing, he says, "Open your eyes."

I do as he says.

My mouth drops open. "Yenyen—" My breath catches in

my throat. There are no words to describe this dress. I know, in that moment, that this is it. This is The One. The bodice is swathed in the softest, most delicate lace that looks like it was sewn by fairies using spider silk. The skirt is a gorgeous frothy affair that somehow remains light enough for me to move around in. The entire thing hugs my body in all the right places and accentuates my curves in a way that is at once sexy and conservative. I feel as though I'm wearing a cloud. Tears rush to my eyes. "It's perfect," I whisper.

Yenyen waves me off, but it's obvious he's fighting off a huge smile. "Shall we show your family?"

Here we go. Deep breath. I don't know what I'll do if they say they don't like it. I steel myself, tightening my hands into fists. I'll fight for this dress. I've acquiesced to their never-ending laundry list of complaints, despite many of the dresses I've tried on being perfectly fine. This one isn't just perfectly fine, though. It's actually perfect. And I won't let them ruin it for me. I won't. I—

"Ta-da!" Yenyen cries as he yanks open the bedroom door with a flourish.

I grit my teeth, awaiting the cascade of complaints, but there are none. In fact, there is nobody around. The sofa and chairs arranged in a semicircle in Ma's living room are empty.

"Aduh," Yenyen cries, throwing up his hands. "Yenyen can't work like this. You know how important a good entrance is? This isn't just a dress; it's an experience!"

"I'm so sorry. I don't know where they went. Maybe to the bathroom?" I'm about to call out for them when footsteps thunder down the hallway.

"Meddy? That you? Sudahan ya?" Ma calls out.

"Yes, she is done!" Yenyen snaps. "Please take your seats so your daughter can show you her beautiful wedding gown."

"Eh, tunggu! Meddy, you close your eyes!"

"What?" Yenyen's face is turning red. His whole moment is being ruined, poor guy.

"Just go with it." I pat him on the shoulder.

"Unbelievable!" he snaps, but takes control of himself and arranges my skirt and train so it cascades flawlessly across the hardwood floor.

"Ready or not, ah?" Second Aunt shouts.

"Yes." I close my eyes, half-dreading what I'm about to see. Ma and the rest of my aunts come out of Ma's bedroom giggling like schoolgirls. But before they get to the living room, Yenyen mutters, "This feels wrong," and rushes over to the hallway to see them.

His gasp can be heard all the way over in Santa Monica. "Those are *not* the dresses Yenyen brought you!"

"No, it's the dresses *Jonjon* brought them," someone else says regally.

Okay, not even the strongest-willed person can keep their eyes closed through this. I crack one eye open just as a tall, thin man wrapped in a tight-fitting snakeskin suit emerges from the kitchen.

Yenyen gasps again. "Jonjon. How dare you!"

"What's going on?" I say.

"Hello, nice to meet you. I'm Jonjon, you might have heard of me? Voted most avant-garde fashion designer in Indonesia? I was featured in *Tatler* and *Vogue*?" He extends a hand dripping with various chunky rings. Unsure what to do, I shake it limply. "Your family asked me to design their gowns for your wedding."

"But Yenyen designed their gowns!" Yenyen cries.

Jonjon snorts. "Those lumpy brown sacks? I don't think so. These ladies deserve better. Ready to see them?"

"Wait, wait!" Yenyen grabs a wool blanket off the couch and throws it around me. "Okay, when the time is right, throw off the blanket with a flourish, ya?"

"Um. Okay." I hug the blanket tight around me and nod at Jonjon, half-dreading what I'm about to see.

"Behold!" Jonjon waves grandly, taps on his phone, and tinny pop music plays as, one by one, my family struts down the hallway.

I turn around. And stare in shock-horror at the spectacle before me.

Big Aunt, Second Aunt, Ma, and Fourth Aunt are all decked out in the most blinged-out, most aggressively purple dresses I have ever laid eyes on. Ever. How do I describe the particular shade of purple? It's as if flamingo pink and electric blue had a baby and then that baby snorted a line of coke and proceeded to punch you in the face. It is a *lot* of purple. And it's a *lot* of different kinds of material. I'm talking taffeta, and embroidery, and sequins—oh god, so many sequins. With every move my mother and aunts make, crystals and jewels flash and threaten to blind me. And that's not even the worst part.

"What are those things on your heads?" My voice comes out hushed with horror, but Fourth Aunt must have misheard it as awe, because she simpers and flutters her fake lashes at me.

"Aren't these just gorgeous?" She pats the—the thing on her head gently. "It's called a fascinator. They are a must-have for English weddings. We're going to fit in so well."

"With that *thing* on your head? I mean, what—I—but—" I sputter.

"Aiya, you hate it!" Ma wails. She turns to her sisters. "I tell you, I say, Komodo dragon is not good choice, we should have gone with flamingo!"

My mouth opens and closes, but no words come out. What

does one say when faced with four women wearing ten-inch-tall Komodo dragons on their heads? Well, not actual live ones, at least. I think. "They're not real, are they?" I don't know that I'd be able to forgive my family if they were.

At this, Jonjon smiles smugly. "They look real, don't they? I understand why you'd think they are; the craftsmanship is flawless, isn't it?"

Again, no words come. The dragons are in various positions, each one weirder than the last, but also somehow compatible with each woman's personality. Big Aunt's dragon is standing on its two hind legs, the front ones akimbo, like an Asian auntie who disapproves of your life choices. Second Aunt's dragon is—of course—stretched into some bizarre Tai Chi pose. Ma's is sitting down, primly sipping tea. Yes, there is an actual tiny teacup in its paws. And Fourth Aunt's is doing karaoke.

I turn to Yenyen. Maybe he can play bad cop for me and shoot this whole ridiculous getup down in flames. Like me, he's also staring openmouthed at their fascinators. He extends an arm and touches Fourth Aunt's dragon gingerly as though expecting it to come to life and take a chunk out of his hand.

"Amazing," he says.

I sidle over to him and whisper, "Don't you mean 'ridiculous'?"

His gaze flicks over to me and I see belatedly that the expression he's wearing isn't so much shock as it is wonderment. "Look at the craftsmanship. The scales, those eyes!"

"You mean how they follow you around the room?" I can't help but shudder.

"It's called the Mona Lisa effect," Yenyen says.

My mother and aunts preen.

"You do realize he's calling the dragons Mona Lisa, not you," I point out. Which is probably a petty thing to say, but really, now. There is no way in hell I can let this happen. I can't have them meeting Nathan's parents wearing Komodo-freaking-dragons on their heads.

"Okay, yang bener ya. Serious time," Big Aunt says, straightening her back and smoothing down the front of her ruffled skirt. "What you think, Meddy?"

I tear my eyes from the tops of their heads to her face, and that's when I realize it: Big Aunt is nervous. It's the first time I've seen that vulnerable look on her face. Well, I guess I have seen it one other time before, when she had to move the body of a man I'd just killed. The naked worry and hope in her face make my chest squeeze painfully. My eyes move from Big Aunt to the others and find all of them wide-eyed with anticipation. Ma is wringing her hands, and Second Aunt looks like she's one mean comment away from plunging into a Tai Chi pose. Fourth Aunt is studying her nails, but now and again, she steals glances my way, and I know then that she's just as nervous as the others.

Well, crap.

"Um." My voice falters. I clear my throat and try again. "Well. Um. More importantly, what do *you* think, Big Aunt? Do you feel good in it?"

She starts to nod, but Jonjon shrieks, "Be careful!" and she jerks her head upright. Her Komodo dragon wobbles precariously for a few tense seconds as we stare with bated breath. Then it rights itself.

Sensing an opportunity, I pounce. "Well, uh—as incredible as they look, if you can't move freely in them, then I don't know if they're a good idea. I want you to feel completely comfortable at my wedding, Big Aunt."

"True . . ." she says.

Hope flutters in my chest.

"Oh, not a problem. On the day of, you just tell your hair

and makeup artist to sew the fascinators to your wig," Yenyen says. "That's how most celebrities get them to stay on, you know."

"Thanks, Yenyen, very helpful," I hiss through gritted teeth. He's supposed to be on my side.

"So you like?" Big Aunt says, her eyes searching mine.

"I . . ." Six pairs of eyes bear down on me like six searing-hot laser beams. I know when I'm defeated. "If you like them, then I like them too."

Ma and the aunties' faces melt into huge grins, and for just this one moment, I'm glad I went along with it. Then common sense returns and I kick myself inwardly. What have I just done? What did I agree to? What is Nathan's prim English family going to think? The thought of introducing my batty family members to his well-dressed, eloquent mother is almost enough to make me break out in hives. Of course, as always, as soon as I think this, the guilt comes in full attack mode. I shouldn't be ashamed of my own family, not even with Komodo dragons on their heads. They've gone through so much for me, like covering up an actual murder. The least I can do is pretend to like their hideous outfits.

But I don't get a chance to say anything as Yenyen crows, "Okay, Yenyen's turn!" and whips the blanket off me. My family gasps at the sight of my dress.

"Wah, bagus, bagus," Second Aunt says.

"Mm, I love it," Fourth Aunt agrees. "Sexy, not trampy."

I turn to Ma. "What do you think?"

Ma is blinking away tears. "Oh, Meddy." Her voice catches and she grasps my hands.

A lump forms in my throat and I nod through my tears at Ma.

"Yes, so very pretty, so beautiful bride," Big Aunt says, patting my cheek fondly. I smile back at her. The Komodo dragon atop her head grins down at me. "You going to make big splash in Oxford."

Well, some of us will, at least. The mention of Oxford fills my stomach with butterflies. Ever since I cracked open *Harry Potter and the Sorcerer's Stone* at age ten, I was hooked. And when I visited Nathan's family all those years ago, he'd taken me on a tour of Oxford University. It had cemented my love for the gorgeous city. It was a no-brainer when he'd suggested having the wedding at one of the oldest and biggest colleges at the university: Christ Church College. With its expansive gardens and magnificent cathedral, Christ Church makes the perfect wedding venue. I'd thought Ma and the aunties would be against it, but when I told them, they'd literally whooped with joy, especially when we offered to pay for their airfare. And, as horrible as it sounds, there's an additional benefit to having a wedding in England—I won't have to invite the rest of my humongous family.

Not that I don't love them; it's just that there are so many of them—all of my cousins and their families, for one, and then my mother's cousins and their families. Chinese-Indonesian weddings tend to have thousands of guests for a reason; everyone is related to everyone else, and if you fail to invite your cousin's cousin's spouse's cousin, there would be such Slighted Feelings. Generations of family feuds have stemmed from this uncle not inviting that cousin's brother-in-law's father-in-law to his daughter's wedding. With a destination wedding, we can just tell the rest of the family that we don't want to impose, and that they shouldn't feel obligated to spend thousands of dollars to travel all the way to England just to watch me get married. In the end, the only people from my side of the family who are attending are Ma, the aunties, and a handful of cousins, which is such a huge relief. None of my aunties' sons are coming. I had a video call with them and we all agreed that the aunties would be so emotional and overbearing that it would probably be best for everyone's sanity not to have them there. The relieved expression on my cousin Gucci's face was so palpable that I couldn't help laughing and taking a screenshot, just in case I needed to blackmail him in the future. They promised that we'd celebrate ourselves when we next had a family gathering. We've somehow ended up with over two hundred guests anyway, thanks to Nathan's numerous business contacts, which appeases Ma and the aunties' need for big weddings.

Ma waves her hand in my face. "Eh, Meddy, hello, you paying attention or not, ah?"

I snap back to reality and jerk back at the sight of her Komodo dragon. Those dragons, I swear. "What is it, Ma?"

"We have surprise for you," she says with obvious glee.

Uh-oh. The last time my mother sprang a surprise on me, I ended up killing it. Or him, rather. "Um. What is it?" My voice comes out thick with worry.

"Wedding vendor! We find perfect one for you."

"What? But—" Too many things crowd through my head. The first and foremost being a childish wail of *But this is my wedding. I want to be the one who decides who to hire!* But before I can shoot her down, I realize something: Ma couldn't possibly have found a wedding vendor. The only ones she knows are, well, us. "Ma, I told you, I want you all to be there as guests, not vendors."

"Of course not us," Big Aunt says, waving me off like I'm a gnat. "Mana mungkin? How we can cater to your wedding when we wearing this outfit?"

Huh. Maybe I should ask them to cater to my wedding after all. Anything to get rid of those dragons.

"I told you Meddy would want to find her own wedding vendors like a normal bride," Fourth Aunt says, glancing up from admiring herself in the mirror. "Right, Meddy?"

The glare Ma shoots her could have melted plastic. Dammit, why did it have to be Fourth Aunt who said that? I can't possibly agree with her. To Ma, that would be a betrayal, and I'd never live it down.

Then another realization sinks in: how could they have found any vendors in England? They don't know their way around the Internet. Well, my mother did catfish a guy for months.

"So, what you think, Meddy?" Ma says, her eyes shining with hope. Big Aunt and Second Aunt stare at me. Even Fourth Aunt looks at me in the mirror.

"I can't agree without knowing who—or what they do. I mean, Nathan and I have been looking for vendors too—"

"Aduh, of course I not expect you to agree to hire them now," Ma says, flapping her hand at me. "What you think, I so unreasoning I expect you to just agree without even knowing who?"

Well, yes, actually. But I don't say it out loud.

"Of course I don't. I very reasoningable. You meet them first, pasti you will love, I am sure."

"Meet them? But they're in England, surely?"

"Ah, no. They in here. But they do destination wedding. And they family business, just like us. And best of all, they family!"

I blink. "They're family?"

Big Aunt nods. "Mereka itu, your grandmother cousin niece cousin sister-in-law. Very close family."

I try to go over the familial connection, but give up after grandmother's cousin's niece. "Do they have a website, at least?"

Second Aunt waves her index finger at me. "No need website. We meet them for dim sum, they can show you all their photos."

"Uh." I suppose I might as well agree to get them off my back. "Okay. But I want Nathan to come along, and if we don't like them, please don't—"

"Aiya, of course we not push you into hiring them if you not like," Ma cries. "What you think we are? Dictator?"

"No, you're Chinese mothers, which is as good as dictators," I mutter, squeezing Ma's arm with affection.

"Oh ho ho, you so funny. My daughter so funny. Wait until you become mother also. Then you understand. Okay, you go undress. We all go undress. Then we go."

"What, now?"

"Of course now! If not now, then when?"

Of course. I should've known. Still, I can't help but smile as I watch my family scurrying out of the living room, Komodo dragons teetering crazily as they move. I turn around to look into the mirror and sigh happily at the reflection of me in my amazing dress. Even Jonjon is grudgingly admiring Yenyen's handiwork. How did I manage to end up with the dreamiest gown that was ever made? This wedding is going to be wonderful.

2

Less than an hour later, I wait outside our favorite dim sum place for Nathan while my mother and aunts go inside to meet this mysterious vendor they've decided we're related to. I can't help the grin that stretches across my face when I spot him walking across the parking lot. I mean, dayum. He is fine. And he's mine, all mine!

Okay, settle down, creeper. I suppose part of me does feel like a creep whenever I see Nathan from afar. I can't help but undress him with my eyes, which I know sounds really gross. But seriously, how can I not? Look at him, all strong jaw and broad shoulders and muscled arms and those pecs and—

"You've got your horny face again," he says.

"I'm just hungry."

"For me?"

"Okay, ew. But yes." I inhale the scent of him as he bends down and gives me a chaste peck on the cheek; the dim sum bunch is mostly made up of Chinese uncles and aunties who openly stare disapprovingly at every young couple, and Nathan knows I'm not comfortable with PDA in front of this particular crowd. Horny eyes, acceptable. Actual kissing, hells no. "So, before we go inside, there's something I need to tell you."

"Uh-oh." His eyebrows knit together with concern and he lowers his voice while taking my arm. "Is it about . . . the thing?"

My stomach knots. I hate that I've put this weight on his shoulders. It's been almost a year since Ma set me up on a blind date with Ah Guan that ended with me and my aunties accidentally killing him. Emphasis on "accidentally." As if that wasn't bad enough, Ah Guan's body was then mistakenly shipped to a wedding at Nathan's hotel, where through a series of mishaps caused by my aunties, it ended up appearing at the altar as one of the groomsmen. Only a magical combination of quick thinking, false bravado, and sheer dumb luck allowed us all to get away with it. To this day, I can't quite believe how fortunate we were that someone like Sheriff McConnell was in charge of the case. His incompetence was vital in ensuring that nobody ended up charged with anything.

Even though Ah Guan's case is closed—declared an unfortunate accident—Nathan still worries that it'll come back to haunt us, and I hate that he worries. Nathan had figured out the truth behind Ah Guan's death in record time and decided to help us cover it up. Though he's never held the incredible sacrifice he's made over my head, I never let myself forget it. I hate that he has to carry this burden because of something I did. "No," I say quickly, and Nathan's shoulders relax. "My mom and aunts found some wedding vendors that are apparently related to us and they're really keen on us meeting them."

"Oh. Is that all? You looked so worried I thought it was going to be something really bad."

"Well, I mean, it kind of is," I sigh. "I've been dreaming about our wedding for so long, and I've been looking forward to searching for the right vendors with you. I wasn't really expecting my family to swoop in and find them for us. Well, I don't know why I wasn't expecting it from them."

"Aw, hey, c'mere." Nathan wraps his arms around me and pulls me closer, to the immense interest of all the random uncles and aunties around us. "It'll be okay. Your mom and aunts are just really excited about the wedding."

"I know." I sigh and rest my head against his chest. An idea begins to form, and I pat his pecs. "Wow, these are getting really big; you've been working out hard. What a manly man you are."

Nathan grins at me. "I know you're just buttering me up, but I am here for this. Please keep telling me what a manly man I am."

"Well, I was thinking, we'll meet with these vendors . . ,"

"Uh-huh?"

I trail a finger down his chest. "And if we don't like them, you put your foot down like the big manly man that you are and tell my family we'll be hiring someone else."

Nathan laughs. "Me? Say no to your Big Aunt? Hell to the no."

I punch him on the arm and he laughs. "We'll do it together," he says, kissing the top of my head.

"Okay," I sigh. "Well, get ready to meet them."

"What, now?"

"Yep, come on, manly man."

"Nathan, over here, Nathan! Nathan!" Ma shouts, standing up and waving madly as we weave through the dim sum crowd. Nathan waves back at her, but she continues waving and shouting his name.

"How come she's never that excited to see me?" I grumble.

"Because I am, in her words, 'the perfect specimen of a man.'"

I roll my eyes. I mean, I agree with Ma, obviously, but Nathan doesn't need to know that. Over the past year, my family has doted on him as if he's their long-awaited prodigal son, and instead of being scared off as I feared he might be, Nathan has quite happily accepted all the attention.

As we near them, I see that there isn't one or two or three new faces at the table, but—

"Five vendors?" I hiss.

Nathan squeezes my hand. "It'll be okay. We'll eat with them and look at their portfolio and then politely but firmly tell them no."

I take a deep breath. I can do this. I'm an adult, dammit. I can stand up to my family, especially for my wedding. And despite all of his jokes, I know Nathan would back me up if I wanted him to.

Everyone smiles and waves when we get to the table, and Nathan and I go around greeting them—Big Aunt first, then Second Aunt, and so forth. Even though I arrived here with Big Aunt and the others, I still need to make a show of greeting them again. After I greet my family, I'm left with the vendors. They're not quite what I expected. There's an elderly woman who looks about Big Aunt's age, three men who could be anywhere from thirty to fifty-five, and a young woman who looks about my age.

The young woman stands up and comes around to shake my hand and Nathan's with a big, friendly smile. "Meddy, it's so nice to finally meet you. I've heard so much about you, and I'm just so excited about your wedding."

Her smile is infectious, and I find myself beaming back at her before catching myself. I don't want to appear like I approve. I squeeze my mouth into a thin line. But then the woman hands me her business card, and I know then that she and I are destined to be friends. Because her card says this:

STAPHANIE WEITING TANUWIJAYA
Photographer
Stop weiting around, we're here for
all your weidding needs!

I chomp down on my bottom lip to keep from laughing.

"That's not a typo, by the way. It really is spelled with an *a*," Staphanie says.

I meet her eye. "I relate very hard to this."

"I knew you would, Meddelin," she says somberly. "When your mom texted me your name, I was like, 'Okay, I need to meet her. She'll understand what it's like to grow up with an unfortunately spelled name.'"

"I do!" I laugh. "I really, really do. Oh god, you poor thing. I'm guessing you get lots of staph infection jokes?"

"Mhmm. And coupled with my Chinese name, Weiting? Forget about it. 'I'm wei-ting for my staph infection to clear up.' I hear that one at least five times a day."

I'm still laughing as we sit down next to each other.

Big Aunt clears her throat and Staphanie and I go quiet. When all the attention is turned to her, Big Aunt gestures at me. "This Meddy, the bride, and that one Nathan, the groom."

The elderly woman nods and smiles in a very grandmotherly way at us. "Wah, cakep sekali ya? Will give you so cute babies," she says to Ma. Ma simpers, and the elderly woman continues, "You must have babies right away, okay, not be like these modern people nowadays, waiting and waiting, later your womb will dry up."

"Ama!" Staphanie scolds. She turns to us. "I'm so sorry. This is my grandmother, she's just, uh, she's—"

The sight of Staphanie's mortification about her family warms my heart. Finally, someone who truly understands what it's like growing up with my family. "It's okay, I understand," I tell her.

"Oh, you so right," Ma says to Staphanie's grandmother. "Yes, I don't know why all these young people they want to waiting, waiting, until they too old to make the baby!"

Nathan places a comforting hand on my back. I can tell he's struggling to bite back his laughter. I'm glad he finds Ma funny, at least.

"Please, eat," Staphanie says, placing a har gow on my plate. I quickly reciprocate by spearing a char siu bao and putting it on her plate. Around the table, our families are doing the same, rapidly picking up dumplings and placing them on each other's plates—a battle to show which family is more well-mannered. Nathan is used to this by now and jumps in with gusto, giving Big Aunt the biggest siu mai and Staphanie's grandmother the fattest cheung fun. Cries of "Aduh, don't mind me, you eat, you eat," and "Wah, you such good boy," fill the air, and soon, everyone's plate is full and the battle ends in a draw. Now we can finally start eating.

Staphanie takes a small bite of her bao. "So, to give you an overview of our company . . ." She gestures at her family. "Like yours, ours is a family-run business. My ama is the wedding organizer—"

"Oh, wow." I don't even have to fake the amazement in my voice. "That's really amazing, Tante." I say, using the formal Indonesian term for Auntie. "Wedding organizing is so complicated, especially when it comes to Chinese-Indonesian weddings."

Staphanie's grandmother nods with barely restrained pride. "You can call me Ama."

Calling someone else "Grandmother" feels like a betrayal of my late ama, but there's just something about Staphanie's grandma that is so grandmotherly. I totally want to call her Ama, even though we've just met.

"Okay, Ama." Nathan gives her his boyish smile. She beams back at him, and I know then that we have found our wedding organizer.

"Ama is known for having the sharpest eye in the industry," Staphanie says. "She doesn't ever miss anything."

"Ooh, that very important," Big Aunt says, nodding her approval. "Yes, sharp eye very important for wedding, because this and that, need to keep track, ya?"

Ama nods and smiles politely.

"Ama used to hunt when she was younger. She has the keenest eye in the industry and doesn't miss a single detail, so don't you worry, you've got the best wedding organizer in the biz," Staphanie says.

I don't bother hiding my amazement. "That's so cool."

Ama does that pursed-lip thing people do when they're trying not to grin too hard, which looks adorable.

"And this is Big Uncle," Staphanie says, gesturing at the man sitting next to Ama. "He does the flowers and decor."

"Hi, Om," I say. Om is Indonesian for "Sir" or "Mister."

He waves me off and says, "No, no, you call me Uncle James."

"Spelled J-E-M-S," Staphanie whispers, and I have to bite back my giggle. "Anyway, Big Uncle's well-known for his lily bouquets—"

"That what I well-known for!" Ma pipes up. "Until my lily guy—uh." She falters as she probably realizes what she's just about to say. *Until my lily guy was killed by my daughter.*

"Until she moved on to peonies," I quickly say, my heart thumping wildly.

"Oh, iya, peonies, yes." Ma smiles weakly.

"Maybe we can see photos of the flower arrangements?" Nathan asks. I shoot him a grateful look.

"Yeah, of course." Staphanie takes out a tablet and opens up the gallery before sliding it over to Nathan and me. "Here you go."

The bouquets and flower displays are beautiful, well-balanced, and artfully arranged to showcase the vibrant blooms. "Very pretty, Om—I mean, Uncle Jems," I say. "Do you have any photos of bouquets with hydrangeas? I have a soft spot for them."

A frown crosses Uncle Jems's face for a second, and I squirm inwardly, wondering if I'm being too demanding. No, right? I mean, it's normal to ask for your favorite flower in your wedding bouquet.

"Yes, of course," Staphanie cuts in, taking the tablet back and scrolling through the photo album. "Um, maybe not in here, but I'll look up our old photos at home and send them to you."

"Okay, thanks."

"Anyway, Second Uncle is hair and makeup," Staphanie says, pointing at the man next to Uncle Jems.

"Uncle Henry," he says, waving at me.

"There's a rogue *d* in the middle of his name," Staphanie whispers. I didn't think I could love her more, but I do. Where has this girl been all my life? She opens up a different photo album and slides the tablet back to me and Nathan.

As expected, Uncle Hendry's handiwork is beautiful and—dare I say it—rivals that of Second Aunt. As though she could hear my traitorous thoughts, Second Aunt actually gets up from her seat and walks over to us, so she's literally breathing down our necks as we look at the pictures.

"Wah, bagus sekali," she says, "you do that curled plait thing very well, that one very tricky, ah?"

Uncle Hendry nods. "Yes, very tricky, but I take lesson and practice on Staphanie hair."

"Mm, yes, I always practice on Meddy hair also," Second Aunt says, still peering down her nose at the photo album. "Oh, this photo!" She plucks the tablet out of my hands and stares at it closely. "This one your photo?"

There is a second of silence as Uncle Hendry stares at her. "Yes?" he answers cautiously.

"Wah! This one I see everywhere on Pinterest! So very popular. Wah, turns out you are the artist behind it!" The admiration on her face is palpable. She's gazing at Uncle Hendry as if he's just saved a child from a burning building. I exchange a glance with Nathan, who's openly grinning and wiggling his eyebrows at me. I can tell he's thinking the same thing—is Second Aunt in insta-love?

Uncle Hendry breaks the eye contact. "Aduh, is nothing, is very easy technique."

"I been trying to figure, you know, how to do the hair like that? And I cannot get it correct, waduh, drive me crazy. I try on Meddy hair so many time, still not look nice. You have to teach me how to do like that!"

Poor Uncle Hendry looks like he's just about ready to jump out of the nearest window. He's no match for Second Aunt. Or any of my aunts, really.

"Ahem," Big Aunt says. She doesn't even bother pretending to cough. "Please ignore my Er Mei, she lupa her manners, asking people to share trade secret. Hendry, you ignore her, okay?"

Second Aunt's lips thin into a tight line, and for a mortifying second, I'm half-afraid she's about to get into it right then and there with Big Aunt. Or lunge into some Tai Chi position. But then she exhales and smiles at Uncle Hendry. "So sorry, my Da Jie is right, I get carry away. You don't have to reveal your trade secret to me." With that, she returns to her seat and slurps her tea very deliberately.

The tension is too much for me to withstand, so I blurt out, "Second Aunt, I'm sure Second Uncle would love to hear all about the Komodo dragon fascinator and how it'll fit in with your hairdos."

"Oh yes, we have traditional British hats for wedding," Second Aunt says.

"Traditional British hats with Komodo dragons?" Nathan whispers.

"Don't ask," I mutter.

"Sounds exciting," Staphanie says. "Second Uncle would love to take a look at them, wouldn't you, Second Uncle?"

Second Uncle nods quickly. "Yes, of course. Maybe I can come your place and see this dragon sometime?"

Second Aunt's smile lights up her entire face. She's practically glowing like a light bulb. "Okay, boleh," she says, and grins down at her teacup, clearly blushing.

Staphanie and I exchange knowing glances before she says, "And last but not least, Third Uncle is our MC."

"Ooh, nice." Again, I don't have to fake the admiration in my voice. The master of ceremonies is one of the most stressful jobs at Chinese-Indonesian weddings. They're basically the wedding organizer's mouthpiece, the one who herds the thousands of wedding guests along and gathers them into appropriate groups for photos, the one who provides entertainment whenever there's a lull, and the one who hosts the reception.

MCs need to be loud and personable and shameless and charming and energetic, and I don't know how anyone does it.

"You can just call me Francis. I'm too young to be an uncle," he says.

"No!" Big Aunt booms, loud enough to make us all jump. "No such thing as calling your elder by first name."

I look helplessly at Staphanie's Third Uncle and say, "How about Ko Francis?" Koko means "older brother" in Indonesian.

"That'll do. You two need to tell me how you met and everything. I bet you have a juicy love story that I can compile into the best speech ever."

Ha. It's too bad our love story doesn't involve saving baby otters, but rather getting away with literal murder.

The longer lunch goes on, the more I realize that I really, really like Staphanie and her family. How can I not? They're clearly just as bonkers as mine. As expected, her photos are wonderful—slightly overexposed like mine are. She captures the brightness of her weddings with soft pastel colors.

"Which camera do you use?" I can't stop admiring her gallery. The colors scream of film photography, something I've always wanted to try but never had the guts to.

"Same as yours, the 5D Mark III."

"Really? Wow. I could never get my pictures to have these pastel shades. I would've guessed the 1D."

There's a beat of silence, then Staphanie laughs. "You're so kind. No, these are not taken by the 1D."

"Well, I'm impressed. You'll have to teach me how to get the backgrounds so smooth on the 5D."

"Mm-hmm, for sure!" She grabs a pork rib and places it on my plate.

If I don't reciprocate—or rather, retaliate—Ma would tell

me off later for being rude. "Stop doing that. You're making me look bad." I put down the tablet and take a har gow for her.

Staphanie grins. "How else can I show everyone that my Ama has raised me well? Also, I really just wanted more food, and if I take food for myself, Ama will tell me I've brought shame to the family."

I laugh, relating to every sentence she just said. "Okay, you tell me which dishes you want and I'll tell you which ones I want."

"Deal."

As our two families chat with each other, Staphanie and I pile all sorts of dumplings on each other's plates. By the time lunch is over, I know that against all odds, Ma and my aunts have actually done something right and picked the perfect vendors for my wedding.

3

Five Months Later

"Oh my god, what do you have in here, Fourth Aunt?" I grunt, struggling with the giant suitcase.

"A body. Ha ha, just kidding," she adds when I don't laugh. She grabs her carry-on—a matching brown suitcase with the letters LV printed all over it.

"Aduh, Meddy, be careful with that, please. It's Louis Vuitton!"

I give her a look. The family business has flourished for the past year, and technically, they can afford Louis Vuitton anything, but I know my family well enough to know they wouldn't spend tens of thousands of dollars on the real stuff. "Is it *really* Louis Vuitton, Fourth Aunt?"

She tuts. "It's a Class One bag, it's just as good as the real stuff! Cost me two thousand dollars, okay? You can take it to Paris and they won't be able to tell it's fake."

In Indonesia, fakes are sorted into different classes. Most Class One stuff is from South Korea and uses real leather sewn by actual leatherworkers. Class Two comes mostly from China, and Class Threes are made in Southeast Asia—Indonesia, Bangladesh, Vietnam, and so on. Class Threes will set you back a few dollars at the most, but then you're dealing with pleather and wonky logos that say Prata and Bluberry. Class Ones cost about a quarter of the real stuff. Still expensive, but more affordable, and they're next to impossible to tell apart from the real ones. They even come with certificates of authenticity.

Ma gives a snort of derision at Fourth Aunt's bags. "This why you can never get rich, because you waste your money on silly thing like this. Big sis teach us more better than this; she teach us to save money."

Here we go again. I steel myself for some sort of snide retort from Fourth Aunt, but it doesn't come. Instead, she just smirks at Ma and sashays off to find a trolley.

There's a beep, and the Uber carrying Big Aunt and Second Aunt arrives. I greet them as they climb out, then go round the back to help with their bags, and—

Oh no.

No wonder Fourth Aunt didn't snark back at Ma. Because Big Aunt and Second Aunt's bags are matching Louis Vuitton suitcases. They might as well take turns punching Ma's heart.

"So nice, yah?" Second Aunt says. "Is Class—"

"Class One, yeah, I know," I sigh, pulling the first piece of brown luggage out. "How come all of you have matching ones except for Ma?"

Second Aunt blinks and stands there unmoving for a second. Big Aunt, coming back with a trolley, snaps, "Eh, why you stand there like patung? Come help."

"Natasya not have same suitcases as us," Second Aunt says.

Wow, no snarky comebacks to Big Aunt. Second Aunt must really be worried.

Big Aunt pauses, then sighs. "When Mimi tell us to buy same suitcase, we should have guess she wouldn't tell Nat. Aduh, aduh. Pasti Nat will get very upset."

Dammit. I suppose it was too much to hope that the peace that had come with the whole Ah Guan ordeal would be permanent. It was nice while it lasted, but now it seems that the old grudges have crept back in. Still, even considering Ma and Fourth Aunt's turbulent past, this is a low blow.

Just as I think that, Ma comes rushing over with another trolley. "Come, put your luggage here—oh." She stands still and stares at the bags. "You all have Louis Vuitton?" Her voice comes out so small I want to run over and give her a big hug.

Big Aunt and Second Aunt glare at Fourth Aunt. "You didn't tell Natasya we all getting the same luggage?"

Fourth Aunt doesn't quite meet our eyes. "Did I not? I must have forgotten."

"How you possibly forget such important thing?" Ma snaps.

I'm on Ma's side here, but even so, I have to make a conscious effort not to roll my eyes at this. I mean, on the scale of what's important, getting matching luggage strikes me as . . . not. But maybe that's just because I'm an only child and haven't grown up fighting silent and not-so-silent battles with my sisters. "It's okay, Ma, you can order a matching set when we come back here."

"But we never travel!" Ma wails. "This my only chance to have matching luggage with my family, but is ruin!"

"You guys go back to Jakarta once every year," I point out.

"That not count as traveling."

"If hopping on a twenty-three-hour plane ride doesn't count as travel, I don't know what does."

Her nostrils flare and even Big Aunt takes a step back from her, but just then, there's a honk, and two cars pull up next to us. One of the windows rolls down and Staphanie pops her head out, grinning at us. Saved! I run over to them.

Over the past few months, as Nathan and I have gone through the excruciating process of planning a destination wedding, Staphanie has been indispensable. She took care of details such as registering with the Oxford county hall so we could actually legalize the marriage, she helped us find the perfect baker for the wedding cake, and she even booked my family's hotel rooms.

"So glad you're here!" I give her a big hug.

Staphanie stiffens, and I kick myself. Is it weird that I hugged her? Maybe she only sees me as a client and not a friend? But then she hugs me back and the weird moment is over. When we let go, I greet her family in order of age, starting with her grandmother and ending with Third Uncle, while Staph does the same with mine. I can't help but notice that Second Aunt immediately sidles up to Second Uncle to tell him she loves his fanny pack. I also can't help but notice that she is wearing quite a bit more makeup than usual.

"You remember to bringing our hats, right?" Second Aunt says.

"Of course," Second Uncle says with a smile.

"You gave your fascinators to Second Uncle?" I say.

"Yes, he say he going to sew more clip on them, make them more secure," Second Aunt says.

"And I did. They very secure now. During wedding they will stay on your head very firm, I guarantee."

Second Aunt practically swoons over that. *Iiin*-teresting. Staph catches me looking, and we grin at each other before going to get more trolleys.

"Can't wait for this trip!" she says. "Everything going okay?"

"You arrived just in time," I whisper. "My mom and aunts were about to start World War III over, of all things, luggage."

"Oof." Staph grimaces with sympathy. "I totally relate to that. My uncles were arguing over who's overpacked and needs to leave stuff behind."

Somehow, that makes me feel slightly better, and again, I feel a wave of gratitude toward Staphanie for being here.

When we get back with the trolleys, our two families are chatting amiably with each other. No signs of Ma almost going nuclear just minutes ago; she's now laughing politely at something Staphanie's Third Uncle is saying. Only the tiniest little sharp glances occasionally thrown at Fourth Aunt betray Ma's true feelings. She's not going to let this one go so easily.

"Looks like your mom's over it," Staph says.

I snort. "Nah, she's just waiting for the right moment to get back at Fourth Aunt. Is it the same with your uncles? Tell me they snipe at each other just as much."

"Hmm, there's definitely a lot of infighting, and they need to prove to each other that they're the manliest of men all the freaking time. Watch." She nods to me as we get back to the group with the trolleys. As if on cue, her three uncles leap into action, pouncing on the bags and yanking them quickly to the trolleys.

"Let me do! You so old, later you hurt your back!"

"Hah, I old? I still stronger than you!"

"You're going to break the wheel! Why don't you just wheel it like a normal person?"

My family and I watch openmouthed as the three men grapple with the luggage, creating far more work for themselves than necessary with all the arm flaps and exaggerated maneuvers. Finally, all of the bags are piled on top of the trolleys and the men step back, chests heaving. As one, they look at Ama expectantly.

Ama nods and says, "Very good, you all good boys."

The uncles' smiles are blinding.

Is this what it's like to have a grandmother still alive in the family? I guess it's sort of like how Big Aunt is with us. There's such a large age gap between Big Aunt and the rest of her sisters that they all look up to her as if she's their mother. Except for Second Aunt, of course. Even as I think that, Big Aunt links arms with Ama, and together, the two gray-haired women totter into the airport. Staphanie and I each grab a trolley and push.

"Are Nathan and your friends excited about the trip?"

"Yep! My best friends Selena and Seb will be flying out tomorrow. Nathan will be here in an hour or so. There's some last-minute work stuff he needed to take care of."

"Well, we *are* inexplicably four hours early."

"It's not inexplicable. I blame it on Big Aunt."

"I blame it on Ama." We grin at each other.

Inside the terminal, we find seats for our elders and betters, gather everyone's passports, and go to the check-in counter. As we go over our seats, the woman at the counter points to a piece of paper and says, "Just as a reminder, these items are prohibited on the flight."

I nod automatically, skimming through the list. Gun, nope. Knife, nope. Aerosol spray, nope. Power pack, nope. Of course I didn't bring any of these things to the airport, I—

Taser.

My hand flies to my handbag, where my trusty Taser lies. The thought of having to leave it here and go to a whole new country without it is sickening. It reminds me of the first and only time I've had to use it. The way it had made Ah Guan's body jerk like a doll. The car crash. And every horrible, gruesome thing that had happened afterward.

"Everything okay, Meddy?" Staph says.

I nod wordlessly, then shake my head. "Uh. I need to—uh. I'll be right back." I grab the stash of passports, but my hands are so sweaty that I almost drop them. I hold on tightly and wander off from the counter, unsure where to go. Maybe I can slip the Taser into my check-in luggage? Would that be okay or would that be breaking the law?

"What's going on?" Staph says, catching up with me. Her face creases with concern when she sees my expression. "Let's go to the restroom." She takes the passports from me and leads me away without waiting for an answer.

Inside, she grabs a piece of tissue, wets it under the tap and hands it to me. "Wipe your face. It'll help."

I press the cold, damp tissue against my forehead and close my eyes. I take a deep breath. Exhale. After a while, I open my eyes and look at Staph's reflection. "Sorry. I'm fine."

"Wanna talk about it?"

I turn the tap on and splash water onto my cheeks. "It's stupid." I open my bag and take out the Taser. The weight of it in my hand makes my heart rate double. I hate the thing, but I also can't be without it. "It's—I just realized I won't be able to take this with me."

"Is that a Taser?" Staph holds out her hand.

"Yeah." I hand it to her and watch as she turns it over in her hand.

"Huh. I've toyed with the idea of getting one, but I'm more of a pepper spray girl myself." She gives it back to me. "And yeah, I'm pretty sure you can't take one of these on a plane."

"I know. I should've realized it sooner, but I've just been so distracted by everything else I never thought—"

"You've had a lot on your plate. It's okay to forget."

"Well, it's not just that." I sigh, leaning against the sink and running my fingers across the angular edges of the Taser. "This thing, it's saved my life. Like, literally saved my life."

Staphanie's eyes go wide. "Wow."

"Yeah. I was on a date, and the guy tried to—uh." I'm revealing too much. I should stop.

"Oh god. I'm so sorry to hear that." Her expression is aghast.

"It's okay. Nothing happened. I just—I managed to get away." My mind can't help careening back to the worst night of my life. I'd saved myself only by Tasing my attacker, who later died of—uh, other reasons.

"Still. To be in that situation in the first place, that must have been terrifying. I was in a similar situation once. Back in college, I went to frat party and—yeah, things got a bit out of hand. Luckily, my cousin had a spray deodorant on him. It works almost as well as pepper spray, you know, especially if you hit them right in the eye."

"Wow, lucky your cousin was there."

Staphanie's smile wavers. "Yeah. We were really tight. He was my age."

"Was? I—oh, I'm so sorry."

"It's okay. Anyway, I haven't left the house without my pepper spray since. Well, except for now. It's illegal in England, can you believe it? But I've packed a perfume bottle in my check-in luggage that's filled with alcohol and cayenne pepper. Tell you what, when we get to England, first thing we'll buy is a spray bottle and I'll give you half."

"Oh no, I couldn't take your homemade pepper spray solution."

Staph laughs. "Yes, you can. There's way too much of it for

myself. What am I going to do, spray the whole of England's male population? Realistically speaking, I won't even go through a single spritz before the whole thing loses its potency and I have to throw it out."

"Okay," I say reluctantly. "Thank you. That helps." Huh. It actually does. Who would've thought? I give her hand a grateful squeeze. "I'm so glad we're friends." It's so weird that even though I've only known her for five months, I feel like Staph and I have known each other for ages.

"Me too," she says. "And now, let's go turn this Taser in before TSA finds it on you and arrests you."

4

Nathan arrives at the boarding gate a scant ten minutes before we're due to board, slightly out of breath, with his hair looking deliciously rumpled.

"Aiya, you finally arrive," Ma scolds, patting his shoulder with obvious affection. "Plane almost leave you. We tell them must wait for groom but they say cannot."

It's true. My mother and aunts have been taking turns for the past thirty minutes letting the gate attendants know that they can't possibly start boarding passengers because Nathan isn't here yet. Unsurprisingly, they haven't been as understanding as my family expected.

"Yes, now we go tell them they should hurry and start boarding, we all here, so rude to keep passengers waiting," Big Aunt says. She turns to go to the gate, and the attendants visibly shrink back as she approaches. Poor things. I don't blame them.

I grin at Nathan. "I'm glad you made it."

"Sorry I took so long. The meeting lasted forever. The board's somewhat uneasy about me leaving for a week." He gives my arm a little squeeze. "Did you guys enjoy the lounge, at least?"

Ah, the lounge. It's the first time any of my family members, including myself, have had the privilege of flying first class. Staph and her family are flying economy and I'd originally thought we'd stay with them until we boarded, maybe get some sandwiches, but Staph had practically pushed me into the first-class lounge and told me to enjoy myself. I didn't know what airport lounges were like; I'd always thought they were sad little waiting rooms, but the moment we stepped inside, my mother and aunts went berserk, and I could hardly blame them.

We'd been greeted by a cascading waterfall that drowned out the usual airport noises, and beyond the partition was a larger-than-life buffet, complete with tiger prawns, caviar, and a full bar. Ma and the aunties had squawked and charged straight for the prawns while I found us a table. Then there were the showers. Again, never thought I'd ever want to shower at the airport, but these showers were beautiful—gleaming marble and rainfall showerheads and warmed, fluffy towels.

"Fourth Aunt had one too many glasses of Dom," I whisper to Nathan, nodding at Fourth Aunt, who's asleep in one of the chairs with her mouth open. As usual, people are looking, though I don't know if it's because she's snoring or because of today's outfit: a shiny, emerald-green dress, neon-orange scarf, and matching emerald-green sunglasses.

With obvious relief, the gate attendant picks up her mic and says, "Flight 382 bound for London Heathrow is ready for boarding. We will be boarding First Class and Business Class passengers first." She's barely finished the last sentence when Big Aunt and Ma charge the counter.

Second Aunt pokes Fourth Aunt's head, and when that

doesn't work, shakes her roughly, shouting, "Eh, Si Mei, ah, bangun! We boarding already!"

I shoot Staphanie an apologetic glance. She and her family must think we're cavepeople, but they're busy grappling with the numerous carry-ons and passports and an assortment of snacks and drinks they've bought outside the gate. Well, at least they're not witnessing this.

Fourth Aunt awakes with a startled snort and leaps out of the chair. "Ah? Yes, ready!" Straightening her scarf, she grabs her (Class One) Louis Vuitton handbag and stalks to the counter, orange scarf fluttering behind her.

"Ready to go?" Nathan says.

I nod, gathering my stuff, and together we board the plane.

First Class! Even my family's usual antics aren't capable of taking away the magic of the experience for me.

"Good afternoon, Ms. Chan, welcome on board," a flight attendant says in a lovely English accent. "May I show you to your seat?"

May he? Of course he may! I smile and follow him to the cabin, where there are rows of beautiful brown leather seats that are too big for me to fill. Amazing.

"Here is your seat, and would you like a warm—"

"Hullo. Eh, hullo, luv!" The unmistakable voice of Big Aunt fills the cabin. I swear, literally every soul on the plane stops to stare.

Nathan and I freeze, and then crane our necks to see Big Aunt, nestled in one of the huge seats, waving at a flight attendant. She comes over with a puzzled smile.

"Yes, Ms. Chan? Is there something I can help you with?"

"Ah, yes, luv," Big Aunt says, still in that strange, awful new accent of hers that makes me want to stab a knife straight into my brain. "I have a hot cuppa, can or not? Thanks, luv."

To her credit, the flight attendant doesn't show any outward emotion. She merely smiles and says, "Of course. One hot tea coming up."

"Toodle pip, cheerio!"

I turn to Nathan in a panic. "I think she's having a stroke."

He laughs and puts our bags in the overhead compartment. "She's fine."

I hurry to Big Aunt's seat and crouch down next to her. "Hi, Big Aunt." *Step carefully, Meddy. It's still Big Aunt, even though, apparently, some sort of deranged British alien has wormed its way into her head and taken over her tongue.*

"Ah, Meddy, Nathan! You okay?" Big Aunt says.

"No," Ma scolds from the seat next to her. "You suppose to say, 'Alright, Nathan, luv?'"

Big Aunt nods somberly, then turns to us and says, "Alright, Nathan, luv?"

My smile is fighting to turn into a grimace. "What's going on? Why are you speaking like that?"

"Surprise!" Ma says. "We all been taking lessons to speak British!"

Big Aunt nods with obvious pride.

"Yes, we all do so we don't make you lose face," Second Aunt says from the row behind them.

It hits me then that for the past few months, Ma and the aunties have been speaking more in English and less in Mandarin or Indonesian. I'd noticed it weeks ago but thought nothing of it. Now I realize they'd been preparing for this trip, so they'd be more comfortable speaking British slang. I'm torn between affection and embarrassment; story of my life. I mean, the fact that they went to all this trouble is so incredibly sweet, but also, argh!

"Speak for yourselves. I only went along with it so I'll be able to impress Prince Harry," Fourth Aunt says. "No offense, Meddy. But I'm just here for Harry."

"He married, you hussy!" Ma snaps. "Married to nice girl, very good girl, not like you."

"Who knows, they might be receptive to the idea of an open marriage."

Ma's face turns an alarming shade of purple, but before she can utter a word, I quickly say, "That's nice, but I don't think the English accents are necessary. Thank you for taking lessons; that's amazing! But I prefer your normal accents."

I elbow Nathan, who nods quickly. "Yeah, Meddy's right. Your normal speech is great. Terrific."

"Aww, bless," Ma says, smiling fondly at Nathan.

"You can't carry off 'bless,'" I say dryly.

"Meddy, don't be such tosser, lah," Second Aunt says.

Nathan's eyebrows disappear into his hairline.

"Did you just call me a 'tosser'?"

"Tosser is mean someone who always toss out the good time."

"That—no. Second Aunt, that is not what 'tosser' means."

"Yes it is, see here, I got put in my notebook, hmm, where is it . . ." She takes out her book and flips through page after page of handwritten British slang, muttering under her breath the whole time. "Bugger . . . bugger off . . . bugger it . . ."

"Stop saying 'bugger,' Second Aunt," I plead.

"Is mean 'booger.'"

"It definitely doesn't mean that," Nathan says, barely able to keep his face straight.

"Then what it mean?" Second Aunt says. And suddenly, it feels like the entire cabin is looking at us expectantly.

Nathan falters. "Uh. It means . . . um." After an interminable silence where not a single eye in the cabin blinks, Nathan mumbles, "Yeah, you're right, it means 'booger.'" The fucking coward.

Second Aunt, Big Aunt, and Ma nod with satisfaction. Fourth Aunt grins at us. I pull Nathan aside. Once we get to our seats and are safely out of earshot, I say, "Let's get off the plane. It's not too late, the gate's still open."

Nathan pats my arm. "It'll be okay."

"Nathan! They're speaking like Hugh Grant!"

"I can assure you they sound nothing like Hugh Grant."

"I know! But they *think* they sound like him. And they keep swearing. What if they call your mom a tosser and tell your dad to bugger off?"

Nathan bites back a grin. "I mean, it would be hilarious."

I punch him on the arm, hard enough for him to wince. "To you, maybe. I would be mortified. Oh god, this is terrible."

"It's hardly terrible. Is there something else bothering you?"

I take a deep breath. "I have this fear of your parents realizing they're nuts and convincing you to call off the wedding."

Nathan laughs. "Meddy, it'll be fine. My parents know to expect some loss in translation. And they love you. Therefore, they'll love your family too, just like I do. I adore your mother and your aunts, you know that."

I sigh, leaning against his reassuring shoulder. "I know. Although I can never understand why. You know they're bonkers, right?"

"Only in the best possible way. Trust me, my family is going to fall head over heels in love with them."

I close my eyes and try to believe him, but somehow, whenever I try to imagine his painfully prim family meeting my ramshackle one, all I can see is a disaster. I'm so sure that, at some point, Nathan will realize that my family and I are a complete mess and decide to escape before it's too late. And then I'll be wrenched out of this wonderful dream and find myself back where I was before Jacqueline and Tom Cruise Sutopo's wedding—alone, crushed under the weight of familial guilt, and worst of all, without Nathan in my life.

5

Despite the unapologetically lush seats, the thought of my family meeting Nathan's keeps me so anxious I can't sleep at all the entire flight. Twice, I'm just about to doze off when I hear Ma or the aunts say something along the lines of "Eh, San Mei, ah, oi could do with a nice cuppa, innit?" Then my heart rate goes up so fast that I get a headache. Oh god, please, please, let them realize how ultra-ridiculous they sound. Who could've foreseen me missing my family's normal speech pattern?

While everyone else sleeps, I stare at Nathan like a complete creep and try to will him to continue loving me, even if his parents end up hating my family. Which is definitely perfectly healthy and respectable and not at all pathetic.

"I can feel you staring," he murmurs, eyes still closed.

"You wish." I turn away quickly. I grab the menu out of the seat pocket and pretend to be engrossed.

He takes my hand and gives me a lazy smile. "Don't worry,

it'll all be okay. Hey, remember the last time we were on this route?"

How could I forget? "I fell asleep and woke up with my head locked at an angle."

The smile grows wider. "You were so cute. I couldn't keep my eyes off you."

"You're such a dork. Go back to sleep." I plant a kiss on his cheek, taking the chance to inhale the scent of him—again, totally normal and not at all creepy—and then go back to the menu. When I next look over, he's fast asleep. Just like everyone else on the flight. I resume biting my nails and thinking about all the ways things could go wrong.

By the time we land at Heathrow, I'm a wreck. Everything passes in a blur: disembarking, regrouping with Staphanie and her family, going through customs, collecting the never-ending row of fake Vuittons, and finally, all of us piling into private cars we've hired for the journey to Oxford. In the car, exhaustion catches up with me and I doze off, my head resting on Nathan's shoulder throughout the one-and-a-half-hour journey from London to Oxford. When the driver says, "We're here," I awake with a start and find to my horror that, yet again, my head is stuck at an angle.

"NOOOO!" Seriously? This again? Right when I'm about to meet Nathan's family again?

Outside the car, my family crowds around me.

"Meddy, luv, what's wrong with your head? Why like that?" Ma says.

"Alright, luv?" Second Aunt says.

"Stop saying 'luv,'" I groan.

"Is sign of affection," Big Aunt tuts. "They showing they love you, call you luv. British people, they full of love."

"I know what it means, I just—ow."

"Aiya, you need warm compress," Ma says, massaging my neck. "Nathan, you suppose to massage her neck, she got stiff neck, just like me, you know? Every day need to massage, aiya, you need to look after my daughter better."

"I'm sorry, Ma," Nathan says, contrite. Ma has bullied him into calling her that ever since we got engaged, and to no one's surprise but mine, Nathan's gone along with it good-naturedly, without a single complaint. "I'll do better."

"What you need is to kerok it," Ama announces.

"Oh yes, kerok!" Big Aunt says.

"What's 'croak'?" Nathan asks.

"I think the English term is 'scraping,'" Staphanie pipes up. "It's where you use a coin or the lid of a Tiger Balm container to scrape the skin until it turns red."

"Oh, gua sha," Nathan says. "Yeah, my dad used to do that to me whenever I caught a cold or wasn't feeling well. It works!"

"I got bring Tiger Balm," Second Uncle says.

"Wah, so helpful," Second Aunt titters, fluttering her lashes at him shamelessly. "Maybe later I come your hotel get Tiger Balm for Meddy."

"Nobody is going to scrape my skin," I say. "The scrapes last for weeks. I'm not going to have huge red welts down my neck and back on my wedding day."

"Yeah, it does tend to look really bad," Staphanie laughs.

Second Aunt looks so disappointed that I feel obliged to add, "But you can still get the Tiger Balm from Second Uncle's room, just in case."

She brightens at that, until Big Aunt mutters, "Tch, lose face, so shameless." Just loud enough for Second Aunt to hear, but not Staphanie's family. Second Aunt's cheeks turn red, but she continues smiling at Second Uncle.

"Speaking of hotels," I say hurriedly, "I'm really tired. Let's all go in and rest, okay?"

"You guys go ahead," Staphanie says. "My family and I are staying at the college, so we'll head over there and meet up with you later, okay?"

"Sounds good." I give Staph a hug and then follow my family into our hotel.

The Randolph is the fanciest hotel in Oxford, a hallowed brick building built in the Victorian Gothic style. It's hard not to be impressed by it. Actually, it's hard not to be impressed by everything in Oxford. The architecture in England is so different from that in Los Angeles.

L.A. is all short, sprawling buildings, whereas Oxford is filled with tall, magnificent, brick and sandstone buildings decorated with tortured stone and marble, crenellations, pillars, and spires. The inside of the Randolph Hotel is just as impressive as the outside, the floors a dark hardwood, chandeliers dripping from the ceiling, everything gilded in rich leather. It's the kind of place where people speak in low, hushed tones of rev—

"Wah, this place surely very expensive, innit?" Ma's voice, loud under normal circumstances, is a shout in the quiet atmosphere. Heads turn. Eyes crawl over us.

"Cor, yes, this place so fancy, ah?" Second Aunt says just as loudly. "You get discount or not, Meddy? If not, maybe can ask for discount, ah?"

I turn to Big Aunt, a pleading look on my face. I can't tell Ma and Second Aunt to speak quietly, or not haggle for a discount, but she can. Big Aunt is a sensible woman. She'll get it. She sees the desperate expression on my face and pats my shoulder reassuringly. I breathe out. She'll tell them to drop the ridiculous accents and that a discount is out of the question.

"You kids choose well," she says solemnly. "We no need ask for discount." Oh, thank god. "This hotel . . ." She nods politely at the receptionists, who are all staring at us, and says loudly, enunciating each word, "This hotel is dog's bollocks."

I can't look the bellboy in the eye when he drops off our luggage. Knowing what everyone in this building must think of them. Of us. Argh.

"Still thinking of what happened downstairs?" Nathan says, toweling his hair dry as he walks out of the bathroom. Normally, I would take a moment to admire his abs, especially when he's only wearing a towel wrapped around his waist, but right now I'm still too stressed out over my family's behavior.

"Like I can ever forget that. 'Dog's bollocks'? I mean, what the hell was Big Aunt trying to say?"

Nathan laughs. "Well, to be fair, 'dog's bollocks' means awesome, so she's not wrong. This hotel *is* pretty awesome."

"You know what I mean," I groan, flinging myself onto the bed and burying my face in the fluffy pillows.

"I know," he says gently. The bed sags slightly as he sits down next to me. He rubs my back and I melt against his touch. "They're just being themselves. Their wonderful, loving selves. You're usually okay with them. What's really bothering you? Is it my parents?"

His parents, Annie and Chris, are just about as different as anyone can get from Ma and the aunts. Sometimes, I even forget that Chris was originally from Hong Kong. His family had immigrated to England when he was just three years old, and he was put through the best boarding schools England had to offer. He's basically a modernized Mr. Darcy now, both in manner and speech. A teeny tiny part of me may have wished, in my darkest hours, that my family had integrated more fully into their adopted countries, like Chris had.

I turn my head to look at him. "Well, yeah. Of course I'm nervous about your parents. Your folks are so polite and well-behaved and—"

"Anal? Walk around with sticks up their arses?"

"No!" I laugh. "They're great. I bet they've never embarrassed you at school events or called anything dog's bollocks. Why does 'dog's bollocks' even mean 'awesome'? What is wrong with you Brits?"

"Hmm. Good question. Well, I'm sure your aunts will say it again over dinner to describe my mum's food or something, and we can have a lively conversation about the epistemology of the term 'dog's bollocks.'"

I groan into the pillows again.

"It'll be fine," Nathan laughs. "They'll fit right in."

"My family has never fit right in anywhere."

"They'll fit right in with my family."

I have to smile at his hopeless optimism. As though the wildly different Asian diaspora experiences weren't enough, his parents are also significantly wealthier than my family. Old money: Nathan's grandparents had made a killing trading in Hong Kong before moving to England. And their wealthy upbringing has always been so obvious to me whenever I've been around them. I mean, they have different glasses for white wine and red wine, for god's sake. Talk about fancy. Ma and the aunts rarely ever drink, except for Fourth Aunt, who drinks everything out of those red party cups because she's a frat boy at heart.

Then my eyes trail down his stupidly perfect face to his stupidly perfect chest and those stupidly perfect abs.

"What are you looking at with that pervy expression of yours?"

I pull him down on top of me. "Just admiring the goods before I marry them."

He pushes a stray lock of hair away from my face and then kisses me slow and deep, and for the next hour or so, I blissfully forget about my family and their strange new accents.

6

Nathan was wrong. I was right.

Normally, I would be happy about this, but right now, I would've given anything for it to be the other way around.

He is wrong about his parents loving my mother and aunts. I can see it in their faces as soon as we arrive at the house. His parents greet me and Nathan with hugs and good cheer, just as I remember them, but when they go to greet my family, they falter. And who can blame them?

Ma and the aunts are wearing hats so wide that we have trouble fitting everybody inside the cabs. And atop the hats are giant silk flowers and fruit. I'd gently prodded and hinted about leaving the hats behind, but they insisted it was a sign of respect to wear hats in England.

"Hullo," Big Aunt says first, pronouncing it "hoo-lo." I know she knows how to say "hello" like a normal human, but here she is, hoo-lo-ing all over the place. "Very kind of you, inviting us to your home, innit? I very chuffed to be here."

Nathan's mother recovers and her smile regains its wattage. "Oh, with pleasure! It's so nice to finally meet all of you. Please come in!"

There is confusion and mayhem as the pineapples and sunflowers on their hats are knocked askew by the doorway. Thankfully, they decide to take the hats off. I exhale. Now that the hats are gone, maybe the rest of the evening will go smoothly.

"I am Friya," Big Aunt says.

"Enjelin," Second Aunt says.

"Natasya," Ma says.

"And I'm Mimi," Fourth Aunt says.

It's always so weird hearing them introduce themselves by their names when I've known them my whole life as Ma and the aunts.

"Wonderful!" Nathan's mother says. "I'm Annie, and this is my husband, Chris. I can't believe we've never met. We've all heard so much about you."

"Drinks?" Nathan's father says, picking up a tray of cocktails and offering it to us.

"Thank you, luv, but we not really like to drink, please not get knickers in a bunch, ya?" Big Aunt says.

Oh god. "I'll have one." I grab a glass.

"Yah, I can't really take the alcohol, I go very red," Ma says.

"Natasya is more of a weed person," Fourth Aunt mutters as she picks a glass.

"Excuse me?" Chris says.

"She's talking about traditional Chinese medicine!" I practically shout, and give Fourth Aunt a death glare that she returns with a carefully blank look.

"Oh, wonderful. Chris here grew up taking TCM, didn't you, Chris," Annie says.

"I did. In fact, one of the dishes I made for tonight is ginseng chicken."

"Wah, you cook?" Ma says. "Ah, sorry, I mean to say, blimey, you cook?"

My head starts to throb. Chris ushers Ma into the kitchen, both of them chatting about ginseng roots and various Chinese herbs. The rest of us go into the dining room, which has been prepared beautifully, each place setting prepped with elaborately folded napkins and two different wine glasses.

"Cor, this so posh, innit?" Second Aunt says.

"Yes, Annie, you are a toff," Big Aunt says.

Oh god, somebody please stop them. Nathan's mother gives them a puzzled smile, then tells us to sit while she and Nathan leave the room to bring out the dishes.

"Big Aunt, Second Aunt, speak normally, please," I beg them as soon as Annie is out of earshot.

"Tch, Meddy, we trying to be polite. What is that saying? When you in Rome, you need to wear toga," Big Aunt scolds. "Now we in England, we in their home, we speak British English. We show that we make effort to learn their way, they will appreciate."

"Yes, it take weeks and weeks for us to learn, you know," Second Aunt pipes up. "We practice in secret so we can surprise you. Don't be ungrateful, Meddy, okay, you be good girl."

Guilt lances through my gut. They're not wrong. I really am being an ungrateful brat. And I know that they've done all of this out of love, to impress Nathan's family for my sake. But still! Argh!

"Yes, I really appreciate all the effort, but this isn't—I'm telling you, this is not how normal English people speak."

"Who say?" Big Aunt snaps, aghast. "The teacher we hire say is the most up-to-date British saying!"

"What teacher?" I say.

"Oh yes, we find teacher on Fiverr," Second Aunt says proudly. "Such good deal. Five dollar one hour. We take many hour!"

Fourth Aunt snorts, obviously enjoying this entire exchange.

Before I can reply, Nathan and his mother come back in carrying platters of food. Ma and Chris follow, each carrying more plates of food, and before long, everything is out. We settle into our seats and admire the spread. All sorts of food, both Chinese and English. There's the aforementioned ginseng chicken, a huge bowl of spicy sesame noodles, a huge cut of roast pork shoulder, a platter of warm Yorkshire pudding, and various other side dishes.

"Cor, that looking scrummy, dunnit?" Ma says.

"Oh yes, look like very good nosh, innit," Second Aunt says.

"Yes," Big Aunt says politely, "very dog's bollocks."

"Err, thank you?" Chris says.

Annie's gaze flicks rapidly back and forth between my family and Nathan, who's trying not to laugh.

"They've been taking British-slang lessons for this visit," I quickly say apologetically.

"Oh? How . . . nice," Annie says, and makes an obvious effort to smile. "Well, please help yourselves. I hope you enjoy the food."

As we help ourselves to the feast, I catch sight of Big Aunt dipping into her handbag. Oh no. I already know what she's going to get before she even takes it out. It's like I'm moving in slow motion. I reach behind Second Aunt to grab Big Aunt's hand, but I'm too late. The bottle of chili sauce is placed on the table with an earth-shattering *thunk*.

Nathan's parents stop mid-conversation and stare at it, then at Big Aunt.

"Is that—" Annie says.

"Is sambal," Big Aunt says. "Indonesian chili sauce, best chili. Please, try some."

Annie's forehead creases into a frown. "I'm alright, thank you. So you carry around a bottle of chili sauce with you?"

"Oh yes, of course. Otherwise I not so enjoy the food."

This is why I can never take my family to nice restaurants. I've tried explaining countless times why it's rude to bring your own chili sauce to restaurants or other people's homes, but they just don't get it. "In Indonesia, everybody bring their own chili sauce everywhere," Ma would say. "Why you call that rude? Is just practical. Everybody like different kind of chili, if host is good, host will provide all the different brands. But we be understanding, don't put that kind of pressure on host. We bring our own."

"Of course we would enjoy your food with or without the chili sauce," I say. "Mmm, this is all so delicious."

"It's part of Indonesian culture," Nathan says helpfully. "Lots of people there take their own chili sauces everywhere they go. I think it's a great idea."

"Yes, wonderful," Annie says weakly as she watches Big Aunt cover her entire plate of food with the chili sauce. When everything is blanketed in the bright red sauce, Big Aunt passes it to Second Aunt, who also drowns her food in chili sauce. When she's done with the now half-empty bottle, Second Aunt passes it to Ma, but to my surprise and relief, Ma refuses it. Thank god, finally, someone showing an ounce of respect—

"I think I get a bit food poisoning from plane, wah, my stomach so pain just now, I had to poop very bad in hotel. I better not eat spicy tonight," Ma says.

Kill me now. Just end this.

Forks and spoons stop halfway to mouths. Nathan's parents stare, openly aghast, at Ma. I want to explain that in Indonesian culture, discussing one's digestion is a completely acceptable part of social interactions, but I don't know how to even begin.

Nathan clears his throat and says, "Yeah, airplane food can be a bit tricky, can't it? So Mum, how's the garden coming along? I heard you planted a new lemon tree?"

Thank god for Nathan. Annie starts telling us about the fruits and vegetables they're growing in the backyard.

"We've got some lovely tomatoes, really tasty," Chris says, "but let me tell you, gardening is hell on my back." He rubs his shoulder as he speaks, wincing.

"Ah, you must do the Tai Chi," Second Aunt says. "Come, I teach you."

"Second Aunt, no—" But she's already out of her chair, marching over to Nathan's dad, who's looking at her like a terrified schoolboy. I can't blame him in the least as Second Aunt orders him out of his chair.

"It's okay," Nathan murmurs, "it'll be good for his back."

"But—"

To my horror, right there in the beautiful dining room, Second Aunt begins to do Tai Chi.

"This starting position. You follow me." She raises both arms.

Eyes wide with a mixture of what looks like fear and uncertainty, Chris imitates her.

"Second position, Parting the Wild Horse's Mane. The horse very wild, you must very gentle, okay?" Second Aunt steps one foot forward, crouching, and combs an imaginary horse's mane. Chris follows suit.

"The food's getting cold," Annie chirps nervously.

"Okay, we go fast," Second Aunt says. "Quick, White Crane Spreads Its Legs. Cepat, ayo, faster. Brush knee, yes, now push! Good. Now, Repulse Monkey!"

Poor Chris tries his best to keep up with Second Aunt's increasingly rapid flow of commands, but as he lifts his left leg, a sudden look of pain crosses his face and he cries out, "My back!"

Nathan jumps out of his seat and catches hold of his dad. Annie gets up and hurries into the kitchen, saying, "I'll get the ice pack!"

"Let's go into the living room," Nathan says to his dad. "You can lie down on the sofa."

Oh dear god. This is even worse than I had expected, and I had been expecting bad stuff. Really bad stuff. But none of it had come close to my family actually injuring Nathan's father to the point where he has to be carted out of the room. We all stand up to follow, but Nathan shakes his head at me and I tell my family to stay in the dining room.

"Aduh, you and your Tai Chi," Big Aunt scolds. "Nah lho, you look what you done."

"Tch, is because I being hurry, if not hurry, won't happen like that," Second Aunt snaps. "Tai Chi very good for your back. I trying to help."

"I know, Er Jie, you trying to help," Ma soothes. "Ah, maybe I make my TCM drink for him to ease with the—"

"NO!" All of us shout this as one.

Ma looks hurt. "I want help. I got bring my TCM herbs, very good for pain."

"I don't think Meddy's future father-in-law would appreciate you drugging him," Fourth Aunt says.

Ma glares at her, Second Aunt glares at Big Aunt, and somehow we have come full circle. "Meddy," Ma says after a while, "you go check on them, gih. You ask him, does he want TCM drink or not. If he want I make."

I nod and creep down the hallway. For some reason, I want to make as little noise as possible. I guess because I feel like we've intruded into their lives like a whirlwind, as usual, and now the least I can do is move like a mouse. As I near the living room, I hear hushed voices speaking and freeze.

"—not quite what I expected," Annie says. "They're uh, very different from your side of the family, aren't they, Chris?"

My stomach twists. A dozen different emotions war inside me. Embarrassment, anger, just everything. Of course my family is different from Chris's family! Just because both of us come from immigrant families doesn't mean we're all carbon copies of each other.

A sigh. "Yes, Mum, it might surprise you to know that not all Asians behave the same way."

"That's not what I meant. You know that wasn't what I meant."

I feel like I need to puke. I was right. She hates them. She hates us.

"Dad, how're you feeling?"

There's a grunt, and then Chris says, in a muffled voice, "A tad better. You two go back and finish your tea. I'll be fine."

"Meddy, how is going? Everything okay?"

I practically jump right out of my skin. How did Ma manage to sneak up on me like that?

"Yeah, I was just about to—"

"Aiya, you take so long. I go and ask myself, does he want TCM drink or not."

"Ma, don't—" But short of pouncing on her and tackling her, I don't know how else to stop my mother. I watch helplessly as she barrels into the living room before I follow, my cheeks burning. I can't quite meet anyone's eye.

"Sir Chris, I so sorry about what happen," Ma announces.

Sir? What in the hell.

"I tell you what make it better, I make you my famous TCM drink, okay?" Ma turns to Annie and adds, "That's traditional Chinese medicine," very loudly, as though Annie were hard of hearing. "You know? Chinese medicine using all-natural herbs and roots and animal, not like Western medicine always using chemical."

Annie nods weakly. "Yes, I think I mentioned before that Chris sometimes takes traditional Chinese medicine. Um, I suppose if you think it might help . . ."

Ma beams, practically shivering with a sense of purpose. "Very sure it will help, pasti, will help! I got packet of TCM in my bag, you wait here—"

"No, Ma," Nathan says quickly. He knows very well what happened to Tom Cruise Sutopo's groomsmen after a dose of Ma's TCM. "Please don't bother yourself, Dad will be just fine."

"Is okay, not a bother."

"Ma, really—"

A gasp from Annie makes us all stop and turn to look at her. She's staring at Nathan as if he's just punched a baby in the face.

"Mum? You okay?"

Annie's expression is that of utter betrayal and pain. Slowly, softly, she says, "You call her 'Ma'?"

Why do I keep thinking that this evening can't possibly get any worse when it so obviously can? Our families are simply too different. Both sides are obviously baffled by the other. They'd been expecting some similarities, given Chris is not only Asian but of Chinese descent like us, but instead tonight has only highlighted how different we are.

We leave quietly not long after that, having not eaten much at all. Nathan says he'll stay here for the night, make sure his dad's okay, and I whisper, "I'm so sorry." He nods and gives me a reassuring smile, but it doesn't reach his eyes. My stomach is just a large, tight knot.

The goodbyes are painful. I'm not sure if I should try to hug Annie. When I step toward her, she visibly stiffens, so I simply stand there and nod at her, smiling apologetically. "Thank you so much for the meal."

The corners of her mouth lift ever so slightly. "Thank you for coming," she says to us all. "We'll see you at the—ah, well, we'll see you at the—the wedding." She spits out the word "wedding" as if it were stuck in her throat, as if she can't believe she's saying it.

And part of me can't believe that there will be one either, especially not after tonight.

7

"I'm so glad you guys made it!" I say for the fourteenth time that night. What can I say, I'm on my fourth Pimm's and I've gone from slightly buzzed to happy, loving drunk.

Selena grins as Seb squeals and hugs me. "Of course," Selena says. "Wouldn't have missed it for the world. My bestie, getting married!"

"Uh, excuse you, Meddy is *my* bestie?" Seb says.

"You guys are adorable," Staph says, taking another gulp of her Pimm's cocktail. "And these are amazing."

"I can't believe you're getting married in one of the most beautiful cities in the world," Seb says, "and I don't get to photograph it!"

"Hush, you're here as my guest."

"Don't worry, I'll make sure to send you all the bad shots," Staph says with a wink.

"Hey!" I groan.

"I like you," Selena says to Staphanie. "Meds, you chose a great photographer. I thought Meddy was never going to be able to settle on a photographer. It's like, you know how they say doctors make the worst patients? Well, wedding photographers make the worst brides. She kept finding fault with every photographer we found. I was beginning to think that she was going to do her own photography." Selena mimes me setting up a camera on a timer and then running back in my huge wedding gown to strike a pose, and we all burst into laughter.

"You are such an ass." I hug her tight. God, I'm so grateful for my friends, especially after the day I've had.

Nathan and I had spent the whole of today on various last-minute tasks: going to city hall to confirm our wedding registration, going to Christ Church College to go over the last-minute details, and sitting with Ama to go over the finer details of the wedding tomorrow. We also picked up Annie's dress from the dry cleaners. She showed it to me at her house, obviously pleased with how the tailoring turned out. It's a lovely dress—a knee-length gray number with little yellow flowers at the hem. It's nice, but next to my mom and aunts' outfits, Annie is going to look so underdressed. But maybe it's not the case that she'll look underdressed, more that my family will look insanely overdressed.

Under normal circumstances, spending the whole day running errands with Nathan would be a pleasant affair, but today, there was an undercurrent of . . . something. I could tell he was stressed out. It felt like there was a wedge between us, an invisible electric fence that would shock us if we overstepped. I asked him once or twice if everything was okay, after which he kissed me on the head or the cheek and told me everything was fine.

It clearly was not fine. I asked how his dad's back was, and he said it was somewhat improved this morning, though he was still in a lot of pain, and my entire head burned with shame and guilt. I asked how his mom was handling it, and his mouth pressed into a thin line and then he said, "She's fine," and changed the subject, asking me how my family and I were. "I'm fine," I told him. "We're fine."

So many fines, none of them real. I can only hope they're just normal wedding nerves. I have shot over a hundred weddings, and more than two-thirds of my couples have required a calming speech from me, or the maid of honor, or the wedding organizer. This is just one of those things. Still, the whole day, that terrible, insecure part of me just wanted to scream, "DO YOU STILL WANT TO MARRY ME BUH BUH BUH BWAAAH?" I am proud of the fact that I managed to squash down that part of me. See, I'm not totally pathetic! I was actually somewhat relieved when we finally finished the last errand and Nathan dropped me off at the hotel. We'd agreed in advance that he'd spend the night before the wedding at his parents' house and I would stay at the Randolph. I'm half happy, half sad over that decision. On the one hand, I have the privacy of the entire room to freak out in. On the other hand, I kind of wanted to freak out together with Nathan.

"Earth to Meddy," Seb says. "What are you thinking about?"

How happy I am that everyone I love is here for my wedding, I want to say. Instead, I blurt out, "I think Nathan's having second thoughts."

"Aww, hon," Seb says, "he's probably just having those typical wedding jitters, you know what they're like, god knows we've had to talk more than our fair share of brides and grooms down off the ledge."

"True story," Staph says, nodding wisely. "And I've seen the way Nathan looks at you. That's marriage-level love, that is."

"They were like that in college too," Selena says. "Can you imagine how gross it was being her roommate?"

"You poor, unfortunate soul," Seb says. "How did you even stand it?"

Selena places her hand on her forehead dramatically. "I don't know how I managed, honestly. Anyway, our point is, you and Nathan are so clearly meant to be. This whole anxiety thing is like what Seb and Staph said: normal wedding-day jitters."

"I hope so." Then I feel absolutely terrible for being a whiny baby and force a smile. "Come on, let's go dance."

The next two hours or so pass by in a blur of us jumping and dancing and more drinks. At some point, we all decide we're done for the night and stumble out of the throbbing club with our arms flung around one another, laughing and talking way too loud. My ears are still buzzing and the world is swaying at my feet.

"I wanna go to a pub," Seb says.

"Yes! Let's go to the Eagle and Child. That was where Tolkien wrote *The Hobbit*, you know," Selena says.

"Really?" I blink, trying to envision Tolkien writing in a pub.

"Well, I don't know if he actually wrote there or if he just went there to get sloshed, but he was definitely a patron. I read they have a plaque and everything."

"I would love to, but I should go to bed. I have to wake up early for hair and makeup tomorrow."

"Yeah, you do," Staph says, "because YOU ARE GETTING MARRIED! Ahh!"

We all laugh and squeal at one another.

"Okay, Selena and I will go to the Eagle and Child. What about you, Staph? You coming?" Seb says.

Staph shakes her head. "I have to work tomorrow," she says, winking at me, "so I'll call it a night too. I'll walk you back to your hotel, Meddy."

We part ways and Staph and I head toward the Randolph. "Your friends are so great," Staph says.

"They really are. I'm lucky to have them in my life. I'm lucky to have you in my life too." I link my arm through hers and she smiles at me. "Are you going to be okay walking back to your hotel alone?"

"Don't worry about me," Staph says. "I'm going to meet up with Third Uncle for ice cream at G&D's. That's not very far away from the Randolph at all. I'll be fine."

"Okay, if you're sure." At the entrance to my hotel, we hug again and then part ways. I go into the lobby, smiling dopily, and rummage through my bag for my key card. My fingers brush up against a box. Dammit! I'd prepared little gifts for both Seb and Selena and, at the last minute, had decided to give Staph one too, because she'd been so helpful with all of the prep leading up to the wedding. I take out the box and then totter back out onto the street, pausing to let the chilly air sober me up a bit more.

This time of night, the streets are almost empty, save for random groups of rowdy, drunk college kids. I spot Staphanie's form in the distance and walk briskly toward her. She's on her phone. I try to call out her name, but my voice is hoarse from shouting in the club and I end up coughing instead. No choice but to jog to catch up with her.

A few paces away, I catch snatches of conversation.

"Yes, it's still on," Staph says, irritation showing clearly in her voice. "No, I'm not drunk, I spat—"

Huh? Scenes from the evening flash through my mind. Staph had carried a bottle of cider with her the whole night, which she'd used to chase down whatever shots we took. But now that I think about it, did she use the bottle to spit the shots into instead of chasing them down? I can't—I don't understand why she would. I slow down my steps so I won't be breathing hard and keep a few paces behind her.

"—I needed to—partying otherwise—get suspicious."

What's going on? I walk even closer to her.

And then Staph says something that makes my blood freeze and my brain short-circuit.

"Yes, target is still—tomorrow. We—take her out—wedding."

I'm so shocked by this revelation that I don't realize she's stopped walking until it's too late. I walk right into her. She turns around and her mouth drops open. It's as though I'm seeing Staph—the real Staph—for the first time ever. Without the layer of professionalism or friendship masking her, she looks different. More sharp-edged, more dangerous. For a second, neither one of us moves, then she slowly lifts the phone to her ear and says, "I'll call you back." She places the phone back in her bag without breaking eye contact. "What are you doing here, Meddy?"

"I—uh, I came back because I forgot to give you this—" I raise my hand and realize with a start that I've squeezed the gift box so hard that it is now the shape of the perfume bottle nestled inside. My breath comes out in a small laugh. "Sorry, I kinda crushed it while listening to you talk about taking someone out at my wedding. What the *shit*, Staph?" I will her to deny it, to tell me I've drunk too much, that I've somehow mistakenly taken some of Ma's pot, but she does none of these things.

She blinks, her eyes wide.

"Are you seriously going to kill someone tomorrow?" My voice comes out shrill and unrecognizable.

And then her hand shoots out, quick as a viper, and grabs my arm. I startle, jumping back—or trying to, at least. Her grip is shockingly strong. I pride myself on being strong too, but that's me at the best of times, not me after seven shots of hard liquor and a full night of dancing. Every instinct of mine is off. I try to pull my arm out of her grip, but she yanks me along like a toddler into a nearby alley. Fear crashes through the alcohol-induced fog and suddenly I'm back in the car with Ah Guan, realizing that I'm about to die. I open my mouth to scream—why didn't I scream earlier, fuck, just how wasted am I—but Staph's hand is over it. I try to bite her and she removes it from my face. I take a quick inhale, but her hand darts back, and before I know it, the breath is knocked out of me.

Jesus. She's broken my neck. Each breath I take is immediately coughed up. I fall forward. Oh god, air. Air!

"Stay calm," Staphanie hisses. "I sort of punched you in the throat. You'll be able to breathe in a few seconds. I think. I hope? Meddy, are you okay?"

No, I'm not fucking okay, you broke my neck, I try to say, but end up coughing again. A few excruciating moments pass and I realize that she probably hasn't broken my neck, because then I'd probably be dead.

"I had to do it, I'm so sorry, I couldn't have you shouting for help. Look, argh, shit, Meddy."

I draw in a shaky breath and don't immediately cough it out. Another gulp of air. Gasp, gasp, breathe. "What"—I gasp, then swallow and try again—"the hell is going on?"

Staph blinks hard. "I—ugh—yes, I'm sorry, we *are* going to take someone out tomorrow?"

The words are clear, but they're also unclear. I mean, I hear each one perfectly fine and know what each single word means on its own, but strung together in a sentence, the words Staphanie is saying might as well be German. Which I don't speak, to be clear. I snort, straightening up, my eyes tearing with mirth. "Because what, you guys are yakuza? Cartel? Mafia?"

There's a moment of uncertainty, and then Staph's face hardens, and she lifts her chin. "Yes, Meddy, we are. We're mafia."

"Ha." The laugh coughs out weakly and dies immediately. Because it's obvious from her face that Staph isn't shitting around. She really does mean it. "But—wait, what? But we went to dim sum together," I say weakly, as though that some-how means something, as though mafia can't go to Top Island Dim Sum on a nice Sunday morning. But really, they seem so normal. "No tattoos," I blurt out.

Staph shrugs. "Ama doesn't approve of tats. She's our matri-arch, in case you haven't figured that out."

"Did you—are you armed?" I whisper. Oh god, am I going to be shot?

She shakes her head. "How the hell would I have smuggled a gun on the plane, Meddy?"

"I don't know! I don't know how you mafia people . . . ma-fia!" I need to stop saying the word "mafia." "But—why us? Why at our wedding? Who are you taking out?"

Staph's eyes soften. "I can't tell you that, but trust me, the person we're taking out is evil. They deserve whatever's coming to them, okay?"

"No. NO! Not okay. What the fuck?"

"Come on, Meddy, be reasonable—"

"And let you kill someone at my wedding?" I snort. "You're crazy. I'm calling the cops."

"You don't want to do that." Her voice is steel.

Shit, I probably shouldn't have said that last part out loud, but in my defense, I am lacking oxygen due to my windpipe being crushed—okay, not crushed but definitely bruised—and also the aforementioned alcohol.

"I'll tell you why you don't want to do that," Staph says.

I steel myself, expecting her to tell me that she'll kill me or Ma or any of my aunties or Nathan. But then she says some-thing that's somehow even worse. "Because we'll tell the police you killed some dude at Santa Lucia, and then you and your whole family, Nathan included, will go to prison for a long, long time."

8

I don't remember the walk back to the Randolph. I don't remember walking up the beautiful staircase, nor passing by the numerous centuries-old paintings, nor making my way down the hallway to the bedrooms. I don't remember passing by my room, not giving the door a second glance, and ending up instead outside Ma's room. I don't remember raising my hand and knocking, but all of a sudden she's at the door, her hair up in rollers, blinking with confusion at me.

"Ada apa, Meddy? Is time for hair and makeup?"

I shake my head wordlessly, and Ma peers closely at me.

"Aiya, you just come back from club? Aduh, so late. Tomorrow you get eyebags, you see later, you will regret it."

Eyebags. Tomorrow. I give a shaky laugh at the thought. Right, because tomorrow's my wedding day, and I should be worrying about things like eyebags and definitely not things like the mafia.

Ma must have realized that I'm barely holding on to my sanity, because her face suddenly turns serious. "Meddy, what is wrong? Ayo masuk." She takes my arm and ushers me into her dark room, pausing to turn on the lights.

Second Aunt sits bolt upright in her bed. "Wha? Time to do makeup, is it?"

"No, Er Jie," Ma says. "Meddy is here, I think something happen."

Second Aunt exchanges a look with Ma. "Oh no, who you kill?"

"What? Nobody!"

Second Aunt shrugs. "Last time you show up middle night looking like this, is because you kill date. Who know, maybe this time you kill groomman?"

"No, nobody died, okay?"

"Oh no. I know what happen!" Ma says, her face contorting in sorrow. "Even worse than Meddy kill somebody. Nathan call off wedding, right?"

"No! Also, how is that worse than me killing someone? Could you guys just—I need a minute." I rush to the bathroom, turn on the faucet, and splash some icy cold water on my face. I fill a glass with the cold water and gulp it down, then fill another and gulp that as well. My reflection stares back at me, eyes bleary, cheeks splotchy, and hair resembling a bird's nest. I'm a mess. But the cold water revives me and I take a deep breath. I'm okay. I'm fine. This is fine. I've handled worse before. Like that night I killed a guy. *Accidentally.*

By the time I come out of the bathroom, I'm only half-surprised to find Big Aunt and Fourth Aunt in the room as well. All the lights are on and Ma is cutting up a mango while Second Aunt makes tea for everyone. Where did she even find a mango at a hotel in Oxford?

"Wedding is off," Second Aunt is saying in a hushed voice.

"The wedding isn't off. I wish we could call it off, but we can't."

Ma gasps. "Meddy, why you say that? Why you would wish for that?"

"I don't—I'm not wishing for it—I just—" And then it all comes out in a torrent of tears. The night of clubbing, me forgetting Staph's gift, me overhearing her on the phone, and her awful revelation. "And then she said if we called the wedding off or told the cops or anyone else, she'd tell the cops about how we killed Ah Guan and they'd throw us all in prison."

Four stunned faces meet the end of this statement. The silence stretches for what seems like an eternity, and then Big Aunt stands up and shuffles over to the desk.

"Big Aunt, what are you—" I stop when she picks up the electric kettle and starts pouring the hot water into respective cups.

"Tea. Tea good for you, help you think," she mutters.

Second Aunt stands up and immediately dives into a Tai Chi pose, while Ma jumps up and fetches the plate of mangoes. Fourth Aunt studies her nails—she has forgone the feathers in favor of rhinestones that run down the entire length of her fingers. I should've expected this reaction from my family, but seeing it actually happen is still pretty unreal.

Second Aunt pauses mid-pose. "So whole family is mafia? Is include Hendry also?"

Big Aunt side-eyes her cunningly. "Of course is include Hendry. Your boyfriend," she says triumphantly, "is no good."

"Not my boyfriend," Second Aunt spits out, lunging aggressively into a different pose.

Big Aunt snorts. "Oh? Not boyfriend? Then what you call going to eat, just two of you? So hussy, later people talk."

"We just run into each other at Starbuck," Second Aunt hisses, pronouncing it "set-tar-buck."

"Since when you go Starbuck, ah?" Big Aunt says.

"Um, could we focus on the whole mafia part instead of the boyfriend-or-not-boyfriend thing? They do illicit things for a living and, uh, kill people who get in their way. And they're using my wedding as an opportunity to kill someone. You got that part, right?"

"Yes, yes, I know what mafia do," Big Aunt says, handing me a cup of tea. How did she recover so fast from the shock of what I just told them? "Daigu bilangin ya. When I little, mafia big problem in Jakarta. Waduh, every night got shouting here and there, and then morning will have dead body on street, right outside house."

"Jesus, what part of Jakarta did you guys live in?" I say.

"Aduh, no matter which part you live in, will have such problem," Big Aunt says. "This big reason why we move. Now you kids growing up so soft, you hear someone is mafia, you get scared."

"Uh, yeah? I think that's kind of the normal reaction to finding out that your wedding vendors are mafia."

Big Aunt just makes a *tch* sound and pops a sliced mango in her mouth, chewing while also somehow sneering. I can't quite tell what she's sneering at—me or the mafia? I turn to Ma. Out of the four sisters, she's the most cowardly. Her cowardice has obviously been passed down to me, the pansy who finds criminals intimidating. But Ma's eyes are aglow as she chews on her mango slice, more excited than scared.

"Eh iya! You remember that next-door boy? Apa ya his name . . ."

"Hugh Grant Halim?" I hazard a guess. I'm starting to feel light-headed. "Tom Hanks Suwandi?"

"Apa sih?" Ma tuts. "What all those ridiculous names? Stop making fun."

"Sorry," I mumble. I guess I really am being an ass.

"Ah, yes," Ma says, snapping her fingers. "His name Abraham Lincoln. Yes, Abraham Lincoln Irawan."

"Of course. Why was I guessing Tom Hanks? US Presidents, obviously!" I'm being horrible and rude and I know it, but really now. Why is my family so calm about the world-shaking news I just dropped on their laps?

"We call him Abi. Oh, he had huge crush on your Second Aunt. Ya, Er Jie? You remember Abi?"

Second Aunt barely pauses her Tai Chi moves. She glances at us while doing Snake Creeps Through the Grass and bites back a coy smile. "Yes, he very in love with me, aduh, so embarrassing, deh, every morning we go to school, he ask me to sit on his bike."

"Something wrong with you," Big Aunt mutters, "is why bad guy always coming to you."

"Er Jie, they can sense your inner naughty girl," Fourth Aunt laughs.

Second Aunt purses her lips and ignores them.

"This is all very sweet," I say with increasing desperation, "but what does this have to do with the mafia?"

"Tch, Meddy, be patient, okay, you don't interrupt your auntie, so rude," Ma scolds.

"I always tell him no, I not some ngga bener girl who will just sit on his bike," Second Aunt says. Big Aunt sniffs and Second Aunt shoots her a glare, then moves into a different position, raising her arms up dramatically. "Wah, Abi become more desperate, every day bring me flower or kweitau, the kweitau always smell so good but I never accept."

"I accepted them," Fourth Aunt pipes up. "I always told him I'd give them to you, and then I'd eat them myself."

Second Aunt freezes mid-position and stares at Fourth Aunt.

"What?" Fourth Aunt says. "Like you said, it smelled amazing, and I was like, what, four years old? I didn't know any better. You!" She turns to Ma. "You were supposed to be watching me, but you were too busy playing in the ditch, looking for tadpoles or whatever, so I was left alone. I had to fend for myself."

"Aiya!" Second Aunt cries. "No wonder why Abi never give up. He think I accept his kweitau! Aduh, you, ya! Cause me big trouble."

"Why, what happened, Second Aunt?" Despite myself, I've gotten sucked into this inane story.

"Well!" Second Aunt huffs. "When he twelve years old, Abi join the mafia. He tell me he do it to earn more money, then can buy me Mercedes."

"Oh no," I whisper.

"You see what happen because you so greedy?" Ma says to Fourth Aunt.

Fourth Aunt rolls her eyes. "Right, some idiot kid joined the mafia because a four-year-old kept taking his kweitau, cry me a river."

"Please tell me Abraham Lincoln grew out of it and did well in school and is now happily married with three children and a dog," I say.

There is silence. Big Aunt chews another piece of mango noisily. Second Aunt plunges into a different position. Ma slurps her tea meaningfully, and Fourth Aunt plucks at her eyebrows.

"Oh no," I moan. "Did he die?"

"Choi, touch wood!" Second Aunt says. "Of course not, you so silly."

I relax a little. "So what happened to him?"

"The mafia get him to do all sort of bad thing. Stealing from his teacher in school. Then steal from principal office, aduh, so bad. He get find out and of course they expel him. Then his family lose face. Sooo ashame! They beg him stop, get out of mafia, mafia so bad, but no, he says must get me Mercedes. So finally they throw him out." Second Aunt sighs and shakes her head dramatically.

"Like, disowned him?" I say.

Second Aunt nods. "So mafia take him in, raise him as their son."

"Wow. Then what?"

"Then he get older, we hear he take over mafia, then become mafia lord, the end," Second Aunt says simply. She stops doing Tai Chi and sits down. "Wah, feels good to stretch. Eh, where is my tea?"

"Wait." I blink. "That's it? That's the story? What the—why would you tell me that story?"

Ma sighs. "Don't you see, Meddy? Because Abi is so . . . he is so not impress, you know? He so small and so quiet and always mooning after your Second Aunt. But someone like him can become mafia lord, so I think mafia not that scary."

"What? That's not how this works! That's why you told me the story, to tell me that even someone as lame as Abraham Lincoln could become a mafia lord? When was the last time you even saw him?"

Second Aunt barely looks up from her tea. "Before he leave neighborhood to join mafia family, maybe he fourteen, fifteen."

"You don't think he would've changed a heck of a lot since then? He's probably really scary right now."

They all laugh. "Oh, Meddy, you don't know what he like. He always so shy, always so polite too, call me Big Sis," Big Aunt says.

I grab my phone, open up a search window, and google

Abraham Lincoln Irawan. My eyes widen. Wow, how did I not know about this guy before tonight? There are over a thousand hits, most of them news articles from Indonesian news outlets.

MAFIA KING ABRAHAM IRAWAN RESPONSIBLE FOR
MURDER OF HERMANSAH CAHYADI

SCOURGE OF JAKARTA ABRAHAM IRAWAN ESCAPES
TO PAPUA NEW GUINEA

I open up the Images section and yep, there are hundreds of photos of him. Just as I had feared, he looks completely and utterly terrifying—he's muscled, sure, but that's not the half of it. There are tattoos all over his body, all the way up his neck and down his hands. He looks like the kind of person who could fuck shit up. "This him?"

My family leans over and four mouths drop open.

"Wah! What happen to him? Ih, look at all the tattoos," Second Aunt says, shuddering.

"Aduh, so scary," Ma says.

Big Aunt nods, eyes wide. "This little Abi?" she whispers. "Oh dear."

"He got hot," Fourth Aunt says. They all glare at her and she shrugs. "What? He did!"

I take my phone away and they all protest, but I lock the screen. "Look, all I'm trying to say is: mafia is freaking dangerous. Look at this guy! You guys thought you knew him, but look how he's turned out. He's killing people left and right. So I think we need to take Staphanie and her family seriously."

Ma purses her lips. "Well, Staphanie and family not look like that."

I sigh. "You have a point, but that doesn't mean they're not dangerous." Seriously, why is she being so chill about this?

"Meddy is correct," Big Aunt says, "we play safe. We go police."

"No, we can't do that," I say hurriedly. "Remember? I told you how they'd tell the cops about us and Ah Guan if we canceled the wedding? We'd all go to prison, even Nathan. Even Jacqueline and Maureen!"

Big Aunt mutters a curse in Hokkien. "Terus gimana? What they want us to do?"

"They want us to have the wedding as planned and pretend that we don't know anything so that they can take out a target."

"What this 'take out' mean? Taking away? Like when you say, 'get Chinese takeout,' like that?" Big Aunt asks.

"No, dear big sister, it means killing," Fourth Aunt says. "They wanna kill someone at the wedding."

Ma, Big Aunt, and Second Aunt all look up from their teacups and pause mid-mango-chew. "This true, Meddy?"

I nod. "Yeah, why do you think I've been freaking out this whole time?"

Ma's face twists in horror and her mouth drops open in a wail. "Aiya! Cannot! How can?"

I nod furiously. Good, it's finally sunk in how dangerous Staph's family is.

"So unlucky!" Ma cries.

I stop nodding. "Wait, what?"

"Kill someone on your wedding?" she snaps. "Will curse your marriage! Later no grandbabies!"

"Um. Sure, yeah. Although the more pressing issue is the murder itself, maybe?" Oh, who am I kidding? The number one issue for my mother will always be grandbabies.

"Tch," Ma says. "Yes, yes, murder bad, but murder on someone's wedding day even worse! Ugh, how can someone so evil want to curse me like that? Curse me to never become grandmother!"

"Alternatively, how can someone be so evil as to want to murder somebody else? But whatever," I mutter, more to myself than anyone. Then I say in a louder voice, "Yeah, totally, would be a shame if Nathan and I couldn't have babies because of it. We should stop them."

Ma nods so hard she resembles a bobblehead. "Yes! We must stop them. Right?" She looks at Big Aunt.

No one speaks as Big Aunt puts down her teacup gently on the table. "Meddy," she says after a while. "Who they want to kill?"

"I don't know," I sigh. "Staph wouldn't tell me. She did say that whoever it was deserves to die, so I'm guessing someone from a different mafia family?" That makes me pause. Good lord, how many mafia members do I have present at my wedding?

"Okay, we go through guest list," Big Aunt says. "You have it?"

"Sure, yeah." I bring out my phone and send the guest list to the family WhatsApp group chat. There are a few moments of silence as we all study the list.

"No one from our side," Fourth Aunt says.

"Mm," Big Aunt agrees, nodding smugly. "Nobody on our side can involve in such thing, we are very good family."

I look down the list of guests from our side of the family and they're right. No one on it jumps out as an obvious mafia target. "Okay, but so's Nathan's family. You've all met his parents, do they strike you as the mafia type?"

Second Aunt cackles at that. "His dad can't even do Tai Chi, how he going to kill someone?"

"Harsh, but yes, that's a good point. And I've met a few of Nathan's relatives; they're all kind of like that—very prim and proper." I look at the list again and it's like a light bulb's suddenly turned on in my head. "Business," I breathe out.

"Eh, what?" Ma says.

"Business people!" I say the words so quickly my tongue trips over them. "Nathan's got lots of investors and business partners—people with loads of money who fly private jets and stuff like that. They're more likely to be involved in shady things."

"Oooh, make so much sense!" Ma says. She pats my cheek with pride. "My daughter, always so smart."

"You and I need to have a conversation about which things make you proud, but thanks, Ma."

"So which ones, his business investors and partners?" Big Aunt asks.

I scan the list and pick out a few names that I recognize. "Braian Tjoeng. I think he owns—"

"Tjoeng! Oh yes, that very big developer, second biggest in Indonesia. Very billionaire," Big Aunt says.

"Okay, so that's one. Lilian Citra—they're quite close and he treats her with such deference, I think she must be one of his biggest investors. And Elmon Negorojo—I think his family owns coffee plantations on Indonesia's islands."

"Oh, those island, some of them grow coffee, some grow palm trees, then some grow cocaine, who know?" Ma says. "Too many island for government to know."

"Er." I try to imagine Elmon, a bespectacled, quiet guy, as a drug lord. "Maybe? Anyway, these are the only three I can think of who are big enough to become mafia targets."

"Okay, good," Big Aunt says. "We can handle."

"Um. How?"

"Tomorrow, we protect them. We make sure nothing bad happen to them. We catch Staphanie and family when they try to murder, then we catch, haiyah! And then send them to police. Once police find out they are mafia trying to kill someone, no matter what they tell police, police won't believe."

They all nod at this, looking very resolute, and my heart swells to fill my chest. My family, always so ready to jump to my rescue. I don't deserve them. "Thank you, Big Aunt. That's a good idea. Yeah, we'll do that. We won't let them kill anyone."

"Of course not," Ma says, a fierce fire burning in her eyes. "Nobody come in between me and grandbabies!"

PART TWO

◆

MAKING SURE YOU ENJOY YOUR WEDDING

(Is it even a wedding if nobody gets killed?)

9

I wake up with butterflies fluttering in my stomach, a bubbly feeling of excitement that makes me open my eyes with a big smile. I'm marrying Nathan today! I reach for my phone and grin when I find messages from him.

Nathan (06:32AM): [Sends an image]

The image loads and when it opens, I can't help giggling out loud as if I'm all of twelve years old. It's a screenshot of his contacts list, and I'm no longer listed as Meddelin Chan, but as "Wifey."

Nathan (06:33AM): I couldn't wait to change it. ☻

God, how is he this adorable?

Meddy (07:02AM): You are adorkable.

Nathan (07:02AM): There you are. Can't wait to see you. Can't wait to marry you!

My grin is so wide that it actually hurts my cheeks.

Meddy (07:03AM): Me too. Okay, gtg get ready. See you later . . . hubs! 😘

I close the chat window and frown at my WhatsApp notifications. There are . . . a lot of messages in the family group chat, complete with the usual indecipherable emoji game.

Second Aunt (06:45AM): Meddy U awake already or not?? We already in Christ Church room. Makeup person here already. The U-Kno-Whu. 🤕 ✉️ 🎉

Ma (06:46AM): Is Second Uncle. Makeup person is Second Uncle. Aduh, so scary, have mafia touch my face . . . !

Second Aunt (06:47AM): Aiya why U say on the chat??! Later polise will see!!!! 😡 😫

Fourth Aunt (06:48AM): Yeah, the cops would totally be looking through our phones and this will be incriminating. 🙄

Ma (06:49AM): How to delet message????

Big Aunt (06:50AM): You klik on message, then got say delet then you choose delet. 👊 ☠️ 🤖

Ma (06:51AM): How? I not see delet where got? 👍🏻 🤠

Ma (06:52AM): Ah I see it I think.

Ma (06:52AM): [Ma has left the chatroom]

Fourth Aunt (06:53AM): Typical. Of course she had to make a dramatic exit. 🙄

Second Aunt (06:53AM): Eh, Nat say she exidentelly leave. U add her back can or not?

Fourth Aunt (06:54AM): Sorry, don't know how to. 🙇🏻‍♀️

Big Aunt (06:55AM): Meddy can you add your mama back or not ah?

Second Aunt (06:56AM): Yes Meddy will kno how. Meddy U wake up now okay Meddy.

Big Aunt (06:57AM): Meddy hello pls wake up good morning hello.

It goes on for a while, all of them incessantly sending messages to wake me up even though I've obviously turned my phone to silent mode. I slam the phone face down on the bed, the butterflies in my stomach mutating into killer wasps. Mafia. Shit.

The events of last night rush back, and suddenly I feel ill, all that cheap alcohol bubbling up in my stomach. I make it to the bathroom before I start to dry heave into the sink. Oh god. How could I have forgotten? Staphanie and her family are *fam-*

ily. Like the fucking Sopranos. My wedding photographer, the person I'd thought was a friend, someone I trusted on a personal level, is a literal gangster. I feel so violated at the realization that while I thought of her as a real friend, she'd been working me as a job.

I splash freezing cold water onto my face and gargle mouthwash. In the bright light of day, without the blurring effects of alcohol, I realize that that was one question I had failed to ask Staphanie. It seems like too big of a coincidence. The knot in my stomach tightens. There's only one possibility: that it wasn't a coincidence. They must have sought us out, gotten hold of Ma or the aunties and then wooed us into hiring them. I glare at the mirror, hating myself for falling for their trick. How could I have been such a terrible judge of people? After Ah Guan, I thought I was more careful, I thought I'd developed some sort of radar for baddies. But nope, here I am, as naive as ever.

And now my wedding is going to be an event where a target—literally another human being—is taken out. "Taken out" sounds so flippant when I put it that way, as if I'm talking about a date rather than someone getting killed.

Oh god. I didn't even think about how they'd do it. Shoot the person in the head? My breath shudders out of me and I squeeze my eyes shut. I see it all the time on TV and never bat an eyelid, but now the thought of it sickens me. Or maybe they'd stab the person? Or break their neck? I try to think of Staphanie twisting someone else's head to the point of breaking and find, to my horror, that I can very easily imagine her doing it. I see her in my mind's eye, face resolute, coming up behind some unsuspecting man while he mingles and eats canapés during cocktail hour. I imagine her sliding a little knife out and bringing her arm up smoothly until the blade is at his throat. She drags it swiftly across his throat. Blood spurts, people scream—

Shit.

I breathe out shakily. No. Don't think like that. We'll be there to stop her and her family. Whatever happens, we will stop them. I quickly finish washing up, shrug on a pair of jeans and a shirt, and make my way to the lobby. Outside, I catch a cab to Christ Church College, where we've been provided a room specifically to get ready for the wedding. Staphanie's already arranged to have all of our dresses steam-ironed and hung inside the Christ Church room. I grimace at the thought of Staphanie running all these errands. So helpful. So deceitful.

Ma opens the door and noise spills out, my aunts squawking as usual, but this time, a man's voice is also mixed into the chaos, just as squawky as theirs. "Meddy! Aiya, you sleep so late."

For a second, all I can do is stop and stare. Ma is in full-on Chinese-Indo hair and makeup—everything big, everything larger than life. Her face is caked with powder—her skin ultra-white, her eyelids heavy with fake lashes, her eyebrows extra dark and thick. Her hair, normally embiggened by meticulously applied rollers, is now so huge it looks like she's wearing a cloud. And on top of the pouf of hair is the dreaded Komodo dragon fascinator sipping its tea.

"What you think?" Ma asks nervously, patting her hair gently. "Too pale? More blush?"

"Uh . . ."

Ma doesn't wait for me to reply before turning around and walking back inside the room. The dragon's tail nearly takes my eye out. I hurry after her, grimacing as I take in the chaotic scene.

At the dressing table, Second Uncle is clipping wads of fake hair onto Big Aunt's head, his teeth gritted with obvious annoyance as Second Aunt looks over his shoulder. As he inserts a large pin into Big Aunt's hair to secure her fascinator, Big Aunt yelps. "Aduh, you pinch scalp!"

"Need to make sure the dragon very secure," Second Uncle mutters, stabbing another pin into her huge hairdo.

"You do it wrong!" Second Aunt snaps. "You see, this what happen when no-good gangster think you can do highly skill profession like hair and makeup artist! You see? YOU SEE?"

Oh god. Please tell me not even my family is crazy enough to speak like this to THE ACTUAL MAFIA.

Who am I kidding? Of course they are.

Big Aunt is watching her reflection with quiet displeasure and pressing her temple with one finger. Now and again, her gaze flicks upward to shoot Second Uncle a cold glare, but her lips are kept firmly shut.

Fourth Aunt is lounging back on the sofa, applying her own makeup. "No offense, Mister, but I'm not going to trust some fake makeup artist with this masterpiece," she mutters as she slathers on foundation with expert ease.

And now I realize that Second Uncle probably knows nothing about hair and makeup. It feels like a large rock is crushing my chest. All those beautiful images they'd shown us at dim sum, all the hair and makeup examples and the bouquets and everything, they must've just been stolen off the Internet. I recall, now, how Second Aunt had recognized one of the images. Of course. They must've just saved photos from Pinterest and put them in their portfolio.

Rage boils through my veins. In addition to being ruthless criminals, my wedding vendors are also *plagiarizers*. Ugh!

"You even know how to use curler? Hanh? You know or not? I think you not know!" Second Aunt nags. "You think so easy is it? Just because you big man, so gangster, you think you know how to use lipstick wand?"

Second Uncle doesn't reply to the onslaught, but from the way he *tch*-es under his breath and how knotted his forehead is, it can't be long before he snaps and—I don't know—does whatever it is that mafia members do when they snap. Maybe pull out a machete from his back pocket and start hacking away at us there and then? That's gotta be a possibility. Right?

I hurry over, giving him a small nod. I should be nice to him, given the worrying possibility of a machete attack, but I can't quite bring myself to smile at him, knowing who he really is. "Hey, Second Uncle."

He glances at me and goes, "Hmmh."

Second Aunt and Ma's mouths drop open and their faces go red. "That is not how you greet bride!" Second Aunt scolds. "Bride is your customer, and customer always right. You are usually first one to see bride on wedding day, so you set tone for wedding. You must greet bride with big smile, like this, see?" Second Aunt waves her hands across her face and stretches her mouth into a Joker-esque grin.

Second Uncle exhales slowly. "Enjelin, I tell you, I sorry—"

"Hanh! You sorry? You sorry why? Nothing to be sorry about, kok!" Second Aunt turns away from him abruptly.

Ah. I see. Second Aunt is being even more in-your-face than usual because she's hurt. The past few months, she and Second Uncle have been—I don't know—dating? Well, not dating, because the Chinese-Indo community doesn't believe in "dating." They call the stage between friendship and marriage "pendeka-tan," which translates to "getting closer." The past few months, she and Second Uncle have been getting closer to each other, and the realization that he's mafia with ulterior motives must've really stung. My heart aches for her.

"Second Aunt . . ." I have no idea what to say. I'm sorry your sort-of-kind-of-boyfriend turned out to be mafia?

Second Aunt harrumphs. "I just teaching him, he want to be fake hair and makeup artist, he have to do properly. Everything you do, do it well, otherwise don't bother doing, that is what I say."

"It's a very good philosophy," I say in my most placating voice. "Very relevant. Um, Second Aunt, I know this is a huge favor for me to ask, but um—no offense to you, Second Uncle—but since, uh, my makeup artist has turned out to be a . . . a fake makeup artist, could you possibly do my makeup, Second Aunt, pl—"

Second Aunt's whoop nearly deafens me. Her face brightens up immediately, erasing all traces of heartbreak. "YES! Of course! Aduh, I want asking you, but I scared, I thought maybe, oh no, Meddy won't want, but aduh, the thought of some gangster doing your makeup, aduh, Meddy, it break my heart, adu-duh—"

"Don't talk so much," Big Aunt cuts in. "You better quickly do it."

Second Aunt's mouth snaps shut and she shoots Big Aunt a glare. "Yes, yes, okay. Come, Meddy. You sit here." She takes my arm and pulls me to a chair at the small dining table and pushes me into it before taking a step back and studying me. She tilts her face this way and that, muttering for a while, then claps her hands. "Okay, I know perfect look for you."

There's a knock on the door, making all of us jump.

"Hello? Everybody decent?" Selena calls out.

"It's Selena and Seb!" I hop up. But before I can move toward the door, Second Uncle reaches out and grabs my arm tightly.

"Remember," he growls, as my family watches, shocked, "no telling truth about my family."

Cold fear stabs into my belly.

"How dare?!" Ma cries. "You let go my daughter now!" Even Fourth Aunt is getting up from her chaise longue, looking concerned.

There's another knock, and this time Seb's voice comes through the door. "Helloooo, we come bearing coffee and scones."

Second Uncle narrows his eyes at me, ignoring everyone else. "Understand?"

Somehow, I manage to nod. He lets go of me and I sag with relief, my heart thundering against my rib cage. Jesus. That went from weird to really fucking scary in the space of a single second. Ma rushes to my side.

She puts an arm around me. "Meddy, you okay?"

"Yeah, I'm fine, Ma. Don't worry." I take a deep breath. I can do this. I can pretend to be calm and lie to my best friends on my wedding day. This is totally fine. Through the mirror, Big Aunt gives me a grim smile and a small nod. I know it's her way of telling me to be strong. I've got this. We've got this.

I open the door to find not just Selena and Seb, but also Staphanie, who brandishes her camera in my face.

She grins wide like a shark as Selena and Seb hug me. "Happy wedding day, Meddy," she says. "This is going to be FUN."

10

By now, the room has become unbearably crowded. The college has given us the largest suite room, but even so, put four loud aunties, one surly, potentially dangerous uncle, two exuberant friends, one deranged fake friend, plus myself into an enclosed space, and the noise level reaches a pitch that makes me want to jump out the window. Maybe I'd feel differently if none of the mafia crap was happening. Maybe I'd actually feel happy and carefree and not at all like I'm about to burst into tears at any given moment.

I stand back in a daze as Seb, Selena, and Staphanie breeze past me and loud, happy greetings fill the room. My family greets Selena and Seb like their long-lost children, telling them how grateful they are that they flew all the way here just for me. Everything they say seems so heartfelt and genuine. How are they so good at pretending that everything's okay? Meanwhile, here I am, frozen at the door.

The click of a shutter startles me. Staph lowers her camera. "The nervous bride to be," she muses.

I stare at her. She looks so different in the light of day. I try to remember her as she was last night—sharp-edged and raw and as dangerous as a viper. Now she's wearing natural makeup, her hair is tied back neatly, and her clothes say, *Don't mind me; I'm just part of the background.* She looks so sweet and young and totally incapable of killing anyone. I had wondered, as I tossed and turned in bed last night, full of anger and self-hatred, how I could've missed it all. Over the past few months, Staph and I had gotten close to each other and I'd stopped seeing her as my photographer and started seeing her as my friend. Surely I should've realized it sooner?

But now, seeing her in person after her revelation, I know that I didn't stand a chance. She is so good at hiding what she truly is. She looks as wholesome as a ray of sunshine, as comforting as a warm loaf of bread. In fact, if Second Uncle hadn't just accosted me minutes ago, the sight of Staph now would've made me question if I'd imagined everything that happened last night. I mean, I was pretty wasted; it's possible that I'd dreamed it all up.

Staph's eyes widen, her smile unmoving, and she tucks a stray lock of hair behind my ear. "Big smile, Meddy. Don't want to make people wonder," she says in a low voice.

Yep, definitely did not imagine last night. I snap out of my daze and shy away from her touch before brushing past her.

A loud pop slices through the noise and my heart jumps to my throat. Gunshot! For a second, I'm frozen, all sorts of things flying through my mind. Did she shoot me? Where's the pain? Am I about to feel it? Shit, shit—

Cheers and applause come from inside the bedroom.

"I think that was a bottle of champagne," Staph says drily as she walks past me and into the bedroom.

Champagne. Of course. I straighten up, trying to catch my breath, and make my way back into the bedroom. Just as Staph predicted, a bottle of champagne had been opened and Seb is pouring it into several glasses. Selena rushes over to me with two flutes. She places one in my hand and waits until everybody is holding one.

"To my best friend, Meddelin Chan," she says. "May you have the best wedding there ever was in the history of weddings. You deserve it."

Everyone cheers and I smile weakly. The best wedding. Right. I'm about to down my glass but change my mind and take a small sip instead. If I'm supposed to foil the mafia's plan and keep some poor sod alive, I'm going to need all of my wits about me. You wouldn't know that from my family, though—all of them, Big Aunt included, down their glasses quickly. I guess they're nervous too, even though they're hiding it so well.

"Wow, Auntie, your fascinator is . . . fascinating," Seb says to Ma.

"You like?" Ma grins and blushes. "Is latest design, you know. Very what-you-call-it, advance guard."

"Avant-garde. Yes, it certainly is." He looks sideways at me and I shrug. Can't believe I was so worried about the stupid Komodo dragon hats. Now, I couldn't care less about them. At least the whole mafia plot has put things into perspective for me.

"Ah, that very nice," Second Aunt says, plonking her champagne flute on the table. "Now, excuse, excuse." She steers people out of the way. "Meddy, you come sit here. Time for makeup."

I nod and sit in the chair she's pointing at. Selena frowns. "Why are you doing her makeup, Auntie? Isn't Staph's uncle supposed to be doing it?"

Oh, shit. Why indeed. With the exception of Seb and Selena, everyone in the room pauses, looking startled and lost.

"Um, yeah, why are you doing her makeup?" Staph says, and there's the tiniest edge in her voice that I wouldn't catch if I weren't looking out for it. "I thought everything was going according to plan." She throws Second Uncle an accusatory look and he shrugs in reply before making his way toward me.

The thought of having this man who's just threatened me in front of my family touch me is unbearable. As he reaches out toward my face, I jump up with a shout. "NO!"

Okay, now everyone is definitely staring, and Seb and Selena are wearing what-the-hell faces.

"Sorry," I say quickly. "I just—I changed my mind. I—Second Aunt, I really want you to do my makeup. I've always loved and admired your handiwork and I'm so sorry, I know I asked you to be here as my guest, but please do my hair and makeup?"

"Aww!" Selena says. "That's so sweet."

Second Aunt rushes over, barging into Second Uncle.

"Yes, of course, sayang. Okay, you just sit, ya, I get makeup bag."

Second Uncle shrugs again and turns to Fourth Aunt. "I can do your hair now."

Fourth Aunt looks up from her compact mirror with such a venomous look that my skin crawls. I swear she's about to pounce on him and tear out his throat with those ridiculous fingernails of hers. "I can do my own hair, thank you very much."

Clearly exasperated, Second Uncle looks around the room. Both Ma and Big Aunt are done with their hair and makeup and are pointedly ignoring him. Ma is puttering about, making more tea for Seb and Selena, and Big Aunt is sitting primly, her back straight, studying the room with quiet judgment.

"Um, if the family's done with their makeup, maybe you can do mine now?" Selena says, inching forward with a hesitant look.

She doesn't know he's a fake makeup artist. The thought of him touching her face is equally unbearable. "I'm sure Second Aunt would love to do your makeup," I say.

Second Aunt comes back into the bedroom, frowning into her makeup bag. "Aiya, I missing so many things. I got no proper tool kit, you know, no complete color palette. I didn't bring because—"

"Second Aunt, you'll do Selena's hair and makeup too, right?" I say.

"Hah?" She looks up and waves us off. "Yes, of course, can."

"Uh, no," Staph says with finality. When we all look at her, she forces a smile and says, "Sorry, guys, I hate to point this out to you, but we don't have all day to do hair and makeup, and if we have to wait for Second Aunt to do everyone's makeup and then do her own makeup, we'll be running late."

"That makes sense," Selena says. "Let's do this, Uncle Hendry!"

I'm about to stop her when Staph shoots me a look. I swallow my protest and watch with bile in my throat as my best friend sits down and Second Uncle starts combing her hair. I can't bear it. I turn away and close my eyes, reminding myself that Selena will come to no harm. He's not going to do anything to her. She's not part of their plot.

Someone touches my hand, and I open my eyes to see Ma standing next to me. "More tea. You have more. I put ginseng in it so you have energy for wedding, okay?" She pats my shoulder gently. "It be okay, Meddy. I know you nervous, but is okay."

Tears prick my eyes and I blink them away. How does she do it? How is she able to take the worst situations and have such faith that they'll turn out okay? I sip the tea gratefully as Second Aunt massages some product into my hair. Taking a deep breath, I watch the entire room in the mirror. My family is here. My two best friends are here. I'm about to marry the man I've loved the whole of my adult life. I'm going to be okay.

Then another click attracts my attention. Staph is going around taking pictures of everything, and another awful realization sinks in: Does she even know anything about photography? I know that it's nothing compared to the whole "mafia is blackmailing us into letting them kill a wedding guest" thing, but WOW, the thought hits me hard.

I mean, not to toot my own horn, but the photographer is one of the most important people at a wedding. Get a shitty one and couples will live to regret it for many years to come. I belong to at least half a dozen wedding forums, and in terms of vendor hire, this is by far the thing that couples most often regret skimping on. If the food's bad, they tend to forget it after a week or so. If the cake is awful, they usually have fun posting photos of it on Twitter, #NailedIt and so on. But if the photography is bad, they come to these sites and lament how they will never have good images of their special day to show future generations, and my heart always aches for them.

And now I'm about to be one of these brides who will have shitty pictures because my freaking wedding photographer is a shitty fucking *fake*. My hands tighten into fists and I have to stop myself from launching out of the chair and punching the ever-living crap out of Staph. Okay, I guess my priorities, like Ma's, need work.

"Can I take look at your camera?" I call out, making sure my voice comes out all pleasant.

Seb groans. "Uh-oh, it begins."

"You owe me five bucks," Selena says, laughing.

I frown at them. "What?"

"We had a little bet to see how long it'll take for you to try and take over the photography," Seb says. "I said an hour; Selena said pretty much right as soon as it starts."

Ah. Well. I'm annoyed by this for two seconds before I realize that I might as well lean into the role of a bridezilla so I can exert some form of control over Staph. I stretch my mouth into a grin. "Yep, guilty as charged. C'mere, Staph. Let me see those photos."

I'm rewarded by a scowl from Staph, but she catches herself and smiles through gritted teeth. "Of course." She marches over and places her camera in my outstretched hand.

I turn it over critically. As promised, she really does have a 5D Mark III, which makes me wonder if she's had one all along or if she bought one just to pass as a photographer. Big investment, if it's the latter. My gut sours with fear. The camera's just another reminder of how far they're willing to go to carry out their plan. I shake it off and go into the menu, scrolling through the photos she's taken so far. There are only about five, and they're all mediocre. I want to smash this fucking thing in her face.

"Did you even bother to learn how to use it?" I hiss. Or try to, anyway. Second Aunt, without any regard for the tension between me and Staph, has started painting my lips.

Staph leans over with a sardonic smile. "I didn't think you'd want to be reminded of today."

Good point. Yes, please regain some perspective, self. But still, this brings tears to my eyes. It's embarrassing how incredibly selfish and silly I'm being, but damn, this is what really drives home the fact that my wedding is being turned into a sham. I might as well try and be proactive somehow. "Take lots of pictures." I can barely get the words out, I'm so spitting mad.

Staphanie arches a brow.

"Pictures mean everything to me." And also, the more photos she takes, the more chances I have of her capturing something incriminating.

"You go away now," Second Aunt hisses quietly at Staphanie. "Here." She grabs the camera roughly out of my hands and shoves it at Staphanie. "You go pretend to photo-photo, okay? Go."

With a shrug, Staphanie walks away. Second Aunt crouches so she's face-to-face with me. "Meddy, you be strong, okay? So what, she not know how to use camera? My wedding, I only get less than ten photo, but all the good memory intact inside my head. And you and Nathan will surely get many good memory."

For her sake, I force a smile. "Thanks, Second Aunt." Though if Staphanie's family carries out the plan and really does kill someone at our wedding, I find it hard to believe that Nathan and I will have many positive memories of today.

11

Once my makeup and hair are done, Second Uncle and Seb are shooed into the living room so that my family can help put me in my wedding dress.

"You do realize I'm gay, right?" Seb protests.

"I no care," Big Aunt declares. "You gay or not gay, no boy seeing my niece naked!"

Second Aunt and Ma nod and make shooing motions at him. Selena grins and waves at Seb as he stalks out.

I can't help but get all emotional again as Big Aunt and Ma lift the fluffy dress off the mannequin. My dress, like most Indonesian-designed wedding dresses, has so many layers of tulle that even without the mannequin, it's able to stand up on its own. I hold on to Ma's hand as I step into it, and then comes the arduous process of hooking the corset in tight. It takes Ma and all three of my aunts to get it done. Then they do up the dozens of buttons and Second Aunt attaches the long lace veil to the back of my hair.

"Done," Second Aunt says, her voice as gentle as I have ever heard it. Ma and the other aunties crowd around me as I turn to face the mirror.

My breath catches in my throat. I have seen so many brides in my line of work, all of them beautiful in their own way. There's something about brides that pulls my gaze to them. I just want to stare at their dresses and their pretty nails and their meticulously done makeup, which is a lot less creepy than it sounds, really.

And now I'm one, and it's indescribable. My wedding gown is a vision, hugging me snugly around my waist before flaring out in gentle waves all the way to the floor. I take in a shaky breath.

"You look ah-may-zing," Selena says. She glances at her own reflection and frowns. I don't blame her. Second Uncle has followed the Indonesian style of makeup artistry—everything has to be a highlight. So now, like Ma and Big Aunt, Selena is sporting really thick, dark, hyper-arched eyebrows, voluminous fake lashes, and huge, luscious lips.

"You look great too," I say. I mean, she does, in a Kardashian sort of way.

"A bit too strip club," she mutters, but then shrugs. "Ah, well, it's fine, I can carry it off."

"Yeah, you can."

"Oh, Meddy," Ma says, with a hand on her chest. She's blinking hard to stop the tears from falling. "My baby, you so beautiful." My three aunts all nod with teary smiles. I reach out to Ma and we hold hands for a while, not speaking, just smiling at each other and savoring this sweet moment.

The click of a shutter jerks me back to the present, and we all turn to see Staphanie, who takes another picture.

"Smile!" she says.

Except for Selena, who grins widely at the camera, my family and I scowl. The shutter clicks. "You guys all look great," Staphanie says. "Anyway, sorry to break up the moment, but it's time for your First Look session."

Oh god. In all the excitement/awfulness, I've all but forgotten today's schedule, including the First Look.

First Looks are exactly what the name sounds like—the moment that the bride and groom first see each other on their wedding day. In recent years, more and more couples have opted to do a First Look session because it's a much more intimate way of seeing each other for the first time, rather than at the altar in front of hundreds of guests. The other reason why I adore First Look sessions is because from the photographer's point of view it's a much better way of capturing the delight on the bride and groom's faces as they see each other in complete wedding attire. Of course, I doubt my photographer has given any thought to finding the best angles or anything. Not that I'm bitter about that.

I lift my skirt and walk over to my luggage, unearthing a gift I had gotten for Nathan. I take a deep breath. "Okay, I'm ready."

When we leave the room, Ma and the aunties are all busy squeezing themselves into their neon purple dresses. Staphanie and I walk wordlessly down the hallway, our footsteps matching the increasing beat of my heart. Right before we get to the staircase, Staphanie suddenly stops walking and taps me on the arm, so I stop as well.

She speaks in a low voice. "I'm sure I don't have to remind you of the absolute importance of keeping this from Nathan."

I don't say anything.

"If he finds out, we will report all of you to the police immediately."

"But why? He's the groom; he has the right to know."

Staphanie stares hard at me. "I think you know damn well that unlike you and your sleazy, scheming family, Nathan wouldn't go along with it. He'd want to do the right thing and call off the wedding. He'd ruin everything."

God, how much I'd give to be able to pop her in the face right now. But even in the haze of anger, I realize that Staphanie has touched on the truth. And isn't that why I haven't already told Nathan? Because deep down inside, I knew he wouldn't let this go on. I grind my teeth and force out the world's tiniest nod. "I won't tell him."

"Good."

We resume walking. At the stairs, Staphanie calls her grandmother, who's helping to coordinate Nathan's arrival at the meeting place so that we don't accidentally run into each other. Staphanie nods at me and we walk slowly down the stairs and into the beautiful cloister.

Right before we step out into the pristine cloister garden, Staph stops and says, "Don't make me do anything I'll regret."

My stomach squeezes so painfully I think I might puke, while my chest leaps in anticipation. Goddammit, make up your mind, body. I take another deep breath, then walk out into the garden.

Nathan is waiting behind an olive tree. When he hears my footsteps, he turns around, and the delight on his face is enough to make me tear up. His eyes widen, his mouth drops open into a perfect O, and he crosses the garden in two strides and picks me up like I'm a doll.

"Oh my god," he laughs, spinning me round. "Oh my god,

oh my god. Meddy, you look amazing." There are actual tears in his eyes. He puts me down and kisses me. "Mm, I love kissing your teeth."

That cracks me up, despite everything. I lean in and hug him tight, so tight. My beautiful, wonderful groom. And oh god, he truly is beautiful, especially in his tux. He looks like a Disney prince come to life.

"I can't believe we're here." My voice cracks just a little. So much has happened in our past that I never really let myself believe that this could happen.

"I know." His voice comes out just as heavy with emotion.

Staphanie moves around us, taking pictures. I glance at her with mounting irritation, and she peers at us over the camera. "Don't mind me, guys. Just pretend I'm not here." Ugh. Having her in the bedroom with my mom and aunts was annoying enough, but having her here in this particular moment is so infuriating I want to break off an olive branch and beat her with it.

"—sleep okay?" Nathan's saying.

I blink and turn my attention back to him. "Hm?"

"I asked if you were able to sleep last night."

"Oh, yeah." It's a struggle to keep my face straight. "Yeah, slept like a baby."

Click, click.

I have to stop myself from glaring at Staphanie. "You?"

"Took me a while to fall asleep, but once I did, it was fine."

Click.

My frustration boils over and I turn to Staphanie and snap, "Could you stop that, please?"

Staphanie lowers the camera from her face and looks innocently at us. "I'm sorry, stop what? Taking pictures?"

I grit my teeth. Now that she's said it like that, it seems ri-

diculous that I would ask her, the photographer, to stop photo-
graphing us.

"Everything okay?" Nathan asks, holding me close to him.

"Yeah, sorry, just camera shy." I force out a laugh. "As it
turns out, it's a lot more nerve-racking to be on this side."

Nathan smiles at me. "It kind of is, isn't it? I've got more
sympathy for celebrities now."

Well, I'm not about to let this chance go. "Yeah, it's really
stressing me out." I turn to Staphanie with my most apologetic
face. "Can we have some privacy, please? Just for a bit." Then
I recall her threat and add, "I promise we'll be well-behaved."

Her smile tightens and for a moment I wonder if she'll lose
her cool, but then she nods and says, "Sure, of course. You're
the boss!" She starts to leave, then stops. "Don't take too long,
though, or else Ama will freak out and who knows what she'll
do." She widens her eyes at me meaningfully and then leaves
the garden.

I turn back to Nathan, who's frowning slightly.

"Is everything okay?" he says.

"Yeah! Totally! Why wouldn't it be?" Jesus, tone it down,
self.

Nathan narrows his eyes at me, smiling quizzically. "Uh,
because you just told our photographer to go away? I know
you, you're all about the wedding photos, and I'm not just saying that because you're a wedding photographer, I'm saying it
because you have, like, some weird fetish about photos with
brides in them."

"I think you mean admirable dedication."

"Oh, right, that," he laughs. "But really, what's going on?
You know you want ten thousand pictures of you in that dress.
God, look at you. You are beautiful. How the hell did I get so
lucky?"

My insides are at war. Half of me is crooning *awww*, and the other half is tearing its hair out and going, "THIS IS A DISASTER!"

"I just wanted some alone time with you, is all. There's plenty of time for pictures later."

In response, Nathan bends down and kisses me. By the time he pulls away, we're both slightly out of breath. "I have something for you," he says, walking over to a table and picking up a box.

I open it. "A UCLA mug?"

"Not just any UCLA mug. You remember that time we made mug cakes at the dorm? I made you the kimchi-and-hot-dog mug cake and you were like, 'Ew, gross!' and then proceeded to finish the entire thing."

"Yeah, of course," I say, as if I hadn't ruminated and obsessed about every single day spent with Nathan for years after we broke up.

"This is that mug. I went back to the kitchen afterward and, uh, took it."

"You stole from the dorm?" I say with mock horror.

Nathan grins. "Yeah. Because I knew I was in love with you, and I just had to have it because it was in your hands. I even thought about not washing it. But I did, just to be clear."

"Wow, that is so sweet and yet also so creepy." I laugh.

"Sweet and creepy, that's my brand."

This man, I swear. Every time I think I've revealed the innermost layer of him, there's another one hidden underneath that takes my breath away. What amazing deed have I done in past lives for me to deserve him? I must've been a nun. Or maybe a war martyr. Or a really good, loyal doggo. Because this, right here, me and Nathan as a couple, this is a reward of some sort, and I don't want to lose it. Shit, could I be any more selfish?

But is it selfish to want what I've dreamed of for years? I'll just—I'll go along with my family's strategy. It'll be fine. We'll totally be able to outsmart the actual mafia and foil Staphanie's plan without anyone finding out.

"I have a gift for you too."

Nathan grins and rubs his palms together, and I punch him on the arm before giving him the box. I watch his face as he opens it, smiling as his eyebrows raise at the sight of the beautiful midnight-blue watch inside.

"It's not a Chopard or a Patek Philippe," I say apologetically.

"Those are overrated." He takes the watch out and turns it over. The back has been engraved with just one word: "Meddy's." He laughs and puts it on immediately. "I love it."

My chest constricts at his unabashed, boyish grin. I should tell him the truth. Even though it'll ruin everything and land us all in prison, I don't want to start my marriage by lying to Nathan. This is not how weddings are supposed to go: with the bride's family plotting against their own wedding vendors, who are planning to murder someone. I should end the charade now.

"Nathan, there's something I—"

There's a commotion, a sound of rushing footsteps and vague shouts, and we turn just in time to see Ma and Second Aunt run out from the cloister, both of them gasping for breath.

12

"Meddy, ah, you are here!" Ma says, as though I would be anywhere else. "Ah, hi, Nathan, wah, you looking very handsome today, ya?"

Nathan's eyes are as wide as I've ever seen them, though I'm not sure if that's because of Ma and Second Aunt's sudden appearance or because of their appearance, period. The latter is a lot to take in. Even for me, and I've already seen their outfits. The violently violet dresses, combined with the Komodo dragons and the huge hairdos and the stark makeup and matching sequined heels, are even more overwhelming than before. I nudge him and he blinks.

"Thank you, Ma," he says, recovering quickly. "You and Second Aunt look . . . um, very fascinating."

"Is called a fascinator, luv," Second Aunt says, primping her Komodo dragon. "Very English, ya? You tell Meddy, she not believe this English tradition."

"Um . . ." Nathan turns to me with wide, slightly panicky eyes. "Yeah . . . it is a fine English tradition . . ."

"Anyway," I hurriedly cut in, "did you need me for something?"

"Ah, yes," Ma says. "Meddy, you come up to the room, okay?"

"Uh, sure. I was just—when I'm done, I'll come up."

"Okay, sure, of course, yes, yes, you take time, yes," Ma says, backing away with a manic grin.

I turn back to Nathan.

"Okay, no more time!" Ma says, rushing back to us.

"What?" I say.

"What your mama trying to say is, we got a bit makeup problem upstairs," Second Aunt says.

Uh-oh. I've got a real bad feeling about this.

"Wait, but aren't you the makeup expert?" Nathan says.

"Ah, yes, but the thing is . . ." Second Aunt falters. I can practically see her mind working frantically to come up with a convincing lie. "The makeup problem—the problem is Meddy face."

Nathan looks at me. "Her face looks fine. Better than fine," he says with a tender smile.

"Ah, yes, it look fine now, but later no good, will turn red. Then swell up. Then get spots, then—"

"What?" Nathan cries. "That sounds like you need medical attention."

"Ah, no, no, maybe just a bit swell up, anyway, you come now, we remove it, okay? Okay, bye-bye, Nathan, you good boy, so handsome." Second Aunt grabs my hand, Ma takes the other, and the two of them practically drag me away.

Before we get to the cloister, Ma whispers, "You get rid Staphanie, she cannot come inside bedroom, you listen, okay?"

"I—okay, yeah." I know better by now than to argue with them, especially when it's so obvious there's something wrong. Their sense of urgency has infected me and now my heart's thumping and I'm pretty sure I'll end up with pit stains on my wedding gown.

As soon as we get out of the garden, I see why Staphanie hasn't come out with Ma and Second Aunt; Big Aunt is there, and to any passersby, it would look like she's holding Staphanie's hands in a kindly way. But as I get closer to them, I see that Big Aunt is gripping Staphanie's hands so tight that her knuckles are white, and Staphanie looks like she's torn between anger and calling out for help. They both sag with relief when they see us. Big Aunt lets go of Staphanie and she rushes over, looking furious.

"Did you tell him?" she says. "Because, I swear, if you did—"

Nathan comes striding in from the garden. He smiles when he sees us, dimples appearing in full assault. "Ah, you're all still here. Looking good, Big Aunt. I like your dragon." Hah, at least one of us has gotten used to the Komodo dragon. "Hey, Staphanie. Hey again, you." His eyes soften as he steps toward me.

"No, no," Big Aunt says. "No time for romance. Later will have time. Now no time. You go away, okay, bye-bye."

Nathan raises his hands in a gesture of surrender and laughs. "Okay, Big Aunt. See you all at the cathedral!" He leaves the hotel, whistling as he walks through the cloister.

I turn to Staphanie. "Does he look like someone who just found out the freaking mafia is at his wedding?"

Staphanie chews on her bottom lip, glaring at Nathan's retreating back. She exhales slowly. "I guess not. Why are the three of you down here?"

"I need fix Meddy makeup," Second Aunt says.

Staphanie narrows her eyes. "It looks fine to me."

"That because you not know makeup," Second Aunt sniffs. "Her face is disaster."

"Harsh," I mutter.

We make our way up the stairs and Staphanie follows us all the way to the suite. How the hell am I going to stop her from going inside the bedroom? Of course, now that we're back at the room, I belatedly realize I should've asked her to stay behind and take photos of Nathan on his own. Duh. Too late for that now.

Music blares from the living room, overwhelmingly loud. I notice that the bedroom door is shut. Seb and Selena look up from their phones.

"How did it go? Did he cry when he saw you? Was it the best moment ever?" Seb shouts over the music. He's photographed enough First Look sessions to know what to expect.

"I still think it's weird that you guys chose to see each other before the ceremony," Selena says. "I'm a traditional girl; I want to see my future bride or groom lose their shit at the altar when they see how gorgeous I look."

"It went well. Uh, why's the music so loud?" I say. "Can someone turn it down, please?"

"No!" Big Aunt shouts. "Music loud is good luck."

I narrow my eyes at her, but she's wearing an expression that says, *Seriously, do not question me.*

"Okay . . ." Somehow, I need to try and get rid of Seb, Selena, and Staphanie. "Um, so . . ."

"How did Nathan look?" Seb says. "Mmm, Nathan in a tux."

"He looked fine," I mutter distractedly, still trying to think of how to get rid of them without causing offense. Staphanie is leaning against a wall, pretending to check her camera, but I know she's listening to every word. Once every few moments, she steals frowning glances at Ma and Second Aunt, who are so obviously up to no good.

"He looked 'fine'? Ugh, what is going on with you?" Seb says. Next to him, Selena frowns too, and now Staph is staring as well. Well, crap.

"I—uh. I'm just really nervous, I—"

The rest of my sentence is suddenly swallowed by a wail from Ma.

"I going to lose my daughter!" Ma cries. "Meddy getting marry and leave me to die alone!"

Seb and Selena exchange glances and I'm pretty sure they've made a bet on this happening too, those assholes. I hurry toward Ma just as she's about to crumple to the floor. Second Aunt and I manage to catch her and she sags against us, wailing the whole time about how she's going to die and no one's going to know and then her cat is going to eat her face.

"You don't own a cat," I point out helpfully.

Ma pauses, then resumes crying. "I not even have cat to keep me company!"

Her eyes wild with panic, Second Aunt says, "This no good, her makeup will start running. Come, we take her lie down inside bedroom."

"Let me help you," Staphanie says, reaching out toward us.

"No bother," Big Aunt says.

"No, really, it's fine. Let me get Second Uncle to help—"

"No!" Big Aunt snaps so fiercely that we all flinch. "You stay. This for family to fix."

Clearly frustrated, Staph takes another small step forward, but Seb reaches out and puts a hand on her arm. "I wouldn't go against Meddy's aunts," he says, and Selena grunts in agreement. Ah, if only I could beat my chest at Staph and crow, "That's right, biatch. Don't mess with my family!"

Instead, I make myself focus on helping Ma toward the bedroom, which is no easy task. She's really leaning into me, and in my heavy, huge-ass wedding gown, moving without having to shoulder the weight of a distraught Ma is enough of a challenge. I murmur soothing things to her, reminding her that I've been living on my own for the past year and how we see each other every day, and that Nathan and I will see her most days, if not every day. Ma is inconsolable, and it makes me ache to see her so heartbroken.

Second Aunt knocks on the bedroom door. "Is Er Jie."

The door cracks open and Fourth Aunt peers out. She opens it just wide enough for us to fit through before slamming it shut behind her and locking the door. Well, that wasn't suspicious at all.

"Aren't you being a little bit dramatic?" Fourth Aunt says to Ma by way of greeting.

It's as though the words fortify Ma; she straightens up, barrels past us to the dressing table, shouldering Fourth Aunt aside, and then turns to face us. That's when I realize Ma's face is completely dry.

"Why you stand there your mouth open? Later fly go inside mouth," she says to me.

"Um. Are you okay, Ma?"

"Aiya, I acting, you cannot tell, ya? Because I act so good, right?" Ma grins.

Fourth Aunt rolls her eyes. "I could tell those were fake sobs from a mile away. You were overacting. Typical rookie mistake."

"Oh? You think you can do better, is it?" Ma says, glowering at her.

In response, Fourth Aunt tilts her face a little and looks at the floor. She sniffles. "My daughter—my only baby—she's leaving me forever. All those years I spent raising her have come to this." A single tear rolls down her cheek. We're all watching, entranced despite ourselves, when she bows and says, "End scene." She looks up smugly, dabbing at her cheek. "That's how you convey human emotion in an authentic way."

Ma opens her mouth, but I quickly cut in before they turn this into a full-on acting showdown. "Those were really great performances from both of you, wow." I clap politely. "Anyway, you all wanted me to come here for something? Something important enough to, uh, interrupt my First Look session with Nathan? Not that I'm bitter about that or anything."

"Oh, yes," Ma says. "Come. Ayo, cepat." She flaps her hand at me to come toward the bathroom.

Before I can follow, Fourth Aunt steps in front of me and says, "Don't freak out, okay?"

Welp. That's one way to make me start freaking out. In fact, as I walk toward the connecting door, all sorts of horrific things flit through my mind. What could it be? Did Ma bring a luggage full of hallucinogenic shrooms? Did Fourth Aunt smuggle some boy toy in her (Class One) Louis Vuitton?

Wow, I really do have a low opinion of my family.

Then the bathroom door opens and all my thoughts are silenced. Whatever I came up with, however bad I thought it could be, this is so much worse.

Because there, in the middle of the bathroom, is Second Uncle, pants off, gagged, and tied to the toilet.

13

I don't really know how to describe the sensation of seeing a full-grown man actually tied up a few feet away from me. It's as if a supernova has gone off in my head, obliterating all thought. I stand there, frozen for what seems like hours, staring wide-eyed at Second Uncle as he struggles uselessly against the restraints, before Big Aunt clears her throat and nods at Ma, who rushes toward me with a cup of tea.

"Come, you drink this, help you digestion," Ma says, bringing the cup to my lips.

I snap back to life and shy away from the cup, sputtering, "No, argh! Just—don't. I just—I need time to think." I turn away from Second Uncle and take a deep breath. Inhale, exhale.

"Come, you do the Tai Chi with me," Second Aunt says, but I bat her outstretched hand away.

"It's okay, I'm alright, this is not a big deal, you've all just gone and KIDNAPPED Second Uncle. What the hell?"

Second Uncle starts shouting something behind his gag, and Fourth Aunt smacks him on the head and barks, "Quiet!"

"Jesus, Fourth Aunt!"

She looks at me as if to say, *What's wrong with a little bitch-slapping?*

My mouth flaps open and closed wordlessly.

"Oh, Meddy, you upset," Ma sighs.

"I mean, yeah? Sort of? Kind of hard not to be when there's an actual person tied up to your toilet."

"Meddy, calm down, we explain," Big Aunt says quietly. And when Big Aunt speaks quietly, in that tone, nobody dares to go against her. I've even seen stray cats listen to her when she uses that voice.

I sigh and nod.

"Things get bit hotted when you leave room," Big Aunt begins.

Ma nods and says, "Yes, we—ah—we get into a bit of argument with Second Uncle—"

At this, Second Uncle starts protesting but quickly quiets again when Fourth Aunt raises her hand.

"Wah, he saying all sort of thing," Ma cries. "Very bad thing, so horrible, burn my ears."

"What was he saying?" I ask.

"Aduh, a lot, deh," Ma says. "He say we so bad family, we not know how to raise our children, is why they all leave—"

Hurt flashes across Big Aunt and Second Aunt's faces, and Ma falters.

"I mean, that is mean, yes, but it's just words," I protest. But truth be told, I feel furious at the thought of him hurting Big Aunt and Second Aunt like that. What a low blow, and on a morning when everyone's emotions are already running sky-high. A small part of me is glad that he's tied up to a toilet now.

A small part, though. Tiny. "I'm sorry he said that about you guys," I say to them, but especially to Second Aunt. This can't be easy for her, coming from her non-boyfriend.

Second Aunt sniffs. "Aiya, I no care, so what he say bad thing? He think his family so good, meh? His family is mafia! How can he judge our family?"

I nod. "So then what happened?"

There's silence. Big Aunt and Second Aunt purse their lips. Ma looks down guiltily.

"Then he said the only one who didn't leave has turned out rotten. That was when your mom lost it and threw her tea in his face," Fourth Aunt says triumphantly. "Her hot tea."

Second Uncle nods with renewed vigor, his eyes wide and now flicking back and forth from Ma to Fourth Aunt with equal amounts of terror.

"Aiya, not hot. Lukewarm only," Ma mutters.

"Oh my god, Ma." Should I be torn between hugging Ma and telling her off? I settle for squeezing her hand.

"How can say such thing about you? My Meddy is good girl, most filial girl! You go around world also cannot find such filial girl," Ma says, shooting Second Uncle another death glare before patting my cheek. "And look, you are so beautiful bride. Cantik ya?" she says to her sisters.

"Yes, very beautiful," Big Aunt says. Second Aunt nods proudly, probably admiring her handiwork more than my actual face. As usual, they've all gone and gotten themselves derailed.

"Thank you, I'm very flattered. Anyway, back to Second Uncle. So Ma scalded him with her hot tea—"

"Lukewarm!" Ma snaps.

"Right, lukewarm. And then what happened?"

"Then he so angry!" Ma says. "Waduh, he go crazy, arms going everywhere—"

"Oh, is so scary," Second Aunt says. "We very scare."

"Not that scared. We not Denzels in distress," Big Aunt says disapprovingly.

An image of a distressed Denzel Washington flashes through my head and I have to shove it away to keep from laughing hysterically.

Second Aunt rolls her eyes. "Yes, not Denzels in distress, but still quite surprise."

"Yes, we were surprise, so we think, okay, you cannot do like that, scaring us this way, you very bad man, we better keep you under control," Big Aunt says.

"Keep him under control. By tying him to the toilet. How did you even—you know what? Doesn't matter."

"Oh, is quite easy, Meddy," Ma laughs. "Big Aunt and me, we take one arm, Second Aunt take other arm, Fourth Aunt go and get stocking, tie him up. You know in Jakarta for Eid we often tie up goat for korban, same thing here."

I gape at her in horror. "Korban? As in sacrifice? You're not even Muslim. Why are you tying up goats for Eid?"

"We help our neighbors," Ma says. "We celebrate with them together."

"Right. Uh, anyway, he's not a goat we're about to sacrifice. I mean, I hope you weren't thinking of sacrificing him, whatever that means."

Fourth Aunt grins and slides her finger across her throat, making Second Uncle and me shudder.

"Tch, don't like that, you scare him," Big Aunt says, and Fourth Aunt shrugs, not looking contrite at all.

"I need to think." I turn around and leave the bathroom, because really, what is there to do now that my family has literally kidnapped a man? A man who is part of the mafia, let's not forget. The mafia that's about to take someone out in a matter of a few hours, at my own wedding.

Shit.

Okay. Calm down, Meddy. You've been through worse than this. I mean, technically, murder is worse than kidnapping, and you got through that just fine, so this is nothing! Yeah, this is fine.

"You haven't hear our plan yet," Ma says as they all shuffle out after me.

Oh god. They have a plan. This is going to be bad.

Or maybe not. They did help me resolve the whole Ah Guan issue, after all, so maybe it's time I give my family some credit.

"You have a plan?" I say warily.

"It's obvious, isn't it?" Fourth Aunt says. "We hold him hostage. Tell them to call off their plan, otherwise . . ." She slides her finger across her throat again. Second Aunt nods solemnly, and the dragon on her head bobs up and down.

Clearly my family does not deserve any credit at all.

"Nobody is killing anybody," I groan.

"Yes, very bad luck, killing someone on wedding day," Ma scolds Fourth Aunt. "You stop it, you curse Meddy wedding. Later who know what bad luck fall on her marriage? Maybe husband die? Or even worse, maybe no baby, then how?"

"I'm pretty sure having Nathan die is worse than—" Why am I arguing over this? "Never mind. Bottom line: no killing anyone. I can't believe I have to tell you guys this."

"Yes, no kill," Big Aunt says. Finally, some reason. "Will be so hard to get rid of body here." Okay, so she agrees for the wrong reasons. "Now what we do with him?"

The thought of holding anyone hostage is so beyond my comfort zone that I can't think of anything. I mean, it's not as if I grew up getting taught Kidnapping 101. My mind is a fuzzy, panicky blank. But then, like a sea monster rising from the depths of the ocean, a sudden thought surfaces.

"His phone!"

Four pairs of eyes lock on me. "His phone," I say again, flapping with excitement. "We can go through it, maybe find out who the target is!"

"Wah, very good, Meddy. Oh, so clever, my baby," Ma says, beaming proudly. "She so clever, ya? Ya kan?" she says to the others, shamelessly goading them, especially Fourth Aunt, into agreement.

"Yes, very clever," Big Aunt says. Second Aunt nods, smiling.

"Well, we were kind of distracted by the actual hard work of overpowering him, but whatever," Fourth Aunt mutters. Ma narrows her eyes and Fourth Aunt turns away, but as she does, she gives me a quick wink.

We all file back into the bathroom. "Okay, so we just have to find his phone—" I frown at Second Uncle. "Speaking of which, why doesn't he have his pants on?"

"Ah, yes," Second Aunt says with pride. "We remove so that he too embarrass to run out and call for help. We think out him." She taps the side of her nose slyly.

"Outthink," Fourth Aunt says.

"Outing? What outing?" Second Aunt says.

"I think she just wanted to get his pants off," Fourth Aunt whispers in a very loud, non-whispery way.

"Where are his pants?" I have to raise my voice over theirs.

"In closet, Meddy, we not so messy, leave it out," Ma says.

"Of course not, my bad." I make my way to the closet, and sure enough, the pants are there, folded into a neat square. Grimacing slightly, I pat them down—wow, feels weird to be putting my hands all over some man's pants—and breathe a sigh of relief when I find his phone. I slide it out and brandish it at my family, who clap and cheer for me.

"Now." Fourth Aunt turns to Second Uncle and moves silkily, dropping her voice low. "Tell us the unlock code, or I will take the bluntest clotted cream knife and use it to saw off your—"

"It's a facial recognition lock, no need to saw off anything," I call out, running over so fast I trip on my dress and would've face-planted if Ma hadn't caught me. God, Fourth Aunt. If I didn't know any better, I'd think she's enjoying this. Wait, who am I kidding? She is totally enjoying this. I link my arm through Fourth Aunt's and usher her to one side gently, and all the while, she's glaring at Second Uncle and making "I'm watching you" motions with her index and middle fingers as he watches balefully. When I hold up the phone to Second Uncle's face, he turns away.

"Oh, hell no," Fourth Aunt growls, jumping up. She grabs his head, digging her blinged-out nails into his scalp. He struggles to turn his face away again, but he's no match for Fourth Aunt, and I manage to get the phone to unlock before she releases him and wipes her hands down her dress with a grimace.

I scan the home screen until I find WhatsApp. Everyone in Indo uses WhatsApp. I tap on it, and sure enough, at the top of the list of ongoing chats is Wedding Group Chat. There are 132 new messages.

My family crowds behind me, and as one, we go through the chat messages.

14

Unlike my family's WhatsApp group chat, the messages in Staphanie's family group chat are mostly written in Indonesian, peppered with a few Mandarin characters and sentences here and there.

"Scroll down, Meddy," Second Aunt says.

"I'm not done reading yet," I say. For once in my life, I'm the one who's struggling to keep up with my aunts. It makes me realize that it would be so much easier for them to communicate via chat in Indonesian or even Mandarin, but they stick to English for my sake. Despite the situation, I feel a twinge of guilt and love for my ridiculous family. I shake off the guilt and force myself to focus on the messages, scrolling through a bunch of stuff that doesn't seem to be relevant until I get to the most recent messages, sent a few minutes ago.

Ama: Semua sudah siap?

That's simple enough: *Is everyone ready?*

Jems: Sdh.

Staph: Ya, Ama.

Francis: Ya.

Francis: Hendry ada dimana?

Uh-oh. They're asking where Second Uncle is.

Staph: Masih dikamar. Kayanya masih lagi dandanin keluarga Meddy.

I think he's still working on Maddy's family's hair and makeup. Phew, okay.

Ama: Ingat, kami harus hati-hati, awasin Sang Ratu.

Be careful, we need to watch out for the Queen.
The Queen? "Am I missing something here?" I say, turning round to look at my family. "Is this an Indo saying that means something else? Or does she literally mean the queen, as in the queen of England?"

If they're here to assassinate the actual queen of England, we might be in a lot more trouble than we originally thought. Though how they were planning on assassinating the queen at my wedding, I have no idea.

"The queen?" Big Aunt says. "Meddy, you got queen coming to your wedding? You not tell us?"

"How can not tell us?" Second Aunt snaps. "We wear like this, so ridiculous, in front of queen of England?"

I stare at them. *This* is when they finally realize the ridiculousness of their outfits?

"If we know queen coming, we would add feather," Big Aunt says.

Ah. Ridiculous because the fascinators are featherless, not because of the Komodo dragons. They're all staring at me, and the combination of those displeased expressions and the disapproving Komodo dragons atop their heads is very disconcerting.

"Er, no," I say, finally finding my voice. "The queen of England is not coming to my wedding. I think it's a code name."

"Ooohhh," they say, nodding sagely.

"So who can be code name Queen?" Big Aunt says.

"It must be Lilian Citra," I say, feeling sick to my stomach. "Out of the three people we've singled out from the guest list, she's the only woman." The words are coming out faster the more I recall about the old woman. "I haven't met her myself. She lives in—uh, not sure, actually, I think Nathan might have mentioned Shanghai and Dubai at some point? I've overheard him talking to her over the phone, and he's always so respectful toward her. I think she's someone really, really important. Someone who's a likely candidate to be a mafia target." I open up a web browser and type her name in, and sure enough, the search results are impressive.

The Citras own this mall and that hotel and this plantation and that mine. They're a powerful family headed by an aging matriarch, Lilian.

I show my family the Google images of her. She looks like she's in her seventies, with gently graying hair worn in the typical Chinese-Indonesian way—big and poufy and short. Around her neck is a simple string of pearls, and her clothes are all well-tailored pantsuits à la Hillary Clinton. Altogether, she looks like the exact type of person who'd get the code name "the Queen."

My family nods their agreement. "Wah, yes, look very queen," Ma says. "Oh, look, here she is carrying the ostrich Birkin, you see?"

They all nod and give appreciative grunts. At a snort from Second Uncle, we all look up.

"What? You got something to say?" Fourth Aunt growls. He looks away. "That's right, bitch, we cracked your code. Your code ain't shit!"

"Jesus, Fourth Aunt." I'm about to say more when my alarm goes off, startling all of us. "Sorry, that's just—shit. That was the wedding ceremony reminder. Ceremony's in half an hour. The guests are probably starting to arrive. What if—oh god— what if they plan on killing her as soon as she gets here?"

There's a beat of silence as we stare helplessly at one another, and then Big Aunt says, with utter and complete confidence, "We will watching over her."

"Yes, we go now and protect her," Ma says.

"You can't go out, you're the mother of the bride, you're giving Meddy away," Fourth Aunt says. "You've gotta stay in here until the ceremony starts."

Ma looks like she's about to argue, but Big Aunt nods and says, "Si Mei correct. You stay here, is okay. We go out and we protect this queen, we be okay."

I'm about to say something, though I have no idea what, when there's a loud knock at the door.

"Open up!" Staph calls out, her voice tinged with frustration. At this, Second Uncle starts yelling, but the sock in his mouth muffles his voice, and Ma leaps at him and yanks his ear like he's a naughty kid until he stops shouting.

"The guests are arriving," someone else says from outside. Seb. Crap.

We all file out of the bathroom and close the door behind us. "Are we really going to do this?" I say.

My family nods.

"Okay." I make sure Second Uncle's phone is on silent mode before sliding it into one of the bedside drawers. "Ma and I will go to the antechamber, and you guys will protect Lilian." I reach out and hug all of them, blinking back my tears. "Thank you."

"Aiya, is no problem," Big Aunt says. "We must making sure you have perfect wedding day. No murder."

"Amen to that," Fourth Aunt says.

With one last hug, Ma and I walk slowly to the door. The wedding is about to begin.

15

There is a chamber where Ma and I can wait that leads into Christ Church Cathedral. It's basically a waiting room, but it feels wrong calling it a waiting room because waiting rooms aren't supposed to be this majestic. It has marble floors, beautiful paintings on the stone walls, an impressive vaulted ceiling, and floor-to-ceiling stained glass windows. As soon as Ma and I get in, I rush to the windows to try and get a view of the quad. I finally find the least blurry spot and peer through it.

Just as Seb said, the guests are arriving. My heart leaps when I spot Nathan, looking so tall and gallant in his tux. He's flanked by two groomsmen and they're all beaming and looking like they fell out of some Oxford rowers brochure. God, I am going to marry the hell out of that man. Then I feel guilty for having such a raunchy thought in a cathedral. Then I feel even guiltier for having a raunchy thought while my family is out there trying to stop a literal assassination attempt.

"Wah, look at fascinators," Ma says from the next window down. "Oooh, what is that one? A swan?"

I squint at where she's pointing. "Pretty sure that's a flower, Ma."

"Really? Oh yes, you right. Hanh," she sniffs. "Flower. So biasa."

I bite my tongue before I can tell her I wish she'd gone for biasa—average—too.

"Oooh, that one interesting! Look like tiger—"

"Also a flower."

"Hmm." Ma pats her Komodo dragon and looks at me with a worried frown. "How come no one wearing animal on hat? Jonjon say is all rage in England."

And now I'm presented with a conundrum: tell Ma the truth—that Jonjon probably lied because he wanted to do something outrageous and avant-garde to get his name out there—or lie to save her feelings.

"That's because this group is pretty conservative when it comes to fashion," I say.

Ma smiles with such pride that I'm glad I chose not to tell her the truth. It would've killed her to not be able to fully enjoy her Komodo dragon today.

Speaking of killing . . .

I peer back through the window. No Lilian in sight. I allow myself to relax a little, but then I spot Staphanie in the crowd, standing out among the pastel outfits in her all-black photographer clothes, and my stomach clenches once again. Staphanie is making a good show of pretending to be a photographer, that conniving little professional killer. She's working her way through the crowd, smiling and nodding at people while taking their pictures.

Meanwhile, Ama is standing on the fringes of the crowd, and from here, I can see her mouth moving; she's talking into an earpiece. The vise around my chest tightens, especially when I realize I have no idea where Staphanie's other two uncles are. They could be anywhere. One of them could be positioned on the rooftop with a sniper rifle trained at the quad. I mean, that's a crazy thought, but they're mafia. Who knows what they're capable of? What's Ama saying? She must be giving instructions to her family, getting them into position to strike—

And oh god, just as I think that, Staphanie approaches Nathan and his parents. My hands curl into fists as she places her hand on Nathan's arm, and argh, I just want to plant my fist right in that smarmy face of hers. The face that has smarmed at me for months and pretended to be my friend—

I need to focus. Her betrayal isn't the important bit here. Yes. Thanks to the Ah Guan incident, I understand that my mind keeps flitting and settling on the unimportant bits of the situation only because it can't handle the terror of the real problem. But understanding this and knowing what to do about it are two completely different things.

I can't help the flare of jealousy as Nathan's mother smiles fondly at Staphanie. They only met yesterday, and yet she's hit it off so well with Nathan's parents. Much better than my family and I did. *She's a killer!* I want to shout at them.

Gosh, I am really bad at focusing on the actual stuff that matters. Okay. Where are my aunties?

Just as I think that, the crowd shifts, heads turning, and I know exactly where they are. They're making their entrance. Oh, man. I can only imagine the whispers that are going through the crowd right now. I can almost see the ripple of surprised expressions.

Fourth Aunt comes out to the quad first, because of course she does. She sashays down the stone steps and onto the grass field as if it's a red carpet, waving and beaming at everyone else.

Even from here I can see the miniature faux mic that her Komodo dragon holds in its paw, and I can hear snatches of Fourth Aunt's voice as she greets the other guests in her newfound English accent. Oh god.

Big Aunt and Second Aunt walk out after Fourth Aunt. Well, I say walk, but really, Big Aunt strides as per usual, like a North Korean dictator marching out to greet his army. Her Komodo dragon stands as erect as ever, gazing down with disapproval at everyone. Second Aunt glides out next to her, the sly fox hiding in the tiger's shadow.

I catch a glimpse of the looks of sheer horror on Nathan's parents' faces before they plaster on polite smiles and greet my aunts, and I swear this moment is a knife twisting in my guts. I know it's wrong, but oh god, so much secondhand embarrassment. The shame. I could cry, I really could. Okay, but perspective, I remind myself. In the larger scheme of things, this isn't so bad. I mean, who doesn't have embarrassing family, amirite?

Well, Nathan, for one.

Okay, my thoughts are clearly not being helpful. No matter how embarrassing my aunts are, they're about to help me prevent a murder, so . . . Yanno. Be grateful for them, I remind myself as I watch my three aunts strike a pose for Staphanie and all the guests gape at them. In the bright daylight, their shiny purple outfits are blinding. I wonder if Staphanie would know to adjust for the added exposure—oh, who am I kidding? She's probably got her camera set to Auto.

Then my aunts suddenly perk up and their heads turn as one, like meerkats. Ma utters a low gasp.

"I think is her," Ma says, flapping her hand at me. "Look, Meddy, is the queen."

And sure enough, Lilian Citra, Nathan's biggest investor and the target of Staphanie's family, has arrived.

She wears a pale blue pantsuit that's obviously tailored to fit her perfectly, along with a matching fascinator that is somehow both modest and eye-catching. Everything about her screams class. Even the way she walks speaks of both power and grace. Wow. Somehow, I understand why this woman is targeted by the mafia. I can totally imagine her being involved in a massive business deal worth hundreds of millions of dollars, or maybe even ordering politicians to make laws that will hurt crime lords. The need to protect her burns even more fiercely when I see her.

"Oh god," I mutter, because Staphanie has spotted her as well and is walking toward her with a determined look on her face. Oh my god, is it going to happen now? I can't watch—

The next moment, Fourth Aunt has elbowed Staphanie out of the way unceremoniously and Big Aunt and Second Aunt shoulder their way through the crowd as if they're scything through the Sunday dim sum crowd. They move without any regard for courtesy, shoving both old and young out of the way until they get to Lilian. Then, to my horror, and probably to Lilian's as well, they each take one arm and beam at her as if they're old buddies of hers.

Lilian must be way too polite to ask them who the hell they are, because the three of them walk arm-in-arm through the crowd and into the cathedral. I turn to Ma.

"Wow."

Ma nods. "Mm."

"I mean. Wow. They basically just abducted her."

Ma shrugs. "Not abduct, maybe more escorting. Why she wear pants? She is quite manly, ya?"

I bury my face in my hands.

16

How do I describe the moments before my entrance? Gut-curdling nervousness? Fireworks of excitement? Both?

As Ma and I make our way from the waiting room to the outside of the cathedral, my knees keep buckling and I hold on to Ma's arm so tight I'm reminded of the times when I was a little kid and was scared of this and that. I was a pretty cowardly kid. Maybe it has to do with growing up with five boy cousins who ping-ponged back and forth between being fiercely protective and complete asshats. Because I was their girl cousin, they had to make sure that I didn't get frogs put in my water bottle, except for the ones that they'd put in themselves. Anyway, I remember countless moments when I clung to Ma just like this, as if she were my life raft.

I glance at her, taking in the fine wrinkles at the side of her eyes and mouth, and my heart aches with so much love. I tug at her arm, and when she turns, I give her a tight hug.

"Love you so much, Ma."

"Tch, apa sih?" She laughs and pulls away. "Why suddenly say such thing?" Ah, yes, now I remember why I don't tell Ma I love her more often, because she doesn't quite know what to do with it.

Seb and Selena are waiting outside the doors to the cathedral, along with Nathan's two groomsmen, Ishaq and Tim. Their faces brighten when they see us and they each give me a huge hug. I close my eyes and breathe in the familiar fragrance that Selena has worn since college, letting myself take a bit of strength from the hug from my oldest friend.

"You ready?" Selena says.

I nod, and the music swells as the doors open.

"See you in there," Ishaq says, and walks down the aisle, followed by Tim.

Seb and Selena kiss me on the cheeks and then walk inside arm in arm in time to the music.

"Ready," Ma says.

I link my arm through hers and squeeze my bouquet as though I were grasping a sword handle. Given that all our vendors have turned out to be fakes, my bouquet is surprisingly beautiful. Even Ma, florist extraordinaire that she is, begrudgingly noted that the mix of hydrangeas and lilies and peonies is not bad work for an amateur. I suppose I've got that little thing to be grateful about. Together, we step inside the cathedral.

I've been here before, of course. Years ago, when I first visited Nathan's parents in England, he'd taken me on a tour of the different colleges. I had gazed in awe at the huge Norman columns and the magnificent vaulted ceilings and the elaborate stained glass windows and golden altar. But now, I see none of these things. I don't see the guests, who are all on their feet. I don't see Staphanie's family, who must be lurking in the shadows like snakes waiting to strike. Well, except for Second Uncle.

The only thing I see is Nathan, who's beaming at me and brushing back tears. At the sight of his tears, mine start to fall as well. It's like a dam of emotions that I can't hold back. As Ma walks me down the aisle, Nathan and I both cry tears of happiness, of relief that after everything, we're finally about to be married.

Ma kisses my cheeks and goes to take her seat at the pew, and quite suddenly, I'm alone at the altar with Nathan. He lifts my veil so gently, like I'm a present he can't quite believe he's opening, and stares at me with open adoration until the priest clears his throat. We jump and grin guiltily.

"We are gathered here today . . ."

I let the words wash over me, throwing elated glances at Nathan. He is incandescent with joy. He's not even pretending to pay attention to the ceremony. He's just beaming at me the entire time, his eyes shining with tears, his hands tight around mine. The priest's words fade away. All our surroundings fade away. We might as well be the only two people in the entire world right now. In this moment, the only thing that matters to me is Nathan. And I see him again as that fresh-faced college kid, his jaw less defined than it is now, making him look more vulnerable and boyish. I see us with textbooks, pretending to study while sneaking glances at each other. I remember our first kiss at the frat party, with the string lights above us like multicolored stars. And I recall, with a stab of heartache, how it felt to lose him.

Then we're both suddenly aware of expectant silence. With great reluctance, we break eye contact and glance at the priest, who gives a minuscule sigh—dude knows we haven't paid any attention to a single word he's said—and says, "It's time for your vows." He hands Nathan his mic. Nathan clears his throat, looking nervous for the first time I can remember. It makes him look so young and sweet, I just want to pounce on him.

"I, Nathan Mingfeng Chan, take you, Meddelin Meiyue Chan, to be my best friend, the love of my life, and my lawfully wedded wife. You are my soul mate, my mind mate, my every-thing. Meddy, I promise to be the best husband I can be. I promise to share all of me with you—the good and the bad and the in-between. I promise to be true to you . . ."

A lump forms in my throat. He has always been true to me, but I haven't always reciprocated. In fact, there have been so many times in our relationship when I was either hiding things from him or actively lying to him. Tears rush to my eyes, and this time they're not tears of happiness but of guilt. On our wedding day, I am yet again lying to him. I blink them back and focus on the rest of his vows, while my mind is a swirl of love and sadness and anxiety.

". . . to support you in the pursuit of your dreams in the best way I can. I choose you, Meddy, to be my person, just as you have chosen me to be yours, and I will spend the rest of my life loving and cherishing you."

Smiling, I lean into him, starting when the priest clears his throat again. "Now it's your turn to say your vows, Meddelin." The audience laughs and I blush. Nathan passes me the mic.

My voice comes out small and the priest signals me to speak up. "Uh. I, Meddelin Meiyue Chan, take you, Nathan Ming-feng Chan, to be my lawfully wedded husband. Nathan—" Emotion overcomes me and my words can't get past the thick lump in my throat. How do I convey in words everything we've been through? I stand there for an excruciating moment, at the edge of breaking down in sobs. Nathan gives me a small nod, and somehow, I manage to speak. "Nathan, I have known you for so many years. I knew you as a teen, and I know that your kindness goes back a long way. You have grown from a sweet, caring boy into a generous, loving man, and I am so lucky to have been given a second chance to be with you. I promise to be the best wife to you . . ."

Again, that stab of guilt. My gaze flicks to the audience, where I see with a start that Lilian is sitting in the front row, flanked on both sides by my family. Ma and the aunts are dabbing at their eyes with their matching violet handkerchiefs. The guilt comes in full force. How can I stand here and promise to be a good wife when I'm keeping such a huge lie from him?

As though she can read my mind, Fourth Aunt raises her eyebrows ever so slightly at me and gives a single nod. *Carry on. You can do this.*

I take a deep breath and force myself to keep going. "I promise to be there for you through the best and the worst of times. I choose you, Nathan, to be my husband today and every day from now, until the very end."

My voice wobbles at the last word, but it doesn't matter. I've managed it. Nathan wipes his eyes as I hand the mic back to the priest. We exchange rings, and I marvel at how the gold band looks around my finger. How final and how beautiful that feels, to have found my forever partner.

"With this, I declare you husband and wife. You may now kiss the bride."

At last, we step into each other's arms and I melt against his comforting warmth as our lips meet. No matter what happens after this, I at least have this moment to come back to as one of the highlights of my life. And somehow, I will find a way to be truthful with Nathan.

17

One of the few things we did keep from Chinese-Indonesian tradition is the bit where we give thanks to our parents. Nathan and I descend from the altar, and we go to his parents and kneel in front of them before hugging them. It's apparent from Annie and Chris's faces that they're uncomfortable with this, but they go along with it and give us stiff hugs. When we get to my side of the family, Ma sobs openly as we kneel in front of her. Big Aunt and Second Aunt put their arms around Ma, and I lay my head on her knees for a few heart-wrenching moments. I close my eyes, wishing I could be a little girl once more, seeking comfort from my mother's lap. The tears flow freely as I hug her with a fierce strength. Nathan has to blink away his tears too as he hugs Ma, and I can't help noticing that Annie looks anything but happy at the sight.

Everything else after that is a blur. We walk down the aisle hand in hand while everyone claps, and when we get outside, we hardly have time to adjust to the harsh sunlight before the confetti is thrown and our friends and families crowd around us. Hands are shaken and hugs are given. I'm dazed by all of the attention, the never-ending flow of people coming up to us and telling us what a beautiful ceremony it was and what a gorgeous bride I make.

"Congratulations!" Seb says, crushing me with a hug. "Oh, Meddy, I can't believe you're married!"

"I know!" I squeeze Seb tight. Then I hug Selena as Seb moves to hug Nathan.

"Do you need help with anything?" Selena says. "Gotta make sure I'm doing my job as maid of honor."

"Uh, excuse you?" Seb says. "I'm man of honor. You're just a bridesmaid."

"You're both MOHs," I laugh. "And no, I don't need anything, thank you. You're both wonderful."

"We know," Seb says.

"Okay, just holler if you need anything," Selena says, and they go off to mingle with the other guests.

"You okay?" Nathan says, leaning over and looking down at me with an expression that makes my cheeks burn. God, I swear he's almost literally smoldering hot. "Wife?" He grins. "You okay, wife? Wow, that sounds weird. In a good way. An amazing way."

I laugh. "I'm okay, husband. Wow, that does sound weird."

The click of a shutter snaps me back to reality, and all of the fluffy, wonderful, cotton-candy feel of the moment melts away, replaced by an ugly panic. That's right. Staphanie and her family are still here. I let myself get carried away by the ceremony. I'm lucky they didn't try to pull anything then, but now I need to be on guard once again.

Staphanie is a few feet away, aiming her camera right at me.

It feels so violating, somehow, having her lens trained on me, as though she can look into my head with it and read my thoughts. Huh, I wonder if this is how people usually feel about me when I'm working.

"How about a picture of the newlyweds?" she says.

"Sure." Nathan puts his arm around my waist and I stiffen. "You okay?" he says again.

"Yeah, I just—" Just what? Just don't want to have my photos taken by a fake photographer who's planning a murder? Only minutes after our wedding vows and here I am about to lie to him. Again. "I—um, can we talk?" I say in a low voice, faking a smile as Staphanie raises her camera.

"Say cheese!"

You asshole, I want to scream, *no self-respecting photographer says "Cheese" anymore!* Is it bad that I find myself raging at Staphanie most when she does the photography badly and not when she, you know, tries to pull off an assassination attempt?

"Now?" Confusion crosses his face. "Sure, is something wrong?"

"Time for a close-up!" Staphanie says, stepping so close to us there's no way she won't hear whatever I say to Nathan.

I struggle to keep myself from—I don't know—screaming or grabbing that wonderful camera of hers and beating her over the head with it.

"Ah, photo-photo!" Big Aunt says, appearing from nowhere. She grabs Staphanie's arm and wrenches her away from me. "Come, you take photo-photo of us, ya?" She's about to drag Staphanie bodily away when Ama steps toward us. What is it with these older aunties and their ability to seemingly appear out of thin air?

"Aduh, be careful, ya," Ama says, smiling politely at Big

Aunt. "Staphanie camera very fragile." She reaches out and places a hand on Big Aunt's wrist. To any passersby, it looks like an innocent gesture, but I'm close enough to see that Ama is squeezing Big Aunt's arm.

Big Aunt smiles at her. "Oh, yes, of course, I know is very easily break, like bones, you know? So easy break, maybe not so easy fix. Is why I hold on to her, so she not have accident, maybe fall?"

Staphanie's eyes are as wide as mine probably are. She stares at Big Aunt in open horror before looking at her grandmother, who raises her chest, nostrils flaring.

"Oh, you so kind and caring, but my granddaughter very careful, you no need worry about her, ya?"

"Um, is this a normal Chinese-Indo thing?" Nathan whispers to me.

"Yeah, this is totally normal!" I whisper back. "It's a— uh . . ." Whenever people question my family's weird behavior, I always have a simple answer at the ready, something that will satisfy even the most curious. I turn to it now. "It's a superstition thing."

"Ah, okay." Nathan nods.

Great job, Meddy. So much for being truthful to your newlywed husband.

Still, how the hell do I explain what's going on right now? I don't even know what's going on; I just know I need to stop it somehow.

"Big Aunt, um, how about you accompany me to uh—ah, oh, you know what? I have a gift for you I'd love to give you. It's in my room."

"Oh, such filial girl," Ama says, and I swear her voice comes out dripping with venom. "Yes, good idea, now we have break, people go to Masters Garden for cocktail hour, ya, you have time maybe touch up makeup, give gift for family, then you come back to cocktail hour, okay."

"Great!" I say with false brightness. I widen my eyes at Big Aunt, silently pleading with her to let go of Staphanie's arm.

With great reluctance, Big Aunt releases her grip on Staphanie and Ama releases her grip on Big Aunt. The two women grin wider at each other, their mouths stretching hideously, then Ama abruptly turns away, taking Staphanie's arm.

I turn to Nathan and see him standing there with a bemused expression. He knows. He must know something's wrong; he's not stupid.

"Is everything okay with your fami—"

"Nathan, Meddelin, oh, bless, it was a beautiful ceremony!" Annie comes over and kisses our cheeks. "You look lovely. Doesn't she, love?" She turns around, presumably looking for Nathan's dad. "Oh, where's your dad gone now? I wanted to take photos with you two."

Big Aunt taps me on the arm and says in Indonesian, "I'm going up to check on you-know-what."

"Wait!" I whisper. I can't let her go up on her own to check on Second Uncle. What if something goes wrong? What if the cleaner arrives to clean the room while she's there? Or worse, what if the room's being cleaned right this very moment? I frantically try to remember if I'd had the forethought to put the Do Not Disturb sign on the door. I mean, I don't know the first thing about kidnapping anyone, but "Check on your kidnappee regularly" has got to be one of the top five rules. Maybe even top three. And I can't fob that off on Big Aunt. "I'll come with you. To give you your gift, remember?"

She looks like she's about to argue, but I quickly turn back to Nathan and say, "I need to go back to the room for a bit, is that okay? I just have something for Big Aunt, and I want to uh, touch up my makeup—"

"Yeah, of course." He smiles and kisses my forehead. "Though, for the record, you look perfect."

"Thank you. Annie, I'll be back down real quick, and we'll get those photos done."

Annie's about to speak when Big Aunt says, "Meddy, how can call elder by name? So rude!"

"Oh, er, that's quite alright, dear," Annie says.

"Not alright. Your ma will heartbreak!" Big Aunt tuts. "We will talk this later. Okay, toodle pip, cheerio. We go now." She takes my arm and leads me away. I throw apologetic glances at Annie, who's standing there looking very confused. Nathan's visibly trying to hold back a smile as he bends his head and says something to her. At least he seems like he's no longer thinking about the weird exchange between Big Aunt and Ama.

Once we're out of earshot, Big Aunt says, "You go first, so people not keep come and congratulate you. I go get your mama. Second Aunt and Fourth Aunt stay here, watch queen."

The reminder of Lilian's precarious position sends my stomach plummeting. It isn't that I have forgotten as such, but it's such an unreal thing to have to think about today of all days. But yes, Big Aunt is right. Not all of us should go back up to the room. Some of us need to remain here to PREVENT A HUMAN FROM GETTING KILLED. I nearly laugh out loud at the sheer craziness. I skirt the edge of the crowd, smiling, accepting all the congratulations as politely and quickly as I can. It's easy to spot Lilian—all I have to do is look for the Komodo dragons bobbing above the crowd. I can't believe those stupid dragons are actually turning out to be useful. Ma and Second Aunt have attached themselves to her like limpets, practically putting their arms around her. She looks slightly overwhelmed but, to her credit, seems to be taking it all in stride.

Big Aunt comes back with Fourth Aunt in tow and says, "Your ma busy take care Lilian, so we just go up with Fourth Aunt, ya?"

Fourth Aunt takes my left arm and Big Aunt takes my right, and together, we walk briskly toward the room to check on the man we've kidnapped. My heart gives a particularly painful squeeze as Fourth Aunt locates the room key. I swear I'm going to perish from heart disease at age thirty if life continues to be this bonkers. I'm not built for this much anxiety. Finally, she unlocks the door and opens it. And gasps.

18

The thing about tying an actual person to an actual toilet is— well, the thing is, it is really bloody hard to do. It's like guns; you see them all the time in movies, so you kind of just take them for granted and never really stop to think about how terrifying they are in real life. Whenever I see a kidnapping scene in a movie, I rarely spare a thought for the logistics of it. Like what kind of knots you have to use, what bits to tie to where, and so on and so forth.

So I probably shouldn't be shocked at the sight of Second Uncle no longer tied to the toilet but instead standing next to the bedside table in the bedroom. His hands are still tied, but he's managed to get the hotel phone off the hook and has apparently called someone.

When he sees us, he screams, "Mafia! Die! I die, ko—"

His shouts end abruptly when a Komodo dragon smacks him in the head. Big Aunt quickly follows Fourth Aunt's lead, tearing off her own dragon to throw, and Second Uncle freezes with his hands up. "No, not dragon—"

Then Fourth Aunt follows up with a blood-curdling war cry and pounces on him.

"Oh my god!" I'm frozen there, half-crouched, my arms out as if I'm about to do something, but what? What the hell do I do?

Big Aunt rushes past me—Big Aunt, my sixty-something-year-old aunt, is rushing past me. Good god, do something! Still, my body refuses to comprehend the commands my brain is throwing its way and I stand there uselessly as Big Aunt zooms straight into the fray. She pauses long enough to pick up the electric kettle, and that's when I spring into action. If she swings that thing at their heads, she might actually kill someone.

"No!" I leap forward. I trip on my huge dress and fall into the struggling mass. The world is shaved down into teeth and claws.

Second Uncle isn't a huge man, but he's still an adult male with everything to lose, and he's not going down without a fight. He flings his body in wild arcs, and though his hands are tied, he's still able to swing his arms up and down, if not sideways. Fourth Aunt has her arms around his waist and is practically biting him. I reach out and grab something—anything. My hands go around one of Second Uncle's arms, and I have to keep from flinching at the contact. He's radiating panicked heat. It feels so wrong, but I grip him tight. Then, as though in slow motion, I see Big Aunt swinging the electric kettle down on his head. A burst of adrenaline rushes through me and I yank Second Uncle to the side. His foot slips, and he falls over with a wail. A wail cut short as his head smacks against the wall with a loud *crack*.

Then, silence.

Oh no. No, no, no.

It takes a while to realize that I'm just standing there going, "No, no, no" repeatedly. Big Aunt takes my arm and shakes me gently. My gaze snaps to hers. "Did I—is he—have I just killed another man?" Unreal. The words are absurd. They can't possibly be real.

Fourth Aunt picks herself up off the floor, breathing hard, and grabs her Komodo dragon. That's what she's worried about? The thought makes me want to laugh hysterically. She uses it to prod Second Uncle's head. It lolls lifelessly. Lifelessly, because I have taken away his life. Oh my god.

"Stop that, Meddy," Fourth Aunt snaps. That's when I realize I've been doing a sort of low moan the entire time.

"Sorry, I just—I'm a bit shocked because—oh god, is he—?"

She shushes me as she wraps a hand around his wrist, then shrugs. "Can't feel a pulse. Well, Meddy, looks like we've got a situation on our hands."

"No!" Not again. The world crashes around me. I think I might pass out. I'm going to—wait. Last time, we couldn't feel a pulse either. Maybe we just suck at finding pulses. I rush to the dressing table, find a small compact mirror, and hurry back to Second Uncle. Please, god, let this work. I open it and hold the mirror to his nose.

And it fogs up.

"He's breathing!" I whoop before sagging back, half in tears. I have never felt such relief, ever.

"Wah, Meddy, you very smart," Big Aunt says from the bathroom. The tap is running. When did she even get to the bathroom?

"What are you doing, Big Aunt?"

"You seem very panic, so I making some tea, ya?"

"I—what? With the kettle you were about to brain him with?"

She turns off the tap and comes back out carrying the full

kettle and her Komodo dragon. "Yes, very useful, electric kettle. So he okay? Good, good. I thought maybe you kill him."

I stare wordlessly as she places the kettle gently on its stand and turns it on. Then she goes to the dressing table and stares sullenly at her fascinatorless head. "How put it back on? Need so many pin here pin that." With a sigh, she puts the Komodo dragon down on the dressing table. Then she picks it up again and shoves it into one of the drawers. "When I see it, it just make me sad," she mutters. "Because now my outfit ruin, all because Second Uncle."

Fourth Aunt clears her throat. "Well, the good news is, he's just knocked out, he'll be fine."

"We don't know that. He might have a concussion," I say.

"Aduh, he okay, no problem, we give him tea and will be fine," Big Aunt says.

I'm about to argue when a horrible thought hits me. "The call. He was calling someone when we came in."

Big Aunt and Fourth Aunt freeze, their eyes widening. "Shit," Fourth Aunt mutters.

My first thought is that he called the cops, but then I recall that he said "ko" into the phone. "Save me, ko," or something like that. "Koko" means "big brother" in Indonesian. "He was calling Big Uncle," I say.

"Ssh," Fourth Aunt puts a finger to her lips, and we all stand there for a second. I'm about to ask what's going on when I hear it—footsteps hurrying up the stairs.

"Aduh, and just about to make tea," Big Aunt complains.

Fourth Aunt walks briskly over to the electric kettle, picks it up, and stands behind the door. She catches my eye and puts a finger to her lips.

There's a loud knock on the door, the kind of knock that says, *Open up or else.*

"Open the door! I know you're in there!" Big Uncle's voice booms.

Ignoring the nauseating twist in my gut, I peer through the peephole. "He's alone."

Fourth Aunt nods at me and whispers, "Then open the door."

"Don't—" I have no idea what to say to her. "Uh—try not to kill him?"

She shrugs.

I open the door, then jump back as Big Uncle barrels through the doorway. "Where my brother?"

"No shouting," Big Aunt snaps, and somehow, against all reason, Big Uncle pauses.

A flicker of something crosses his face. It takes a moment for me to realize what it is: fear. He's scared of Big Aunt. Then his gaze moves to me and the fear melts into a sneer.

"You," he snarls, "you not do enough damage?" He steps toward me and I step backward.

"You stop there, you not move closer," Big Aunt says in her most authoritative voice, and again, Big Uncle hesitates.

"Hendry dimana?" he says.

Big Aunt's eyes shoot to the other side of the bed, where Second Uncle lies unconscious on the floor. Big Uncle follows her gaze and his eyes widen, and now his fury has been well and truly replaced by fear.

"I—is he—sorry, Lao Da, I didn't—" He takes one step back, and that's when Fourth Aunt silently slinks out from behind the door and brings down the kettle on his head.

There's only a small, underwhelming *thud*, and the next thing I know, Big Uncle topples over like a fallen tree. He smacks onto the floor so hard it makes even Fourth Aunt grimace.

"Do the mirror thing, Meddy," Fourth Aunt says as she walks past his prone body and replaces the kettle on the stand.

She flicks the switch and smiles with satisfaction as the light comes on. "Still works! These Brits know how to make their kettles last."

This isn't real. This can't be real, my mind warbles, but somehow my body listens to Fourth Aunt and steps gingerly toward Big Uncle. I crouch low and, with a trembling hand, hold the compact mirror to his nose. A moment later, it fogs up. I sag with relief. "He's alive."

"Good, no bad luck," Big Aunt says. She pats Fourth Aunt on the hand. "Very good hit, Mimi. You knock him out so fast, very good."

Fourth Aunt simpers, practically preening.

"I'm sorry, am I the only one freaking out about the two men we nearly just killed?"

"Tsk, I didn't hit him hard enough to kill him," Fourth Aunt says. "If he dies it's his own fault for having a thin skull."

"No, if he dies, it's literally our fault!" I flop onto the bed and quickly discover that flopping isn't an option in my humongous dress. The fluffy material makes me slide off the bed, and it takes quite a bit of maneuvering before I'm able to perch on the bed. "What are we going to do with them?"

"Well, tie them up, for starters," Fourth Aunt mutters. "Ugh, why is this electric kettle taking so long to boil?"

"Patience," Big Aunt says. She's already taking out the packets of tea and is placing them primly into the teacups.

"Can we stop with the tea for a second and figure out what to do?" I snap.

Big Aunt and Fourth Aunt's heads snap up and they both shoot me such a look of displeasure that I want to shrink back into the giant folds of my dress and disappear. "Sorry."

"Hmm," Big Aunt sniffs. No doubt she's going to tell Ma later about how disrespectful I was. How the hell does she still have this effect on me at such a time? How is she this formidable? Even Big Uncle was scared of her.

Speaking of which, I should secure him before he wakes. I push myself off the bed and stand there for a second, lost. I have never had to tie up another person before, and I don't really know where to start.

"Uh, I need something to tie Big Uncle up with." I nearly laugh at the absurdity of the words. There's a sentence I never thought I'd say.

"Cable ties are in the front of my luggage," Fourth Aunt says in the flippant tone of voice one might use to say, "Please pass the ketchup."

"Why do you have cable ties in your luggage?"

She levels a straight gaze at me. "No offense, Meddy, but I don't trust that your mother won't try to steal my makeup. It's Chanel, you know. So yes, I secure my makeup bag with cable ties, is that okay with you?"

"Yeah, of course," I squeak, withering under the Fourth Aunt death glare. Why did I even question her? I unzip the front pouch of her luggage and locate the pile of cable ties. "Um, I think these are too short to go around his ankles."

"Oh? Tsk, we must've used all the long ones on Second Uncle."

We stare at Second Uncle for a while, and this time, I notice black cable ties twined around his ankles and arms and wrists. How the hell did I miss that before?

"So what can we use now? Bedsheets?" I gnaw on my lip.

"Bedsheet will not work," Big Aunt says with such conviction I half-wonder what she and her ex-husband had been into in the bedroom. Ew, gross, brain. Why would you even spit that out at me now?

"Ah, I know!" Fourth Aunt says, and to my horror, she bends over and reaches up under the hem of her dress.

"Um, Fourth Aunt, what are you doing?"

Instead of answering, Fourth Aunt wriggles and grunts and tugs. I turn away, trying to shut out the weird noises coming from her.

"Ta-da!"

I chance a glance back and see that she's holding up a pair of nude-colored pantyhose proudly. "Da Jie, you take yours off too," she says.

Thankfully, Big Aunt says, "I will go bathroom to take off." I breathe a sigh of relief as she shuffles into the bathroom.

Fourth Aunt tosses her pantyhose at me and I catch them, cringing slightly at the warmth.

"Oh, don't give me that look, Meddy, those are new."

Yeah, but less than a minute ago, they were on your thighs and crotch and—

I shake off the thought and give her a weak smile before kneeling down next to Big Uncle. Okay. How to do this? I thread the pantyhose under his ankles and wrap it round and round. Uh, and then . . .

"Tsk, not like that, Meddy," Fourth Aunt says, marching over and grabbing the pantyhose out of my hands. She twines them deftly around Big Uncle's ankles, making an elaborate knot that looks so secure the only way out of them would be to cut them off.

"Wow, where did you learn to do that?"

She winks at me. "Well, I dated this one guy who was into—"

I clap my hands over my ears and go, "La la la la," until Fourth Aunt shuts her mouth. "Sorry, Fourth Aunt, I don't think I'll ever be okay with hearing about your sex life."

"Prude."

"Apa sex life?" Big Aunt says, popping her head out of the bathroom.

"NOTHING!" we both shout.

Big Aunt narrows her eyes at us and goes back inside the bathroom. Fourth Aunt breathes a sigh of relief. Moments later, Big Aunt comes out and hands us her pantyhose, which Fourth Aunt uses to tie Big Uncle's wrists in under a minute.

"Let's tie them to the radiator," I suggest. But doing it is easier said than done, especially in my lovely, multilayered dress. God, my dress. All these layers of tulle and exquisite lace. It seems silly to worry about it, but seriously, a huge part of me is going, "Don't get it dirty or torn!" Not to mention the fact that it is really hard to carry a full-grown man while wearing an unforgiving corset.

Big Aunt and Fourth Aunt do their best to help me, but by the time we manage to drag him to the wall, we're all out of breath. I take one of Fourth Aunt's cable ties, loop it around the radiator pipe, and secure Big Uncle's wrist to it. We go over to Second Uncle and do the same to his wrist after tightening his bindings.

Then we stand up, exhale, and study our handiwork.

"Okay, can. This good enough," Big Aunt says, turning her attention back to the electric kettle.

Fourth Aunt goes to the dressing table to wrestle her fascinator back onto her head while I stay there, staring at the two men who are now tied up to the radiator in my bridal room. How the hell did we get here? I look at Big Uncle's slack face. His mouth is hanging half open. I keep thinking of the expression on his face as he burst into the room.

He had been really scared of Big Aunt, which is most definitely weird, right? I mean, people are usually intimidated by Big Aunt. She exudes this aura of "Don't try me, kid; I will take off my sandal and beat you over the head with it." Not that she's ever done that to me—oh no, not pliant, submissive me—but she has done it plenty of times to my cousins, especially her younger son, Russ. So the fact that Big Uncle had been so uncertain around her isn't out of the ordinary. But it had been more than just uncertainty; he had been *fearful*. The look that had crossed his face was real animal fear—survival fear—not "Uh-oh, she might take out her feather duster and whack me across the legs with it" fear. And he had called her . . .

"Lao da," I say.

Fourth Aunt laughs, glancing up as she stabs the final hairpin into place. The kettle boils then, and she pours out hot water into three cups. "Haven't heard that one in a while."

"Lao" technically means "old." In Chinese culture, age isn't just a number, but also a measure of reverence. The older you are, the more revered, the more powerful. "Da" means "big." I'm pretty sure Big Uncle wasn't just calling Big Aunt "old and big," but something else. "What does it mean?"

"It means 'boss,'" Fourth Aunt says, grinning. She hands the first cup to Big Aunt. "Here you go, Lao Da."

Big Aunt takes the cup with a purse of her lips. "You boil water too long, it get too hot. You know should not let water boil with these leaves, they cannot take too hot water."

Fourth Aunt rolls her eyes. "Yeah, yeah."

"Wait, but I thought 'boss' is 'lao ban'?" I say.

"'Lao da' is like an informal way of saying 'boss,'" Fourth Aunt explains. "It's used when you're with friends, or—"

"In a gang?" I say. "Is it what they call gang leaders?"

There's a pause. Big Aunt finishes taking a sip of the tea and nods. "Yes, Meddy, usually gang leader we call 'Lao da.' Show respect, but not so formal like in office." She catches me staring at her and frowns. "Ada apa?"

"Uh. He called you that."

"He call me that?" Her frown deepens. "Where got? I not remember. When he call me that?"

Fourth Aunt snorts with laughter. "Oh, yeah! He did, didn't he? When he came in and saw his brother on the floor, he was like, 'Sorry, Lao da!' Ha! That's funny, isn't it, Da Jie? Lao da. Wait until I tell Er Jie about this. She's going to love the fact that someone called you 'Lao da.' And by 'love,' I mean she's going to absolutely hate it."

"I think maybe you not tell her," Big Aunt says, but she says it in a tone of voice that clearly means: *Oh yes, tell Second Aunt, and make sure I'm around when you tell her so that I can see her reaction.*

"Hang on, I think you're missing the point here," I say, raising my voice to be heard above Fourth Aunt's cackle. "Um. The point is . . . he called you Lao Da, which is weird, and he seemed really scared of you, Big Aunt, like fearful. Like he was scared that you were going to actually hurt him." I glance down at his prone body and add, "I mean, he wasn't wrong. But um, I think there's something more here." There's something niggling at the back of my head, something that's calling out to be heard, oh god, what is it—

"Oh my god," I gasp.

Both my aunts peer at me with raised brows. "Yes?" Big Aunt says.

"Second Uncle!" I cry. They both jump and look at him, and I say, "No, he's not up. I just remembered what he said when we came in the room! He said, 'Mafia!' I thought he was talking about his own family, but he wasn't. He meant us. They think we're mafia!"

19

Silence.

Big Aunt and Fourth Aunt might as well be statues, they're sitting so still. Then Fourth Aunt throws her head back and howls with laughter. "Oh my god, that is the most ridiculous thing I have ever heard. Can you imagine us as the mafia?"

All too easily, I want to tell her, but decide it would be wisest not to say that. "I mean, kind of? Look at Staphanie's family. Would you have guessed that they're mafia? I didn't, but well, here we are. And you were telling me how Abraham Lincoln was really sweet and nerdy and now he's apparently a mafia lord."

"Yeah, but there's like—" Fourth Aunt flaps her arms for a few moments before dropping them. "I mean, there's got to be a—some sort of tell, you know? It's obvious we're good people."

"Are we?" I throw a very meaningful look at Big Uncle and Second Uncle.

"Okay, they're the bad guys, we're the good guys; there's a very clear distinction here," Fourth Aunt says.

"Right, but they also know that we killed Ah Guan. Remember? That's what got us into this whole mess in the first place. They probably think we offed him or something. I mean, technically, we did. By accident, but still."

Fourth Aunt's mouth opens, closes, and presses into a thin line. She turns to Big Aunt and says, "Da Jie, what do you think?"

Big Aunt runs her finger along the rim of her teacup, frowning slightly as she mulls. Softly, she mutters, "Is explain what I hear Ama say. She say, 'Rén bùkě màoxiàng.' Is mean . . ."

"Don't judge a book by its cover?" I hazard a guess.

Big Aunt's frown deepens. "Aduh, no, Meddy. Where got book? I say 'ren,' is mean person. Cannot judge person by face. Aiya, I tell your Ma, must send you to Chinese school early, but she not listen. You see, now you think person is book."

"No, I didn't mean it that way. It's just a saying in English, it can also apply to—never mind. Okay, so she said don't judge a book—I mean, a person—by their appearance. What were you guys talking about when she said that?"

"Not to me. I hear her say to Staphanie in bathroom when we meet for dim sum. I not know what Staphanie saying, and then Ama say that to her. Then she say, 'People can look like good family but then turn out they dangerous.' Then I come in and they both smile-smile and become quiet. At the time I thinking, oh, maybe Staphanie have boyfriend not come from good family, and Ama warning her not so gullible, fall for bad boy."

Of course they were talking about us. It makes so much sense. It applies perfectly to us: we seem like a good, normal family on the surface, but beneath that, we're all teeth and claws and dirty fights to the death. And since they already know we had something to do with Ah Guan's death, it's not such a big leap to think we're mafia, especially if they also run in those circles. They must meet so many other mafia families.

What's one more?

A mirthless laugh bubbles out of me. I barely recognize the sound. "They think we're mafia." It sounds absolutely ridiculous when I say it out loud. "They think *we* are mafia," I say again, just to have another feel of the words. Nope, still completely nonsensical.

"You know, that might be the only reason we're all still alive right now," Fourth Aunt says, studying her nails.

"What?" My head snaps up so quick I almost pull a muscle.

"Yeah, like, I'm pretty sure Abraham Lincoln mentioned that mafia families have a sort of code, like if they want to go to war with another family, they need to get the green light from the other families, that sort of thing. Like a board vote, you know?"

My head is spinning. "Wait. There's a lot here. I don't even know where to begin. I mean, there's a mafia board?"

"Tch, not board, maybe more like arisan, you know?" Big Aunt says.

"Arisan? Isn't that like the ladies who lunch?"

"Ah, yes, very rich tai-tai, they gather once every month, have lunch at very high-class restaurant," Big Aunt says. "I got tell you that I was invited to join one or not? The group very high-class one, you know, even got the daughter of the Jofi Corp."

Fourth Aunt snorts. "Like we'd have been able to afford to join that arisan. You need to put in money toward the arisan. The kind of arisan the Jofi Corp daughter would join would probably cost a few grand a month."

"Just to have lunch with friends?" I goggle at them before shaking my head. "Anyway. Okay, so there's a mafia arisan . . ."

"Yes, what you think mafia wives all do? Of course got mafia arisan," Big Aunt says. "The men outside all killing-killing, the women inside eating fine dining and decide who husband should kill."

"Which is not us, because they think we're one of them," Fourth Aunt says.

Big Aunt's eyebrows rise and the corners of her mouth twitch. If I didn't know any better, I'd think she was a bit tickled by all of this. "Are you trying not to laugh?"

Big Aunt purses her lips and doesn't meet my eye. "Well, I just saying, all those tai-tai, they seem a bit . . . how you say, relief when I refuse to join their arisan. At first I think maybe aiya, they look down on me . . ."

"But now you think they were relieved because they thought you were such a big, bad mafia boss lady?"

Again, the corners of Big Aunt's mouth threaten to lift, but she purses her lips into an even tighter rosebud to keep from grinning. "I not control what people think of me. If people think I mafia boss, then I cannot help."

"Da Jie, you'd make the best mafia boss," Fourth Aunt says, refilling Big Aunt's teacup. "Can you even imagine? You'd be like, 'Harun disrespected me on the phone. Cut off his ear.' You'd be fabulous at it."

Big Aunt waves her away and takes a sip of the tea with obvious enjoyment.

Frustration and anxiety bubble through my chest. Why are they so relaxed? It's as though they've forgotten that today's my wedding day and every second we spend in here is a second I miss of my actual wedding. Plus, people are going to start looking for us soon, if they haven't already. "Okay, can we focus?

Staphanie's family, who is actually mafia, thinks we are mafia. What should we do about that?"

"Have fun with it!" Fourth Aunt crows.

I shoot her a death glare and she goes, "What?" as if she hadn't just suggested messing with the actual mafia for shits and giggles.

"Maybe—okay," I mutter, pacing about the room. Or trying to pace, anyway. I keep forgetting I'm in a ridiculously huge dress that doesn't allow for much movement in small spaces. "Right. So maybe it was all a misunderstanding." Hope dawns and I very nearly cry with relief. "Maybe they think we'd be okay with them assassinating Lilian because we're in the same line of work as they are. Maybe if we just told them that we're not mafia, they'd let us go? Maybe they'd call the whole thing off!" Tears of hope spring to my eyes and I grin madly at my two aunts, hoping like hell that they'll agree with my logic.

"Or maybe, like I said before, the only reason why they haven't just bumped us all off is because they don't want to start a war," Fourth Aunt says in a flat voice, stabbing a dagger into my hope balloon.

Big Aunt sighs. "Oh, Meddy, you still must learn so much, ya. Mafia not work like that. Is more like Fourth Aunt say, if they think you mafia, they respect you more. If they think you not, then they know they can kill you and no consequence."

"But there are consequences! You can't just go around killing civilians. The cops will get you!"

"The cops," Big Aunt snorts in the tone someone might use to say, "Pfft, the clowns."

"Yeah, the cops! Especially here in England. They're not going to be okay with a little murder spree going on in good old Christ Church College."

"Don't be daft, Meddy, of course Staphanie's family won't

bump us off right now. I'm talking about later on," Fourth Aunt says. "When everything's done and dusted and we're all back home in L.A., we'll get picked off, one by one. They'll make it look like an accident to the Americans, but the Indos will get the message."

I gape at her. Somehow, in my naivete, I'd thought that if we just made it through today, we'd be okay. This whole thing would be behind us. But she's right, of course. Why wouldn't it follow us long after the wedding is over? Of course the mafia wouldn't just let us walk free, especially since we know what they've done. The realization is suffocating. Literally. I find myself wheezing, my breath coming in and out in an awful whistle.

Big Aunt grabs my face with both hands and yanks me firmly down so I'm staring right into her eyes.

"Stop that, Meddy," she says, using the Voice.

I gulp and stop breathing, staring like a trapped animal.

"You hold yourself, not panic like that, malu-maluin aja," she says sternly.

Embarrassing? I want to laugh. No one's around except us— okay, and the two knocked-out men—and she's worried about saving face?

"We not run around like chicken. No. We handle it. We will show them, we are even more powerfulest family than them."

It's as though Big Aunt has been waiting for this moment all her life. Right in front of me, she changes. Her back straightens. Her enormous bosom rises majestically. Her chin lifts, ever so slightly, and her expression changes into one that is self-assured and speaks of easy violence.

And I find myself staring at a mafia boss lady.

20

Big Aunt and Fourth Aunt coach me on how to behave more like a gangster before giving up and saying, "Well, you could pass as the princess who has no idea how the family business is run, I suppose."

"Thanks, Fourth Aunt."

She grins and rubs her hands together, reminding me of how eager she'd been to see Ah Guan's body that terrible night.

After checking the bindings on the men one last time, we leave the room in time for cocktail hour. I walk behind my aunts, grabbing the heavy skirt of my dress and struggling to keep up with them as they stride down the hallway. Even the way they walk is different. How the hell did they change themselves so effortlessly? Big Aunt has always had an air of self-assurance about her, but now that air has sharpened into something that is, quite frankly, terrifying. And Fourth Aunt, well, she's practically scampering with glee. I can very easily imagine her leaping out of some poor sucker's closet deep in the night with a dagger in her hands.

We walk through the quad and into the Masters Garden,

where they've set up for cocktail hour. The place is breathtakingly beautiful. When I'd last seen it during our tour, it had already been impressive—a vast lawn lined with centuries-old stone walls and greenery, flanked by the majestic Christ Church College in the background.

Now, there's a beautiful white tent set up, inside which there are canapés and drinks, and it seems like there are bursts of flowers everywhere. Huge arrangements of hydrangeas, peonies, lilies, and roses line the borders of the garden, so gorgeous I can't help but stare as we get closer. Everyone is mingling and having a great time. Off to one side, a live band has set up and is playing something I don't recognize but that makes me want to kick off my shoes and dance barefoot on the dewy grass. Staphanie and her family may be fake vendors, but apparently they have good taste in music. The entire place has morphed into a magical fairy-tale garden.

If only I could enjoy it the way I was meant to.

A cheer goes up when the guests spot me, and I give them a weak smile.

"There you are," Nathan says, coming up to me and giving me a kiss. "I was starting to wonder if you got cold feet and ran away," he jokes, but his eyes are truly concerned, making my stomach twist painfully.

"Sorry, I was just—uh, I had to pee, so I had to get out of my dress and, um, it's a whole thing."

Nathan laughs. "I didn't even think of the logistics of going to the bathroom. I'm sorry it was such an ordeal for you. Have I told you that you look . . ." He sighs happily, twining his arms around my waist and pulling me close. I turn my face up toward his and our lips are about to meet when someone says, "Got you!"

I jump, my forehead smacking into Nathan's jaw. "Ow!" he cries, grabbing his chin.

"Shit, I'm so sorry, are you okay?" I say, reaching out for him.

"I'm fine." He waves me away.

"Sorry, didn't mean to scare you like that," Staphanie says with a look that conveys the exact opposite.

The familiar, dark fear clutches at my chest, tightening around my lungs and making it hard to breathe. But then I recall what Big Aunt and Fourth Aunt had told me. About needing to convince them that we, too, are mafia. That we're not helpless civilians. That we, too, have sharp teeth.

I mean, obviously I don't, but I make myself stand up straight and meet Staphanie's gaze straight on. "You didn't scare me."

A frown crosses her face, but with Nathan right there, all Staphanie can do is fake a smile and say, "Oh, good. Everyone's been wondering where you've been."

"Had to go pee. Kind of hard to do in the dress," I mutter.

"Ah," Staphanie says. "Well, are you guys ready for portraits?" She turns to Nathan. "Your parents have been asking about them."

"Oh yes, I forgot to mention. Mum's very eager for us to do family portraits soon, before my Nan passes out from too much champagne," Nathan says, smiling apologetically. "Is that okay? Is your family ready for photos?"

"Sure, yeah, of course."

As Nathan goes to get his family, I crane my neck to look for mine. Big Aunt and Fourth Aunt have located Ma and Second Aunt and pulled them away from Lilian for a bit. They must've filled them in on the two men who are currently bound and gagged in the bridal room—because of course there are two men bound and gagged in the bridal room—because Ma and Second Aunt are gaping in the universal expression of "WTF?"

As I watch, Big Aunt and Fourth Aunt whisper urgently to them, and Ma looks dubious while Second Aunt nods and then shifts her position so that she's standing in a way that somehow conveys belligerence, much like a surly teenage boy. I guess they've just been told of the plan to act like mafia. Ma wrings her hands for a bit, shifting between this position and that position, brushing down her dress, patting her Komodo dragon hat, and fussing until Fourth Aunt snaps at her. Then she straightens, glowering at Fourth Aunt and looking very much like she could kill another human with her bare hands.

Big Aunt goes to Lilian, who's sampling a few of the hors d'oeuvres, and puts her arm around hers. Lilian looks confused, but Big Aunt says something to her and her face breaks into a huge smile and she nods. My family surrounds Lilian, and together, they make their way toward me.

It's a struggle to keep the polite smile on my face as they near. How do I describe the sight of them? Even before the whole disaster with Staphanie, my family would have looked ridiculous—okay, that's mean—eye-catching, what with the matching radioactive-eggplant dresses and the towering Komodo dragon fascinators. But now, the look is compounded by the fact they're trying to pass for mafia.

Each of them seems to have a different idea of how mafiosi behave. Big Aunt is striding like a twentieth-century aristocrat who's just received word that her granddaughter was caught being fresh with a commoner. She's giving strong Maggie-Smith-in-*Downton-Abbey* vibes. Second Aunt is swishing her arms fluidly, as if she's about to launch into some deadly Tai Chi move. Ma is glaring at everyone who glances their way, and Fourth Aunt is strutting, literally strutting, like she's pounding down the catwalk in Milan. Her lips are pouted and she's glaring at everything with her trademark "I'm fierce" face.

It's like watching the Four Horsemen of the Apocalypse descend upon you. My insides writhe, especially as heads turn to watch them. It's as though they've got a magnetic hold on everyone's gazes. No one can look away, and who can blame them?

I'm suddenly aware of Staphanie next to me. With a huge effort, I tear my gaze away from my family and study Staphanie from the side of my eye. She's frowning at my aunts and mom, and I can't decipher the meaning. Is she convinced they're mafia? Then I recall belatedly that I'm not supposed to make her think they're mafia; I'm supposed to make her think *we* are. I need to seem tough too.

Quick, think of something to say. Something badass that the daughter of a mafia family would say.

What the hell would the daughter of a mafia family say to her wedding photographer who also happens to be mafia and is holding her wedding hostage?

All sorts of movie clichés rush through my head.

Say hello to my little friend? What little friend? I don't have a gun on me, and that one's always struck me as kind of weirdly sexual.

Your ass is mine? Is it? Do I even want it? Also kind of weirdly sexual.

"I don't know what your family's trying to pull, but it's not going to work," Staphanie says in a low voice.

My teeth clack together in frustration. "You're messing with the wrong family," I hiss. Wow, that came out really weak. I should've said, "You're *fucking* with the wrong family." "Fuck," I add for good measure.

Staphanie gives me a weird look before frowning at my family. "Where's Big Aunt's fascinator?" she says suddenly.

It's so far off from what I thought she'd say that for a second, I completely blank out. "Huh?"

"Her hat. Where is it?" Her voice comes out tinged with impatience. "She's going to ruin the pictures if she doesn't have it on."

"Oh right, *that's* what's going to ruin the photos, not the fact that my photographer's a complete fraud."

Staphanie shakes her head, muttering something under her

breath, and taps something on her phone. "Is Second Uncle still up in the room?"

My heart thumps like a wild animal against my ribcage. "I don't know. How would I know that?"

She frowns. "Weren't you just there?"

"Oh, right. Yeah. I mean, sure. Whatever." Wow, I am so bad at this.

Staphanie narrows her eyes.

"He wasn't there," I say quickly.

"What do you mean, he wasn't there?" Staphanie growls.

"I mean, I don't know, I think Second Aunt said some really horrible things to him this morning and told him to go." It hits me then that I should lean into the whole "My family is mafia" angle. "You know how forceful my family can get," I add in the most cryptic voice I can muster.

Staphanie's frown deepens. "What do you mean?"

I'm saved from having to reply by my family arriving like avenging angels. Close up, they're even more intimidating. I swear they're practically sweating murder vibes.

"You don't seem to be taking very many pictures," Fourth Aunt says in a syrupy sweet voice.

Without taking her eyes off me, Staphanie lifts her camera and clicks the shutter. "There," she says. She smooths down the front of her pants and takes a deep breath. Then she leans toward me and mutters, "I don't know what you think you're doing messing with us, but you're going to regret it."

If it weren't for Lilian, I would grab that Canon 5D Mark III and smash it into her face. Well, I wouldn't, because of all the guests. And also the fact that I'm a complete coward through and through. I'm not even passive-aggressive; I'm more passive-passive. I can't be oppressed because I'm basically a human mattress.

Luckily, Nathan arrives with his family in tow, saving us from any further interaction. Fourth Aunt looks just about ready to plunge her blinged-out claws into Staphanie's throat.

"We're all here," Nathan says with his easy, boyish grin. "Picture time!"

Dread fills my guts as Staphanie gives a bitter smile and gestures to her camera. "This is going to be a family portrait to remember."

Group portraits are one of my least favorite parts of weddings. As someone who is naturally soft-spoken, having to corral hundreds and often thousands of guests into a cohesive group is a nightmare. Add smartphones to the picture (ha!) and you've got a recipe for a disaster. There hasn't been a wedding in recent years where I haven't had to (nicely) shout at groups of well-meaning uncles or aunties who rush out of the group to grab pictures with their phones.

Our family portraits are just as bad as expected, what with the number of people involved. Ama is helping to guide Nathan's grandparents into position while Staphanie tags along behind her and whispers something to her. My heart rate triples at the sight of the two of them muttering to each other. She must be filling Ama in on what I said about Second Uncle. Why had I said that stuff to her? What the hell was I thinking?

Finally, Ama calls out, "Okay, is look good, I think ready for first photo." She steps off to the side.

"Yep!" Staphanie says with false brightness. "Looking good, guys!" She raises her camera.

"Um, excuse me?" Annie says.

Staphanie lowers her camera and forces a smile. "Yes?"

"Um, not to be a bother, but this photo is supposed to be the bride, groom, and the grandparents only?"

I look over and find that Big Aunt has positioned herself right next to Nathan's grandparents.

"Oh yes, is okay, innit, mate," Ma calls out. "Big Aunt like a grandma to Meddy, matey, ahoy!"

Oh god. I try to shoot Ma mental messages like, "Stop saying *mate*; you are not a twentysomething guy at the pub!" Also, "WHY ARE YOU SPEAKING LIKE A PIRATE?"

Nathan laughs and says, "That's totally fine. Love having you here, Big Aunt." He smiles at Big Aunt, putting his arm around her shoulders and posing for the photo.

The picture is taken, we thank his grandparents and Big Aunt, and Staphanie calls out the next people. "Next one is bride and groom plus parents from both sides."

I can't help but notice that Ama is walking away. Where is she going? But I don't get a chance to point this out to my family as they all march forward and take their place next to us.

Nathan's parents gape as the four women gather around us.

"Um, hang on," Annie titters, smiling uncomfortably, "not to be a bother, but um, the list does say parents only?"

Fourth Aunt growls, baring her teeth. "I will cut—"

"Aren't photos so fun?" I spring between them, smiling manically. Jesus, what are these words coming out of my mouth? "You all look *amazing*. Just *amazing*!" Someone stop me, please.

"Meddy is so close to her aunts, they're like her parents," Nathan says to his parents.

"Then why bother having a list if they're going to be in every picture?" Annie says.

Fourth Aunt looks at Big Aunt and cocks her head. "You want me to pop this bi—"

"Is okay, we not need to be in all photos, you right, Annie," Ma says.

"No," Big Aunt says. "Not right." She widens her eyes at Ma meaningfully. "We are powerful family, we not giving in."

We are powerful family . . . ? Of course. A mafia family wouldn't back down over something as trivial as pictures. All of the life squeaks out of me and I deflate, watching helplessly as Big Aunt turns to Annie and says, firmly, "We staying as family for photo. No worry, Annie, luv, it will be dog's bollocks."

Annie blinks, looking as though she's just been punched in the face. I can't say I blame her.

"Er, yeah," Nathan says slowly. "Yeah, it'll be . . . dog's bollocks." He's looking really confused, but also suspiciously like he's trying to hold back laughter. I'm annoyed until I recall that to him, this is a normal wedding and these are just normal wedding hiccups and nothing to do with a life-and-death situation. "Come on, Mum, it'll be fine. It's not a big deal. The more the merrier."

Annie smiles weakly as we huddle into a tight group and pose for the photo.

"One, two . . . um." Staphanie lowers the camera.

"What's wrong?" Nathan says.

"Uh." We all follow her gaze to my family, and I pray for the ground to open up and swallow us, because they're all doing the most ridiculous poses I can imagine. Big Aunt is standing ramrod straight, chin up, arms akimbo like a proud dictator overseeing her army. Second Aunt has plunged into a Tai Chi pose that's probably called something like "Grab Your Opponent by the Balls." Ma is openly glaring at Staphanie with anger, and Fourth Aunt has gone full Kardashian—butt out, lips pouting, one arm straight up over her head, the other perched on her hip.

I close my eyes. This is a nightmare. Wake up now. Please?

Thing is, I have no idea if this is part of their whole "act like a mafia family" thing or if this is just them being themselves. I suppose it could be either.

"Oh," Annie says nervously. "Are we doing fun poses, then?"

"Fun pose?" Big Aunt says in a stern voice. "What is . . . fun pose?" She says the word "fun" as if it's a completely alien concept.

Annie stares at her.

"Just take the picture," I beg Staphanie.

She shrugs and raises the camera. I force a smile, focusing on the reassuring warmth of Nathan's hand on my back as the shutter clicks. I try not to think of what the final photos will look like. Plus, there are other, more pressing things to worry about right now, like where the hell is Ama and what is she up to?

Fortunately, the next few photos on the list only require Nathan's side of the family. Unfortunately, it means I get even less of a chance to grab one of my aunts to tell them to—I don't know—watch out for Ama, or whatever.

"Is there a reason why your family seems to have adopted Lilian?" Nathan murmurs, watching as my family rushes to Lilian, who looks slightly surprised and unnerved to see them stampeding back toward her.

"Oh, I think they just really connected with her. You know, what with her being a single woman and all," I say, then quickly pat his arm and gesture at the camera to remind him to smile for the next picture.

A flash of movement from the far corner catches my eye. My blood freezes. It's Ama, talking to Third Uncle. From where we're standing, I can't hear what they're saying, but it's clear from Third Uncle's movements that he's close to panicking. He's gesticulating wildly, shaking his head, pacing about. Ama says something and he freezes before hanging his head. I can feel his shame all the way from over here. Then he leaves, looking grimly resolute.

It's clear what's just happened. She's told him to go and find Second Uncle.

21

"Okay, sorry, guys, picture time is postponed for a bit. Bride needs a bathroom break. Oh, wait, I'm the bride. Yeah, I need a bathroom break, okay, sorry! Be back in a bit. Sorry!" I wave apologetically at everyone as I rush to my family, leaving poor, sweet Nathan looking confused.

"Meddy, you done with photo already?" Ma says. "Aduh, why you run here, run there, later you get sweaty your makeup will run. You see, your hair become messy already."

"I have to—can I talk to you all for a second?" Belatedly, I notice Lilian in the middle of the group. Argh. I can't have them leave her, especially not right now, when Ama has just sent Third Uncle to do something nefarious like fetch his sniper rifle. "Fourth Aunt, you stay here. The rest of you, please, I need to talk to you."

"Why me?" Fourth Aunt says.

Because you're the one most likely to be able to actually kill another human, I want to say. But of course, I can't say that in front of Lilian, so instead, I just say, "Please, Fourth Aunt? I'll explain later."

She sighs, pursing her lips.

"Um, maybe I should go," Lilian says.

Instantly, all of us turn to her and say, "NO!"

She starts, eyes as wide as a caught rabbit's. "Um . . ."

"You're such good company," Fourth Aunt says, taking Lilian's arm and leading her away. "Come, let's get more champagne, eh?"

My family gathers around me and I lead them away from the crowd. As soon as we're out of earshot of everyone, I say, "I messed up. I was trying to be all mafia-like and I kind of hinted to Staphanie that we might have done something to Second Uncle." I wince even as I hear the words I'm saying. God, how could I have been so dumb?

Instead of the scolding I'd expected, my aunts and mother simply nod patiently.

"Is not bad idea," Big Aunt says. "Might be scare them."

"Yeah, well, I think it's scared them into doing something! I just saw Ama talking to Third Uncle, and then he went off looking all determined. What if she's sent him to do something really bad like, I don't know, set off a bomb or something?"

"Choi, touch wood!" Ma cries.

"Meddy, why you think got bomb?" Big Aunt says.

I pause. Why would I think there's a bomb? It seems so ridiculous now that I stop to actually consider it. I shrug. "I don't know. I mean, it's probably not a bomb? I just know they're up to something bad, and I don't know how we can figure out what they're plotting. I feel like they've been one step ahead of us this entire time. They've had months to plan this. We've only had one night to come up with a plan to stop them, and now we've somehow got those two uncles tied up in the bedroom—"

I choke on this, unable to say the ridiculous words.

"This Ama, she is boss lady," Big Aunt says.

"Yes, we need overthrow boss lady," Second Aunt says snidely, side-eyeing Big Aunt.

Big Aunt frowns at her. "What you mean by that?"

"Oh, nothing. Just saying if we want taking them down, then we go for snake head. Cut it off." She holds up a hand and mimes cutting something with her second and middle fingers while glaring meaningfully at Big Aunt.

Big Aunt's chest balloons. "Oh, you want to cut snake head, ya? You think you can cut it off and then *you* become the snake head?"

I step in between them and give Big Aunt a terrified smile. "Second Aunt's talking about Ama, that's all. Right, Second Aunt? Right. Okay, so anyway, back to the problem at hand. We need to throw them off somehow. Like, maybe if we could get them to drink too much champagne—"

It's as though a light switch just clicked on inside me. Now I know why they call it a "light bulb moment." Everything really does feel brighter all of a sudden.

"Ma! I got it!"

Ma beams with pride. "Ah, I know you will figure something, you such a smart girl, ya?"

"I need your weed."

Ma's smile freezes on her face. Her gaze moves from side to side, going from Big Aunt to Second Aunt and back to me. "Weed, apa?"

"Come on, Ma. That marijuana you gave the groomsmen at Jacqueline and Tom Cruise's wedding, remember? The ones that got them high out of their minds?"

Ma titters nervously. "Aduh, Meddy, I not know what you talking about. I not take any of that anymore, especially since you tell me they are—what you call it—happy drug?"

"Recreational drugs."

"Oh yes, that. No, I don't bring, I don't drink anymore, of course not!" she warbles.

We all just stare at her. The silence stretches on for eons. Big Aunt sighs and says, "San Mei—"

"Oh, *fine*," Ma snaps. "We go bathroom." She stalks off without waiting for any of us to reply.

Jesus, she has it on her right now? I was thinking we'd have to send her back to the hotel to get it or something. "You carry it with you everywhere?"

"Tch, I not want later maybe cleaner find it and steal it, then how?"

"How did you get it through customs?" I cry.

"I put inside tea box, and then put box inside check-in luggage. Very easy."

She's referring to smuggling drugs through customs as "very easy," a small voice in my head gibbers. This is way too much for me to handle right now, so I shove the thought aside and rush after her. We crowd into the small bathroom. Everything in England is small and I swear my dress fills up the entire space. Ma goes into a cubicle and slams the door behind her. Big Aunt and Second Aunt take the chance to check their reflections in the mirror. We hear grunts, then the distinct sound of something ripping.

"Aduh!" Ma cries.

"Ma, do you need help?"

"I rip my pantyho."

I wince, but as far as things go, that's hardly a disaster. Plus, she's in a floor-length gown, I don't know why she's even bothered to wear pantyhose. There are more grunts, then Ma comes out, looking flushed and slightly worse for wear, her Komodo dragon all askew on her head.

"Nih," she mumbles, slapping down a little plastic baggie onto the palm of my hand. It's warm and slightly moist. Urgh. I do not want to know where this was kept. I hold the baggie up gingerly and Big Aunt and Second Aunt peer closely at it. It's filled with coarse brown powder.

"What's all this stuff?" I say.

"TCM," Ma says. "I grind it all—the ginseng root, lah, the tree bark, the—um—Mary-Joanna—all grind up so take shorter time to cook, otherwise you have to brew for hours, waduh, how to do that in hotel?"

"Okay. Wow, you've put a lot of thought into this." Which is good. The marijuana being in powder form means a faster reaction time. Probably. Good thing Fourth Aunt isn't here right now. She'd definitely make some snide remark about how Ma is so thorough when it comes to her drugs. And, you know, she would have a point.

"We just put a bit in champagne, the bubbles will help react and then bam, they will pusing deh."

"Okay, yeah, sounds like a plan." I grip the baggie tight and head for the door before I pause. "Hang on, I probably won't get a chance to slip this into the champagne without anyone noticing." I keep forgetting I'm the bride, not the photographer who can melt into the background. "Maybe one of you can do it?"

"I do it," Second Aunt says, grabbing it before anyone has a chance to say anything.

"Ahem," Big Aunt clears her throat.

Ma and I stare at the two of them, neither of us wanting to get in between Big Aunt and Second Aunt, round VII. But I can't let this go on too long because it's my wedding day and people will start to notice that the bride is hardly around, which is probably frowned upon or something. Plus, it's a bit shitty to Nathan, given it's his wedding day too.

"Um, maybe you two can do it together?" I say, and immediately kick myself. That is the dumbest idea a human has ever come up with. "Or, uh, let's flip for it!" I pat my pockets, desperate for a coin, and belatedly recall that one, I'm in my wedding gown, and two, I completely failed to foresee the need for coins and do not have any hidden on me.

"No, no, I know how to do quietly, not pull all attention," Big Aunt says, grabbing it. Except this time, Second Aunt isn't letting go.

"Hanh!" Second Aunt barks. "You? Not pull all attention? Hah!"

Ma and I are frozen with fear as Second Aunt gives another "Hah!" for good measure. It's like watching two countries escalate into a World War III situation.

"Maybe Ma could—" I squeak, then jump when the two wrench at the baggie at the same time, and with a horrific snap, the plastic rips and coarse brown powder spills everywhere.

"Aduh!" Ma cries. "You see, you see? Why you two must like that, fighting all the time? Now you waste my TCM! You think very cheap, ya? All the ingredients are so expensive. Like the dong chong xiao cao, that is not cheap okay! Wah, even the yu xing cao—what you call it, the heartleaf—so expensive, you know? I need for my hemorrhoids, otherwise so pain!"

Against all odds, Ma's verbal diarrhea defuses some of the tension between Big Aunt and Second Aunt. They both actually look contrite as they brush the ground-up herbs off their fancy gowns.

Big Aunt can barely look me in the eye. "Big Aunt is sorry, Meddy. Now we not have no drugs."

"Tch," Ma says loudly, marching back into the cubicle and slamming the door behind her.

We stare at the cubicle door. We stare at each other. We shrug. We go back to staring at the cubicle door. Again, grunts come from inside the cubicle. And then little hops, as if Ma's doing jumping jacks. Then a loud bang, which startles us all.

"Ma, are you okay?"

"Yes, yes, just trip and fall against door. I almost get—ungh—ha!" She pants loudly and then unlocks the door and staggers out, holding another plastic baggie with a triumphant smile. This time, I don't wait for Big Aunt or Second Aunt to react before grabbing it myself.

"Eh, Er Jie, zip me up, ya," Ma says, gesturing to her back.

Second Aunt does so, her mouth still half open.

"I can't believe you have two baggies of TCM on you," I marvel. Then I pause. "Wait, how many baggies of TCM *do* you have on you?"

Ma tuts again, sucking in her breath, while Second Aunt grapples with the zipper of her dress. "Aduh, Meddy, of course this my last baggie."

I exchange a look with Big Aunt but decide not to press on. Anyway, my mother being a drug lord has turned out to be a good thing, so maybe I shouldn't make too big a fuss.

"Right," I say, holding the second baggie tight. "Now. We need to decide who gets to do the honors. Of spiking the drinks, which isn't very honorable at all," I add. "Maybe Ma can do it? After all, she's done it before, at Tom and Jacqueline's wedding?"

Ma beams at me as if I've just bestowed a huge honor on her instead of asking her to roofie some drinks. "Wah, me? Really?"

"I feel like you think this is commendable . . ."

Ma snatches the baggie from me. "Yes! Yes, okay, I do. Thank you for trust." She hugs it to her chest, practically shining with pride. Big Aunt and Second Aunt nod with thin-lipped smiles like they're Taylor Swift losing a Grammy to Adele.

"Okay. Well, glad we got that sorted. Maybe Big Aunt and Second Aunt can distract other people while Ma spikes the drinks? That would be very helpful."

They grunt their agreement and we all file out of the bathroom. Ma skips the entire way back to the garden, the Komodo dragon on her head bopping jauntily as she goes. What family gene am I missing? I'm pretty sure I would never be excited about spiking someone's drink.

When we get back to the Masters Garden, I join Nathan while Ma and my aunts go to the drinks table.

"Ah, there you are," Nathan says. "Glad to have you back."

Is it just me, or is his smile a bit forced? I wish I could pull him aside to talk, but I'm immediately distracted by friends and family coming by to chat with us, not to mention Staphanie, who's hovering nearby and taking the occasional photo. Plus, what would I say to Nathan anyway? Where would I even begin with my explanation of this insane day? So instead, I smile back at him and make small talk with our guests, fake-laughing my way through inane conversations about how gorgeous everything is, and oh yes, isn't my dress wonderful, do you know, it's an original piece by an Indonesian designer.

In the midst of all this, I watch out of the corner of my eye as Ma, Big Aunt, and Second Aunt crowd around the drinks table, flapping and occasionally squawking at each other.

After a few tense moments, the little group finally breaks up and Ma carries a tray of champagne flutes with a smug smile. They look around the garden, spot Staphanie taking pictures of Annie and Chris, and begin their approach.

"Staphanie!" Ma calls out with a huge smile. "You working so hard, ya? You such good girl, very good photographer, very good."

God, does the woman not have any subtlety? She might as well be yelling, "I AM UP TO NO GOOD." Staphanie lowers her camera and frowns at Ma. I gnaw on my bottom lip. How in the world did she manage to drug the groomsmen at Tom's wedding in the first place?

Belatedly, I recall that Fourth Aunt had been part of that equation. Of course. Fourth Aunt would be a lot smoother than this. Plus, the groomsmen were already tipsy by then, so the bar was a lot lower. I need to swoop in and help smooth things over.

"Excuse me," I mutter, slipping away from Nathan's side and going to join Staphanie and Ma.

"Meddy, I just telling Staphanie here she doing so good job," Ma says.

"Yes, such good job, such good girl," Big Aunt says.

"Oh, how lovely," Annie says, smiling at the two of them. "And yes, I agree, Staphanie, you've been just wonderful today. Hasn't she, dear?" She turns to Nathan's father, who's obviously not paying attention. He gives an absentminded nod before excusing himself to chat with another guest.

"We have toast now," Second Aunt declares, picking up a champagne flute and shoving it at Staphanie.

"Huh?" Staphanie takes a small step back. "Sorry, I don't drink while I'm on the clock."

"That's what I always say," I pipe in, taking the flute from Second Aunt. "But Staphanie, I insist. I of all people know how hard wedding photographers work, and I think you deserve a little treat." I hold out the glass to her before taking another one off the tray. "A toast!"

"Okay . . ." Staphanie takes the glass from me and lifts it to her mouth. My heart soars.

"No!" someone barks.

I turn to see Ama right behind me.

Ama isn't a large woman; she carries herself with a slight stoop and until now I haven't really had much chance to interact with her. But now I see why she's able to command a whole mafia gang. Why none of Staphanie's uncles have overthrown her, even though the Chinese-Indonesian community is still so devoted to traditional gender roles. Because quite frankly, the woman is terrifying. I can easily imagine Ama killing another person in cold blood.

"No," she says again, plucking the glass from Staphanie's hand. "I forbid. No drink while working."

"Ah, I insisting," Big Aunt says, and takes a step forward so she's face-to-face with Ama. She gives Ama the most pleasant, grandmotherly smile. "Please, do not refuse, otherwise we will be shame." Bringing up shame. Cunning. No self-respecting Chinese-Indo will be able to resist that.

"Oh no, no, if we drink while working, we will be shame," Ama says.

"No, if we not treat our guest well, we will be shame."

"Oh dear," Annie chirps. "We don't want anyone to feel ashamed. I'll drink this on Staphanie's behalf, then." To my horror, she takes the glass from Ama and raises it to her lips.

22

"No!" we cry, but no one is faster than Second Aunt, who snatches the glass out of Annie's hand with the speed of a striking snake. No doubt a move she'll attribute to Tai Chi later on. She looks at the glass for a second and I can almost read her train of thought. What to do with it? Can't let Annie drink it because if Annie gets high and they find out we've spiked the drinks, we'll lose face for sure. Maybe she'll "accidentally" spill it—

But then a look crosses Second Aunt's face. It's a look that every Chinese mother has perfected. A look that says, *For the millionth time, because I am so selfless, I shall sacrifice myself for the family.* It's followed by a very pointed look that says, *Please remember this sacrifice I am about to make. Or not. I'll be reminding you of it for the rest of your life.*

"No, Second Aunt—"

Before I can take the glass from her, she gulps down the champagne.

My mouth drops open in horror. What the shit? Seriously, there are about half a dozen things she could've done that didn't involve drinking spiked champagne, but of course she had to go for the most dramatic option.

"Ooh, are we doing shots? How come no one told me?" Fourth Aunt says, sashaying over with Lilian in tow. She reaches out to take a flute, but Ma pulls the tray away from her.

"No," Ma says.

Fourth Aunt's expression immediately becomes thunderous.

Oh god, no. Not *this* rivalry. I can barely keep up with the amount of shit that's just hit the fan. "Fourth Aunt—"

"I think," Fourth Aunt says, grabbing two champagne flutes from the tray, "Lilian and I would like a drink." She hands one flute to Lilian before downing her own glass.

Lilian raises her glass and Second Aunt, again, snatches it away from her before downing it. Oh. My. God.

Ama must have caught wind of something being off, because she quickly takes another glass and passes it to Annie. Second Aunt's hand shoots out again, a viper snatching a baby chick, but before she can down a third glass, Big Aunt catches her wrist. Their eyes meet, and that same self-sacrificial expression plays across Big Aunt's features. She gently takes the champagne flute from Second Aunt. I can almost hear Big Aunt's thoughts. *Thou shalt not be the only martyr.* Second Aunt gives a small nod, and Big Aunt raises the glass, her face as dramatically resolute as Juliet about to take poison to join her dead lover. She drinks it.

Ama gives another glass to Lilian, and this time, Ma yelps, "Me! Mine! I drink!" She grabs the glass and downs it as well. Ama reaches for another glass, but my senses finally unfreeze and I slap the tray out of Ma's hands.

The delicate flutes rain down on the ground, splashing champagne everywhere. The glass is so thin that they hardly tinkle as they break, but it's enough to make heads turn. Nathan is suddenly behind me.

"What's going on?" he says, his hand on the small of my back. "Meddy, you okay? Mum?"

I gape at him, unable to come up with anything that might pass for a believable excuse.

"I, uh—I tripped on my dress?" Why did that come out as a question? "I tripped on my dress," I say again, firmly this time.

Annie looks aghast, the poor woman, and who can blame her? She places a hand on Nathan's arm. "Nathan, love, would you mind very much accompanying me to the ladies'?"

"Hang on, Mum." Nathan takes my hand and says in a softer voice, his eyes searching mine, "What's going on, Meddy? Are you okay?"

God, could I feel even worse than before? Apparently I can. There is no limit to how terrible I can feel. Just when I think I've hit the very bottom of the barrel, it gives way and lets me tunnel down the pile of shit some more. And there's nothing but more shit.

Moving the corners of my mouth feels like pushing through wet cement, but somehow, I manage to stretch my mouth into something resembling a smile. I bet, like everything, it looks like shit too. "I'm fine," I hear myself saying. I don't even recognize this person anymore, this person who continues lying to the man she supposedly loves, the man she's just married. "I think I've just had a bit too much to drink. I might go sit down for a bit. You take your mom to the bathroom. I'll be fine."

"Nathan—" Annie says.

"One minute, Mum," Nathan says, exasperation tingeing his voice. He takes my arm and leads me away from the crowd.

"Meddy, I know you're keeping something from me. What is it? Tell me and we'll work it out together, okay?"

Tears sting the backs of my eyes. Oh god, what I wouldn't give to be able to just sag into his arms and tell him everything that's happened.

Movement catches my eye. Staphanie. Always at the edges, always lurking, watching for a moment of weakness. And not far behind her is Ama, watching the spectacle like a really hungry hawk who can't wait to strike. I spot Lilian, standing in between Big Aunt and Second Aunt, looking very small and helpless. I just need to get through today, and then I'll be able to be completely honest with Nathan.

"I'm fine, really I am. I'm just not great with crowds. I mean, I'm not great with them when the attention's all on me." Then I say the first true thing I've said all day. "I kind of wish we'd eloped. Left everything and everyone behind and just—you know."

Nathan's eyes soften. "I know. I wish we'd done that too. But we're here now, and we got through the ceremony." He grins at me. "I can't believe you're my wife. Wow, it feels weird saying that."

"It feels weird hearing it." A giggle escapes me, and it feels good. The first real laugh I've had since everything started. Everything will be okay. No one will get killed on our wedding day and we'll all go back home and forget about the craziness of the day. It'll all be—

The murmur from the crowd becomes significantly louder. Nathan and I turn.

Oh god. It's Second Aunt, and she's . . .

"Is she . . ." Nathan mumbles, narrowing his eyes. "Is she making my dad do Tai Chi again?"

23

"Oh no." I don't wait before lifting my heavy skirt and running toward Second Aunt. Just as we feared, Second Aunt has accosted Nathan's long-suffering father and bullied him into doing yet another round of Tai Chi.

"—don't think this is a good idea," Annie is warbling nervously, pacing around them.

"Aduh, Annie, not get your nickies in twist-twist, okay?" Big Aunt says in a singsong voice.

"Excuse me?" Annie says.

"Is what you British say, right? Not twist your nickies?"

"Knickers, I think it was," Fourth Aunt says. "Snickers. Huh." She stares off into the sky. "Snickers . . ."

Annie rushes toward us. "Nathan, oh thank goodness. Please tell them to stop whatever they're doing."

I hurry over to Second Aunt, who's literally pushed Nathan's dad onto his hands and knees on the grass while everyone crowds around, whispering. Oh god, how is this happening? HOW IS THIS MY LIFE? "Second Aunt, stop it. Stop!"

She looks up with bleary eyes. "Eh? Oh, Meddy, good you here. Come, you help me, we must stretch him. You put hands under his armpit, I will pull from his hip."

"We are not going to do anything of the sort!"

Nathan crouches down and helps his dad up. "Dad, are you okay?"

Chris clings to Nathan, his eyes all panicky. "I don't quite know what just happened."

"Oh, darling," Annie says, clutching his arm. "Come on, then, let's get you a chair." Nathan throws me an apologetic look as he leads his parents away.

I smile politely at everyone and say, "Um, please enjoy the canapés and drinks, everyone. Dinner will be served soon." Then I rush to Second Aunt, grab her firmly by the arm, and lead her away from the crowd. Along the way, I grab hold of Big Aunt, Fourth Aunt, and Ma. I have to stop myself from grabbing them by the backs of their collars as though they were naughty kittens. "Okay," I growl when we're safely out of everyone's earshot. "What the hell was that about?"

It strikes me that this is the most impolite thing I've ever said to them, but I don't even care anymore. "Second Aunt, how could you bully Nathan's dad into doing Tai Chi again? Haven't you done enough damage to his back?"

To my surprise, Second Aunt actually looks ashamed of herself. Or, well, she looks . . . something. She blinks slowly. I swear her eyes blink at different times. "Tai Chi good for back," she says finally.

"I know it's good for your back, but remember what happened the last time you tried to get him to do it? I don't think it's for everyone."

"Everyone . . ." she echoes. "Everyone look nice, ya?"

I gape at her for a second before it sinks in, just like the pot in her system. Second Aunt is high.

Fuuuuck.

I look at Big Aunt with desperation. If ever there was a time for Big Aunt to stride in and take over, this is it.

Except Big Aunt is staring off into space.

"Er, Big Aunt? Hello?" I wave a hand in front of her face with hesitation.

"Yes!" she barks, making me start. "We can do buttercream flower for cake! No! Problem!" She swivels her head forcefully and stares directly at me. "Xiaoling, you stir the cream now! Hut-hut!"

Only Big Aunt could get even more authoritative when she gets high.

"Big Aunt, it's me, Meddy."

She blinks. "Xiaoling, why you not moving?"

Oh my god. What do I do now? "Yeah, okay, Big Aunt. I'll get the cream going, okay? You just—uh, you just stay here." I turn to—I don't know, find a hole to disappear into—but a hand grabs my arm.

"Did you hear them?" Fourth Aunt says, her gaze as piercing as a laser beam.

"Yeah, they're high. We need to get them out of here—"

"Ssh!" Fourth Aunt places a finger against my mouth. "Listen!"

I stop talking and listen hard. Maybe she's overheard Ama or Staphanie talking about—

"You hear that?" Fourth Aunt nods and smiles smugly. "They love me."

"What?"

"The crowd!" She releases me and looks around her with sparkling eyes. "Thank you, thank you, everyone!" Stretching her arms out, she bows with a flourish. "I'm so honored that you enjoyed my rendition of 'My Heart Will Go On.' For my next song . . ."

No, no, no.

"I think they high," Ma says.

"I—hang on, you had a glass too. Are you okay? How are you feeling?"

She shrugs. "I okay."

"But how come you're—ah." It sinks in. Ma, who drinks her own concoction every day, probably has built up a tolerance to the marijuana. Which is a relief. Also sort of worrisome. But for now, it's a massive relief.

"I need you to take them back to the room," I say quickly. "They can't be here. They're acting so weird. I mean, much more weird than usual. People are going to notice. Well, they've noticed already. But they're going to notice some more."

"Yes, good idea." But she doesn't move.

"Ma, are you okay?"

"I think I a bit drunk."

Fuuuuck. Of course. My mother's a drug addict, but she rarely drinks alcohol. Of course a single glass of champagne is enough to get her drunk. If I weren't pumped full of adrenaline right now, I'd cry.

"Hey, is everything okay?" Selena says. Next to her, Seb gives a hesitant smile, clearly worried about my family.

"You guys! Oh god. Please, please, I need your help. My family's uh—they're kind of drunk?" We all turn to look at them. "Very drunk."

"Mm, yeah, wow. Reminds me of my last night at college—" Seb says.

"No time for that," I say. "Could you guys just, I don't know, take them back to the hotel, please?"

"Why not the room here?" Seb says.

"Because—" For a horrible second, my mind draws a blank. Why *not* the room here? Because there are two kidnapped men in it, that's why. "Because Second Aunt forgot to take her blood pressure medication, and it's at the Randolph," I blurt out.

"Oh, gosh," Seb says.

"Yeah, of course, we'll leave now," Selena says.

"Thank you, thank you." I squeeze her hands tight. "I'd do it myself, but—"

"Don't be silly, it's your wedding day. You stay here and enjoy yourself," Seb says. "We'll take care of it. Don't worry, I've dealt with more than my fair share of drunk wedding guests. I've got it under control."

"Oh, Seb." My voice wobbles.

"You owe us both a huge one, though," he adds with a wink. "Go, join your wedding party. We'll be back before you know it." He waves me away before linking arms with Big Aunt and saying, "Come on, Big Aunt—hm? Oh, the fondant? Got it covered, don't you worry." He leads her to Fourth Aunt, links his free arm with hers, and walks toward the exit. Selena does the same with Ma and Second Aunt, and before long, they're gone from the Masters Garden.

I breathe a sigh of relief. Great. Now I can . . .

Oh shit. Now I'm all alone with no one else to stop Staphanie and Ama from doing whatever they were planning to do to Lilian. I pick up the skirt of my dress again and hurry back to the crowd, smiling and waving at various guests, not slowing down until I catch sight of Lilian talking to a man. Thank god she's still okay.

"There you are," I say brightly. They both look up at me.

"Meddy, congratulations," the man says. I vaguely recognize him as one of Nathan's uncles. Or maybe he's one of Nathan's business contacts?

"Thank you."

"Everything has been lovely," he continues. "I'm so glad I was able to fly in for the wedding. Did you know that Christ Church College is almost five hundred years old?"

"Yeah, uh-huh." I smile at him while my mind gallops ahead. This is good. I could stay here for a while, making small talk with him and Lilian. That looks totally normal and understandable. People do that at a normal, non-mafia wedding, right? Right. "Yes, I love the um, the history of the place."

Sensing someone who's just as into boring small talk as he is, the man brightens before launching into a conversation about how exciting Oxford is.

I begin to relax, letting his words wash over me. He's talking about crenellations and parapets, and I never once thought of how comforting architecture can be, but here we are. It's almost therapeutic. Lilian's eyes are glazed over and she's smiling politely, probably bored out of her mind, but like me, she doesn't seem inclined to leave his company. Maybe she's grateful for the change of pace from my over-the-top aunts.

Then I catch sight of Nathan talking to his parents. My pleasant haze dissipates and sharpens into anxiety. They don't look happy. Poor Nathan. Of course they're not happy. How could they be after the countless mishaps my family and I have caused? Maybe I should go to him. Maybe I should—should what? Well, I should definitely try to smooth things over with his mom, anyway. That would be the right thing to do. Now is probably a good time, given I can't see Ama anywhere and Staph is walking around snapping pictures of the guests. Lilian will be okay for a while.

"Sorry, excuse me," I murmur, smiling politely at the man before walking toward Nathan and his parents.

As I near them, I see that Nathan's expression is stormy.

Maybe I should let them have their privacy. But just then, Nathan spots me. His face immediately clears and he mutters something to his mother before coming toward me with a smile. "You okay?"

"Yeah, you?"

His smile becomes strained. "I . . . could be better, honestly."

"I'm so sorry." And I am. I truly am. "How is everyone holding up?" I look at his parents, who are hovering nearby, and wave at them. They come toward us, and Annie gives me a smile I've grown familiar with over the years—an uneasy things-are-terrible-but-I-don't-want-to-say-so kind of smile. I'm always seeing them on people who have had to deal with my aunts.

"I'm so sorry about the—um, about everything," I say, gesturing at my surroundings. "It's just been a really hectic day. I promise that my family and I aren't like this on most days."

"Oh, that's quite alright, dear," Chris says, patting my arm lightly. "I know weddings can be very stressful. Did you know Annie and I got married at the courthouse? Nobody else was around. It was a bit of a—er, a rushed wedding, heh."

"Chris!" Annie hisses.

I feel a sudden surge of affection for Nathan's dad, who is now looking very sheepish. "Well, that was our wedding. Afterward, Annie and I shared a pie. Steak and kidney, it was, from a little shop around the corner. We didn't have much then, you see, and Annie ate most of it. It wasn't very nice. I didn't get any steak at all, mostly just kidney that tasted vaguely of ammonia. And then it rained. It was an awful day, really."

I can't help but laugh at this. Annie looks like she's torn between smiling and strangling her husband. Nathan's dad is just one of those people you can't stay angry at for long, I guess. Just like Nathan. I glance up at Nathan and my love for him warms my chest. I link my fingers through his and squeeze his hand. He squeezes back, gazing down at me with an expression that says, "I know. I get it."

"The point is, our wedding day was, well, it was all a bit pear-shaped, really. But it didn't matter, not in the long run. I'm still married to my beautiful Annie, and I'm grateful for that every day. Aren't I, love?" He pulls Annie close to him as I say, "Aww." She relents and kisses him on the cheek.

"You're so full of it," she mutters.

I'm about to say something when my phone buzzes. Since it's tucked into my bodice, the vibrations go all the way through my chest and down my arms, shocking me enough to jump. "Um, excuse me." I release Nathan's hand and walk a few paces away before pulling it out.

It's Ma. I sigh.

"Ma, what is it?"

Her voice comes out in a rapid, panicked staccato, much like a machine gun.

I frown. "Ma, slow down, I can't understand you."

"Meddy! Terrible! Disaster! You come here now!"

Terrible disaster. Of course. Because what else can I expect from today?

PART THREE

◆

HOW TO DEAL
WITH WEDDING DAY
HICCUPS

(Murder: Always a good option!)

24

"Ma, what—" I glance over my shoulder. Shit, Nathan's followed me. How much did he hear? Have I said anything incriminating? I give him a quick, reassuring smile and turn my back to him once more. When I finally speak, I try to control my voice. "Is everything okay? What's going on?"

"Aduh, you come now, deh. Now! Cepat! Emergency! You come alone, you not bring anyone."

The thing with Ma is, she often does things like this to me. Once, she begged me to come home because of an "emergency," and when I got there all breathless, having broken half a dozen traffic laws, it turned out the emergency had been her running out of chili sauce. But now, she sounds genuinely panicked. And not just that: there's a clear undercurrent of fear in her voice. How much of that is because she's drunk and in a foreign country, and how much of that is an actual, real emergency? "Is Seb still with you? Selena?"

"No, they leave already. You come now. Please!"

The word stabs through my chest like an icicle. Ma never, ever says the word "please," especially not to me. It's not generally something that elders say to the younger generation. So for her to say it now means something terrible has happened. I really do need to be there.

"Okay, Ma, I'll be right over."

"Alone! Now!" The call disconnects.

"Everything okay? Did I hear you right?" Nathan says. "You'll be right over . . . where?"

I look up guiltily at him. "The Randolph. My mom's, uh—" My mind short-circuits. If I tell him that my mom is having some sort of emergency, he'll definitely insist on coming with me. And I won't be able to stop him because, of course, he should come with me, unless there is something to hide. Which there is. "My mom's just going through a really tough time over us getting married," I blurt out.

Nathan's eyebrows shoot up in surprise. "She is? But—I—huh. I have to say, I'm pretty taken aback by that because she's been nothing but excited about us getting married. I mean, remember how she accepted my proposal before you could?"

Oh god. That wonderful, amazing, beautiful day. How I long for it. How I wish we could turn back time. I would do so many things differently. But now, I have to—yet again—lie to the love of my life. "Yeah, I think it's just sort of hit her all at once? She was just too carried away by the excitement of the wedding and wanting grandbabies and whatever to really think about what us getting married means. I really need to go to her."

"I'll come with you," Nathan says.

"No!" The word comes out a lot more forcefully than I had planned. "Sorry, I just—I think this is something I need to do on my own."

Nathan frowns.

"It's kind of a mother-daughter thing."

"Okay . . ." he says, his frown deepening. "I gotta say, I didn't think you'd be MIA for so much of our wedding day." Fuck. This is so freaking shitty. I just want to give him the biggest, tightest hug and tell him everything. And I will, just not right now.

"I know, I'm sorry, it's just—my family, you know how they are."

He sighs, shoulders sagging. Now he looks more sad than annoyed, which is even worse. "I understand."

"Um, I hate to do this, but could you um—stay close to Lilian while I'm away?"

The sadness on his face gives way to confusion. "Lilian?"

"Yeah. She . . ." I try to come up with something halfway believable. Anything. My mind spits out a blank. Shit, I really need to get going. "I'll explain everything later, I promise. But please, Nathan. Just make sure she's okay." Wow, that's the closest thing to the truth I've told him all day.

Nathan's mouth opens and closes, but no words come out. Finally, he shrugs and says, "Okay. Yeah, I'll look after her."

"Thank you."

I harden everything inside me and force myself to turn and walk away. Walking away is simple; it's just a matter of putting one foot in front of the other. But I might as well be walking underwater. Somehow, I manage to make my way out of Christ Church College and onto the street, where passersby openly stare at me. I guess a bride walking around on her own isn't something people see every day. Ignoring them, I flag down a cab—thank god they're everywhere in Oxford—and the driver helps push my giant skirt through.

"It's not often I get a bride in my cab," he says as we drive up St. Aldates Street.

I give him a weak smile. I'm giving a lot of them today.

My phone rings again. This time, it's Seb.

"Hey, just to update you: we're on our way back to Christ Church. Um, your family kind of kicked us out of the room. Not that I'm complaining or anything. I mean, it was kind of rude, but—ow, hey!"

"Hey, it's me," Selena says. In the background, I can hear Seb complaining. "So we dropped your family off at their room, and we were kind of hanging around to see if they needed any more help, but then they just started shouting at us to go, so. Yeah . . ."

By now, my stomach is just a leaden ball of dread. "I'm so sorry. Thank you so much for doing that."

"Yeah, of course. No worries. We'll see you back at Christ Church."

"About that," I say. "Um, I'm sort of on my way to the Randolph. But it's fine, you guys go back to the college. I'll be back in a bit."

My breath comes out in a long, endless whoosh once I hang up. What could possibly have caused Ma and the aunties to kick Seb and Selena out of the room like that? Whatever it is, it's nothing good.

By the time I get to the Randolph, all of my nerves are screaming. The driver takes one look at my frazzled expression and tells me, with obvious pity, that I don't owe him anything. I thank him and rush inside.

People look up and eyes follow me as I walk briskly across the lobby and run up the stairs—no way I'd fit inside the small elevator. I try to look as normal as I can, which isn't very, especially not in my huge white dress, but I do my best anyway.

By the time I get to the right floor, I'm out of breath. As far as wedding dresses go, mine is very forgiving and comfortable, but it's really not made for a panicked rush up four flights of stairs. I clamber up the final flight practically on my hands and knees, and stagger to Ma's room. I knock on the door. Noises from inside the room are quickly cut off.

"Ma? It's"—gasp—"it's me." Gasp. "Meddy."

There's a flurry of noise and the door opens. A hand shoots out, grabs me by the wrist, and yanks me inside. I come face-to-face with Fourth Aunt, who kicks the door shut and then pulls me along like I'm some naughty kid.

"Ouch, Fourth Aunt, you're hurting me. Ow, what's going on?"

She stops abruptly and whirls around so our faces are literally inches away from each other. "You need to tell us if this is real or if this is a dream, or if this is, like, the Matrix."

"The Matrix? Huh?"

She sighs impatiently. "Keanu Reeves? Weird simulation?"

"I know what the Matrix is, Fourth Aunt. I just don't know what you're talking about."

"Keanu Reeves." The frown melts from her face and she stares off into the distance. "He's hot. Did you know he's in his fifties? I would totally poke that."

Okay, I've lost her. I try to walk around her, but it's impossible to do so when I'm in my gown and we're still standing in the narrow passageway between the door and the room.

"Um, can I go inside?"

"Oh yes. But can we not with your usual 'Oh my god this is terrible' reaction?"

The clump of panic that's been brewing in my gut threatens to bubble over. "I only do that when things are actually terrible. Are they actually terrible this time?"

"Oh, Meddy," Fourth Aunt sighs, shaking her head at me. "I see you're going to insist on being your melodramatic self."

"I just—never mind. Excuse me, Fourth Aunt." Somehow, I manage to garner up the courage to put my hands on her arms and move her aside, gently but firmly. Then I walk through into the living room. "Ma?"

"In here!" she calls out from the bedroom, and then gives a sort of choked, nervous laugh.

Dread threatens to overwhelm me as I make my way there, but I keep going. One foot in front of the other. I reach the door, prepare myself for the worst, and open it. Ma, Big Aunt, and Second Aunt jump apart guiltily. I stare at the sight before me, my mouth agape, my eyes as wide as saucers. I thought I had prepared myself for everything. But this—

"What. The. Fuck?"

25

They say that your life flashes before your eyes when you're about to die. I don't know that I'm close to death, but my life certainly feels like it's about to come to an end. And it does actually flash before my eyes like some silent film, where the main character isn't even me, but my mom and aunts, who are flapping everywhere. I blink. The silent film vanishes with my mother and aunts mid-nag, mouths open wide.

And there, before me, is reality: Third Uncle bound and gagged on the floor.

"What the fuck?" I say again. This can't be real. I pinch my arm hard enough to make myself wince. And still, he's there, staring with terrified eyes at all of us. "How did he—why did you—but—argh!"

To their credit, Ma and the aunties look abashed at my incandescent anger.

I take a deep breath, trying to sort out my thoughts. But how can I? Where do I even begin? I finally settle on a simple "What happened?"

No one answers. Everyone just glances at each other guiltily.

"Big Aunt," I bark. A small voice squeaks, *You can't talk to Big Aunt like that!* I squash it flat and point at Big Aunt. "What happened? You tell me."

Big Aunt gapes at me and blinks slowly. "Meddy . . ."

"Yes?"

Her face crumples like a piece of paper and she wails, "You are like daughter to meee!"

Oh god, save me from my marijuana-ed aunties. "Yeah, okay, I love you too, Big Aunt. Ssh, that's okay. I'm sorry I snapped at you." I reach out and pat her shoulder in what I hope is a reassuring way. I give Ma a beseeching look, but Ma only nods and smiles benignly and mumbles something about me having four wonderful mothers, isn't that wonderful, isn't everything wonderful?

Suddenly, Third Uncle starts yelling at the top of his lungs. Holy shit, his gag's off. I rush over to him, unsure what I'm about to do, but before I get halfway across the room, Second Aunt, Ma, and Fourth Aunt leap like tigers pouncing on an old antelope and land on top of him.

I don't know who's yelling what, but it's terrible and awful, and I find myself standing at the edge of the struggling mass, frozen. Whenever I've seen fights break out in movies, I've always been super-critical of how slow the protagonists are to react. But here I am, watching three of my family members grappling with a man, and I just . . . I don't know. What the hell do I do? I pick up a lamp from the side table and grasp it like a baseball bat. But still I stand unmoving. How do I make sure to swing it just the right amount? What if I hit Ma accidentally? What if—

A knock. Right at the edge of my hearing. The blood drains from my head. Someone's at the door.

"Quiet!" I half-shout, half-whisper. "Someone's at the door."

The writhing mass on the floor pauses.

"Hello, miss, it's Dan from the front desk?" the person calls out from the other side of the door.

Third Uncle's eyes go even wider and he starts to shout, but Second Aunt swings her leg up in a jaw-dropping feat and mushes her thigh over his mouth. I guess Tai Chi is good for flexibility after all.

"We don't need housekeeping," I call out in a falsely cheerful tone.

"Could you open the door, please?"

I glance over at my mother and aunts and Third Uncle, and Fourth Aunt hisses, "Go. Get rid of him, fast."

With a nod, I make my way out of the bedroom, closing the door behind me. I take a deep breath, blow it out, and pat my hair down before walking to the door. Chin up, polite smile on. Right. My hand trembles slightly as I reach for the doorknob.

"Hi, Dan," I say with forced brightness.

The man standing in front of me looks slightly taken aback to find a bride in her wedding dress opening the door. "Uh. Hello. Miss . . . uh, Natasya?"

"That would be my mother. I'm Meddelin."

"Ah. May I just say, you are looking radiant? Congratulations on your wedding day?" He gives me a hesitant smile.

"Yep, my wedding day. I came back here to do a few touchups to my hair and makeup; you know how it is."

"Ah, yes, of course," Dan says, looking somewhat relieved.

"Anyway," I say. We stare at each other for a moment, both of us smiling with uncertainty. "Um, so. Is there something I can help you with?"

"Oh, right! Yes, well. I'm so sorry to bother you with this, Miss Meddelin, but we've received a couple of complaints about the noise level in your room. Obviously on such a happy occasion I hate to ask you to bring the noise level down a bit, but could you possibly do that?" His smile looks more like a grimace.

"Yeah, of course. I'm so sorry about that. My mother just got overexcited. She's been wanting me to get married for ages. We'll keep the noise down. Thank you, bye!" I don't wait for a reply before shutting the door, sliding the lock in place, and hurrying back to the bedroom. "I got rid of h—oh no. What have you done?"

Ma, Second Aunt, and Fourth Aunt are all standing there looking very, very guilty. Behind them, Big Aunt is still sniffling softly about what a beautiful bride I make and also why couldn't she have had a daughter instead of her useless idiot sons, Hendra and Russ. I look down on the floor, craning my neck to look at Third Uncle, but Ma moves to block my view. Bile rises up from my gut. I swallow thickly.

My voice comes out in a hoarse whisper. "Did you guys—um—did you—is he dead?" Because of course he is. We've nearly killed Big Uncle and Second Uncle, and that was before they all drank marijuana-spiked champagne. My family is dangerous at the best of times. Now, unhinged by drugs and alcohol? Of course they've killed him. It was bound to happen.

"Aiya, no, lah!" Second Aunt snaps. "Why you always think, 'Wah, must be he dead.' You think we just going around anyhow kill-kill people?"

"Uh, sort of?"

"Tch," she tuts. "We knock him out only. Just a bit."

"Oh, well, that's okay, then." I squeeze past them and take a deep breath when Third Uncle comes into view. He's lying on

his back with his eyes closed. Cautiously, I approach him and crouch next to his head. How is this not the first unconscious man I'm checking for a pulse today? It's not even the *second*.

"He's got a clear pulse," I announce with relief.

"I tell you, we not killer," Second Aunt says smugly.

"I mean, we technically are, but okay," I mumble, sitting on the edge of the bed with a sigh. I feel exhausted. I watch as Ma goes to comfort Big Aunt, muttering softly to her. I soften a little. It's hard watching someone as tough as Big Aunt crumble, even though I know it's just a side effect of the drugs and alcohol.

"What're we going to do with him?" Fourth Aunt says.

We all stare at her. "What do you mean? We should probably tie him up and, I don't know, leave him here for now?" I say.

Fourth Aunt shakes her head so violently that her Komodo dragon flings off and lands in one corner of the room. "No, no. Tch, you are so naive, Meddy. We can't possibly leave him here. We can't. We can't!" Of course Fourth Aunt would be manic after drugs and alcohol.

"Why not?"

"Maybe we chop him up—" Second Aunt says.

"*No*," I snap. "No one is chopping anyone up."

"Yes, lagipula here got carpet floor, later you stain the carpet, hotel give you big fine," Ma says.

"I think they'd do more than give us a big fine if we chopped up a living human here," I mutter, "but yes, they'd also probably slap us with a huge cleaning bill."

"Wah, cannot, cleaning bill will be so expensive," Second Aunt says. "Okay, never mind, we think of something else."

Well, at least they've got their priorities straight.

"We've got the perfect opportunity to get rid of him now," Fourth Aunt says. "Look at us, we're all dressed up and gor-

geous. You're in a wedding gown, for goodness' sake. Who's going to be suspicious of a bride? No one!"

As much as I hate to admit it, she's got a point. "What are you suggesting?"

"We get him out of here and dump him in the River Thames, along with his two brothers," she says simply.

My mouth falls open. It's been doing that a lot lately. "I—what—that's murder."

She frowns at me. "They'll probably swim or something."

"What if they don't? What if they don't wake up? They'll drown!"

Fourth Aunt sighs. "The River Thames isn't that deep. They like, do that thing where they push sticks inside, you know, like a gondola? You can't do that if the river's too deep."

"It's deep enough for an unconscious person to drown in."

Fourth Aunt is about to argue some more when there's another knock at the door.

"What?" I bark.

"I'm so sorry, miss, but it's Dan from the front desk?"

Fucking Dan. I point an accusatory finger at my family and hiss, "Don't. Move. And for god's sake do not cut him up while I'm gone." I march out of the bedroom, shut the door firmly behind me, and take another deep breath. I exhale slowly, then cross the living room and open the front door. "Yes, Dan?" I say through a gritted smile.

"We have put together a hamper for you on your special day!" Dan says, brandishing a huge basket filled with goodies.

Okay, I was not expecting that. "Wow. Okay, thank you. That's really nice of you." I reach out for the basket, but he steps back a bit.

"It's really heavy. Mind if I come in and put it down on the desk for you?"

"Yes."

His eyebrows raise. "Yes, you mind?"

"Yes, I mind. Sorry, but my mother's, uh—getting changed into her evening gown, so she's like . . . naked?" I reach out again, but he moves the basket back once more.

"Um, and I'm so sorry for being a bother, but if you could— the noise . . ." He gives me a smile that's more of a grimace.

"Turn it down, right, yes." Clearly the walls here are paper thin. Fourth Aunt is right. We can't risk leaving Third Uncle here. Even if we keep him bound and gagged, if he wakes up, he'd start shouting. Even if the shouts were muffled, whoever's in the room next to ours apparently has superhuman hearing. Dammit. We do have to move him after all.

I'm about to shoo Dan away when an idea hits me. "Dan, is it possible to borrow a wheelchair? Does the hotel provide them?"

"Yes, of course. We pride ourselves on being one of the most accessible establishments in the country. We've had ramps built everywhere, even outside our back entrance."

"Perfect. That's amazing. Good for you."

He preens at the compliment.

"So um, the wheelchair?" I prod.

"Oh yes, right away, miss. Or should I say Mrs.?"

I laugh weakly at the reminder that, huh, it's my wedding day and I've spent most of the day away from Nathan. He leaves the basket with me and hurries off to "procure a wheelchair at once." As soon as I shut the door, the breath leaves me in a huge whoosh. A lump rises in my throat at the thought of the shambles that my wedding day has become, but I quickly shove the thought away. I can't afford to fall apart right now. I'll make it up to Nathan on our honeymoon. Hell, I'll make it up to him tomorrow, or even tonight, once all of this is over.

Taking another deep breath, I go back into the bedroom to tell my family the plan, but it's like trying to explain calculus to a bunch of cats. They blink owlishly at me as I tell them that I've asked for a wheelchair to get Third Uncle out of here.

"Does that sound good?" I say. "Any questions?"

Silence. Did they even understand a word I just said? How long do the effects of weed last, anyway?

"Good idea, Meddy," Second Aunt says.

Finally. "Thanks, Second Aunt."

"Now we just need break the legs."

"Come again?"

She moves toward Third Uncle with her arms out like a zombie. All of my senses scream at me and I jump up, sliding in between her and Third Uncle.

"Hold up! What are you going to do?"

"We need break his legs, ya? So he fit in wheelchair? Wheelchair only for people cannot walk." She explains this to me slowly like I'm a particularly dim child.

"Oh yes, Er Jie, you make good point," Ma says, nodding. "Okay, yes, we break legs."

"Nobody move!" I yell, holding out my arms like I'm Chris Pratt in *Jurassic World* holding off a bunch of raptors. Except instead of raptors, I'm holding back a bunch of meddlesome Chinese-Indo aunties, who I'm pretty sure are more dangerous. "No one needs to break anyone's legs. You can sit in a wheelchair even if your legs are fine!"

"I not think so, Meddy," Ma slurs, swaying slightly. "That no good, that is like lying. You know Auntie Liying do that? She get one of those handicap thingy, you know, put in her car. Then she park in handicap spot. Wah, so bad, I always tell her, you lying to everyone. We cannot like that. So not honor. If other people find out, she will lose face."

"Yes, we not liars," Second Aunt says. "We got face. Come, we break legs now."

"Or we could cut off his legs," Fourth Aunt says.

"That is not how losing face works! Jesus, did the weed turn you all into homicidal maniacs or did you all have this tendency from the very beginning? Listen up. Nobody. Is. Hurting. Anybody. Okay? Got that?"

Second Aunt and Ma nod sullenly. I turn to Big Aunt and Fourth Aunt, who have been strangely quiet this whole time. Big Aunt is still sniffling in one corner about how much she adores me, and Fourth Aunt is touching up her makeup. Well, I say touching up, but really she's slathering the stuff on like it's war paint. The two of them seem completely oblivious to the drama that's just gone down. I guess it's just as well. I'm not entirely confident they would've been on my side, and if it had been the four of them against me, I'm pretty sure Third Uncle would be missing his legs by now.

Luckily, the wheelchair arrives not long after. I hiss at Second Aunt and Ma to stay put and not cut off anyone's legs before rushing to the door.

"Here is the wheelchair you requested, miss!" Dan says proudly. "Is there anything—"

"Great! Thanks, Dan. Bye, Dan!" I practically yank the wheelchair out of his hands before slamming the door in his face. I know I'm being awfully rude, but I can't guarantee that right at this very moment, my mother and aunt aren't in the process of severing somebody's limbs. I shove the wheelchair into the bedroom, breathing hard, and sag with relief to see Third Uncle still intact on the floor. "Okay, great. Let's move!"

It is unfairly hard to move dead weight off the ground. Well, not "dead," knock on wood, but unconscious weight. It is even harder to move unconscious weight when the people you're trying to move it with are drunk/high. Gathering my voluminous skirt and shoving it behind me, I loop Third Uncle's right arm around my shoulders and Ma flings his other arm around hers, but almost immediately she falls over from the weight of it. Second Aunt rushes forward to catch Ma, and the two of them go down with a loud thump that I'm sure will get Dan summoned to our room yet again.

In the end, it takes all five of us to lift him off the floor and into the wheelchair. There's a lot of cussing and squawking involved, and by the time he's in, we're all breathing hard. I crouch down and do my best to loop the rope around his ankles as securely as I can. Then I stand back and stare at our handiwork.

It's not great. His head is flopped back at a severe angle, his Adam's apple jutting out obscenely. It's obvious to any passersby that he's unconscious.

Fourth Aunt must have had the same thought I have, because she pushes his head upright. But as soon as she lets go, it flops back again, his mouth gaping open.

"Wake up, dude, I'm late for my performance," she says, pushing it forward and then letting it drop back again.

"No, what are you doing?" I say, grabbing her wrist. "We don't want to wake him up."

"We don't?" She blinks at him. "Oh yeah, you're right. We don't. Oops. But what about my show? My fans are waiting!"

Her show? It takes a moment for me to recall her imaginary, marijuana-fueled show. "Right, your show. Don't worry, Fourth Aunt, there's still like an hour before the show. We need to figure out a way to wheel him out of here without anyone finding out that he's knocked out, okay? And then we'll go to your show." I grab a blanket off the bed and arrange it on top of him, tucking it securely down underneath him and wrapping him up like a burrito. Okay, at least that covers the rope. And for the head . . .

Inspiration strikes. "Ma, where's your travel pillow? I know you took it with you for the plane ride."

"The plane ride to come England and marry off my only niece," Big Aunt whispers in a heartbroken voice.

"Uh, yes, that plane ride."

"The one come here to marry off my only daughter," Ma wails. The two of them clutch at each other and start crying loudly.

Goddammit. I squash down the part of myself that's aching to hug them and reassure them that I'll always be their daughter and niece. There's no time for that. Instead, I head for Ma's luggage. I rifle through her belongings with ruthless efficiency until I locate the travel pillow, then walk past Ma—who's still wailing—and wrap the pillow around Third Uncle's neck. I step back and survey him again. Okay, it's not great, but it looks less alarming. He looks less unconscious and more asleep. I pull out one of Ma's scarves from her luggage and wrap it around his head, covering his hair. For the finishing touch, I pluck a pair of sunglasses off the table and place them on his face. By the time I'm done, Third Uncle is barely recognizable. In fact, it's next to impossible to tell if it's even a man or a woman sitting in the wheelchair.

"Whoa, what do you think you're doing with that?" Fourth Aunt cries, pulling the sunglasses off his face. "These are Hermès!"

Ma abruptly stops crying. "You buy Hermès? Gila, you so wasteful! Spend money like water and still borrowing money from us all the time! When you will stop becoming so irresponsible?"

Big Aunt dabs at her eyes while nodding. "Is my fault. I spoil Mimi. Just like I spoil Meddy. Now Meddy leaving me."

"Oh my god, it's a Class One Hermès, okay?" Fourth Aunt snaps. "Get it together."

"Aha! Knockoff," Ma gloats. "Tuh kan, I know you can only afford fake. Just like your Louis Vuitton luggage, all fake. Like your face."

"Okay, that's enough," I whisper-shout over the noise. I take the sunglasses from Fourth Aunt before she can argue. "Since they're fake, I think we can use them right now. I'll buy you a new pair, okay?"

"Real ones?" Fourth Aunt says, hope shining in her eyes.

"Of course not!" Ma snaps.

"Uh. We'll discuss that later," I say as diplomatically as I can. I replace the sunglasses on Third Uncle's face and nod. "Right. We're good to go." I check the time and feel sick. There's less than fifteen minutes until the reception starts. "Come on. It's almost time for the reception."

I start to push the wheelchair, but find it impossible to do in my huge dress. I had been able to half-push, half-carry it along from the doorway, but with Third Uncle in it, I can barely get it to budge. "One of you will have to push it. My dress is in the way."

"I do it!" Ma says, grabbing the handles. We all make way for her as she navigates the chair out of the narrow space. She rams one of his knees into the doorway and says, "Oops."

"Careful, Ma." That's going to hurt Third Uncle when he wakes up.

With some more difficulty, we finally get the wheelchair out of the hotel room and down the hallway. Getting it inside the tiny elevator is yet another tricky bit. Ma and Big Aunt go down in the elevator while Second Aunt, Fourth Aunt, and I hurry down the staircase. We arrive before they do and I wait outside the elevator doors, watching the number go down impatiently.

When the doors slide open and I see Ma, Big Aunt, and Third Uncle, I breathe a sigh of relief. I guess I wasn't entirely confident that they'd make it down in one piece.

"Let's go," I say quietly, trying to look nonchalant and innocent and totally not like someone who's in possession of an unconscious person.

It feels like everyone is staring at us as we make our way across the lobby, but I remind myself that all of the attention probably has more to do with our outfits and the Komodo dragon hats than the fact that we're wheeling someone out of the hotel. Probably.

"Shall I call you a cab, miss?" the doorman asks, and I'm about to say yes before I realize that no, we can't bundle Third Uncle into a cab, because then it would become apparent that he's unconscious and tied up. Fuck.

"No, that's alright, thank you. We'll just walk."

The doorman frowns at me. "Are you sure? You'd get that lovely dress of yours all muddy, walking down St. Aldates like that."

"Yep, I'm sure. Thank you!" I push past him and gesture at Ma to follow me.

Outside, we attract even more stares. Of course we do; we must be a ridiculous sight to see—me in my huge wedding gown, my family in their radioactive-eggplant dresses, and Third Uncle looking like an Amish grandmother. I should've gone for an understated sheath dress.

Noticing all of the attention thrown our way, Fourth Aunt claps and grins like a little kid. "Look how many people have come out to watch me sing!" Before I can reply, she lifts her chin, props a hand on her hip, and starts sashaying down the street like she's walking the runway at a Paris fashion show. I'm about to tell her to stop attracting more attention when I realize it's probably a good thing to have her distract everyone from Third Uncle. I think. I really don't have a clue what's best to do in this situation.

We make our way down St. Aldates Street and I try to ignore the numerous cellphones that are being aimed our way. Fourth Aunt waves and throws kisses at the strangers videoing us while Ma, Big Aunt, and Second Aunt cluster tightly behind the wheelchair, obviously uncomfortable at all the attention. My mind is whirring like an overworked machine.

What are we going to do with him? Come to think of it, what are we going to do with the other two men back at Christ Church? Oh my god, we have not one, not two, but three kidnapped men in our possession! We have the entire Tanuwijaya family men knocked out and tied up! Ha. Ha-ha. Ha-ha-ha. Oh *god*.

I mentally shake my mind into stillness. *Okay. It's going to be okay.* I don't know how, but I make myself take a deep breath. Right. Now let it out. Phew. Breathing good. Thinking bad.

Just then, Ma leans over and says, "Oh, Meddy, I have good idea, lho." She wiggles her eyebrows cunningly, looking very pleased with herself.

"Yes?" Despite myself, hope lifts a tentative head. Which is stupid, I know, but still.

"I see in front of Christ Church College got big park."

"The Christ Church meadows, yeah. What about it?"

"Got cows," Ma says, nodding conspiratorially.

"Um, yeah?"

"We dump him in meadow and cow will eat him."

I should've known better than to get my hopes up. Because this is what happens when I do. I struggle to think of how to even begin answering this.

Fourth Aunt cuts in before I can. "Hah! Cows don't eat humans," she says derisively.

Ma glares at her. "Oh? You cow expert, ya? You know," she says, abruptly turning toward me, "Second Aunt and I watch movie last night, wah, about this man like to eat people, aduh, so scary, deh." She's stopped pushing the wheelchair now, caught up in her story.

"Yeah, okay, Ma, keep pushing," I say through gritted teeth.

"And then this guy, right, Meddy, this guy he throw someone in pig pen, waduh! And then he play music and wah, the pig all eat the guy!" Ma shudders. "You see, pig eat people, why not cow eat people?"

I recognize the movie description. "You watched *Hannibal*? That's so unlike you. Anyway, yeah, pigs eat anything. They're omnivores, like us. Cows are vegetarian."

"Not bad idea," Big Aunt says suddenly, looking up from her handkerchief for a second.

Second Aunt snorts and says, "Hah! You think not bad idea, you gila!" Ma shoots her an affronted look, and Second Aunt shrugs. "Sorry, San Mei, but yes, very silly idea. Cow, where got eat human? You drinking too much champagne already, bubble go to head."

"Not that," Big Aunt snarls. "Not cow eating human." At the hurt look from Ma, Big Aunt softens her voice. "Sorry, San Mei. What I mean is, you know, I hear cow can kill human. Not eating them, no, but they can—what's the word—you know, they run so fast and then bam! Running over the human, break all the bone, puncture all the organ, person die. Maybe we put Third Uncle inside meadow and chase cow to run over his body. People think, oh, he just climb into meadow and get running over by cow, so he die, the end."

Huh. That . . . might not be a bad idea. No, wait, what am

I saying? It's a terrible idea! We're literally talking about murdering someone via cow! That's just not—that's not—no.

"We can't kill him. Stop going straight for murder," I hiss at them in a low voice. People are still aiming their cellphones at us as we pass by.

Fourth Aunt waves regally at them before saying, "Can't we just throw him in the river like we decided before?"

"We didn't decide on anything, and stop saying that so loud." I switch to Indonesian. "And did you guys forget the— ugh, what's the word—the other men in the room at Christ Church? Killing Third Uncle still leaves us with the other two."

"Yes, but at least it's two and not three. We can get rid of the other two later," Fourth Aunt points out. "Easier to get rid of two bodies than three, my dear."

Even Ma is nodding at this.

"I can't—no. No! Stop trying to talk me into killing any of them." We finally arrive at the college and I catch sight of Staphanie, standing outside the enormous college gates. I swear under my breath. Shit, shit. What do I do? "Guys, take Third Uncle and go—"

Staphanie spots us and hurries over. Fuck. Of course she's spotted us. She'd have to be blindfolded not to spot us in the crowd. Oh my god, she's going to see Third Uncle and she's going to freak.

I scramble my mind for a solution as she closes the distance, but it's too late. Before I can say anything to my family, Staphanie's right in front of us, just a few feet away from her kidnapped uncle.

26

"There you are," Staphanie says, slightly out of breath. "Listen, whatever you've done to Second Uncle—"

"Whatever we've done to what?" Fourth Aunt says in her normal voice, by which I mean she's basically shouting.

Staphanie looks like she's on the verge of tears. "I really hope you haven't done anything stupid."

"What stupid? Why you say that?" Ma says.

Staphanie shakes her head and her gaze flicks from us to Third Uncle. Third Uncle, who's knocked out and tied up in a wheelchair. I quickly step in front of him, covering him from view. Luckily, Staphanie doesn't seem to recognize Third Uncle. She must be too distracted over Second Uncle's disappearance.

"You were hinting about having done something to Second Uncle," she says.

"Nope, you must've misheard."

"Where were you just now?"

"Um, just now? We just came back from the Randolph." My mind races through the words coming out of my mouth, checking each one to make sure it's an okay thing to say.

Staphanie's brows snap together. "The Randolph? Why?"

"Uh—"

"Staphanie," Ma says, stepping uncomfortably close to Staphanie, who leans back as far as she can. Ma gets right in her face, squinting up at her sternly. I'm pretty sure neither Staphanie nor I am breathing right now. "You got very good skin. Like South Korean star."

My breath comes out in a whoosh.

"Uh. What's going on?" Staphanie says.

"My family's a bit drunk," I say apologetically.

Staphanie's gaze snaps back to me and her mouth thins into a line. "You mean because they were trying to get Ama and me drunk? Is that why your Big Aunt has lost her dragon fascinator?"

"Er, yeah."

Uncertainty crosses Staphanie's face, making her look much younger and, just for the moment, vulnerable. I have no idea what could be going on in her mind. Maybe we just seem like such unlikely killers she's having a hard time putting everything together. One can hope.

She pauses before meeting my eyes. "Look, is Second Uncle okay?"

I almost look away, but I stop myself in time. In as firm a voice as I can manage, I say, "Yes. Depending on how the rest of the evening goes."

Staphanie grits her teeth. Her expression hardens into stone and she gives a small shake of the head. "You don't know what you're dealing with. Anyway. Everyone's been wondering where you are, and the reception's about to start, so let's go."

"Right." The wedding reception. Nathan. Oh, god. He must be so upset and confused right now. "Let's go."

I glance back at my family, standing in a single row with Third Uncle hidden behind them, and wave them off as I follow Staphanie. Please, universe, let them be lucid enough to stash Third Uncle somewhere before joining the reception. They're all looking kind of dazed and uncertain. Not that I can blame them. I feel dazed and uncertain. At least no one's found Big Uncle and Second Uncle, otherwise there would be cops everywhere. The thought isn't a comforting one.

Another thing that isn't comforting? The weird, conflicting feelings of sympathy I'm having for Staphanie. I mean, what the hell is up with that? Just because she's concerned about Second Uncle doesn't mean she's no longer an evil mafia member who's out to kill someone in cold blood. Come on, Meddy, focus on who the real bad guys are here. It's not us. Despite all of the kidnapping and stuff.

"Your time's almost up," I blurt out suddenly. Shit, why did I said that? But then I realize that it's true. There's just the reception left, and a bit of dancing afterward, and then this cursed day will be over and done with, thank god.

Staphanie side-eyes me. "You mean your time's almost up."

"What?"

Staphanie shrugs.

"No, what's that supposed to mean? What're you going to do?" Oh god, this was probably their plan all along. Of course. They've planned to kill Lilian during the reception or maybe during the dancing after, when it's all dark and everyone's drunk. "You disgust me," I spit out. "She's an old woman. Leave her alone."

Staphanie levels a cold gaze at me and quirks her mouth into a smirk. "You'd be surprised at the atrocities old women are capable of."

I'm about to come back with some snarky retort when I realize that she's right. I mean, my family, which consists of older women, did just spend the entire way from the Randolph to Christ Church College discussing various ways of murdering Third Uncle, so.

At the bottom of the stairs leading to the dining hall, Staphanie pulls me to face her. She brushes stray strands of hair away from my face. If anyone were to happen to spot us, they'd think she's just being a meticulous photographer. When she speaks, her voice is low and firm. "I don't know what you've done to my uncles, but I swear, if you've hurt them, you're going to pay for it. Now get in there and act normal."

That's a threat if I ever heard one. I wish I were faster with the comebacks. But I can't think of anything before she leads me up the stairs. And as soon as we round the top of the stairs, all thought leaves my head.

Because there, right outside the iconic Christ Church dining hall, is Nathan. He looks up and smiles when he sees me, but there's sadness in his smile. A touch of exhaustion. With one last meaningful glance, Staphanie leaves us and slips into the dining hall, and now there's just me and Nathan and a whole moat of lies between us. I run to him and give him a tight hug, inhaling the good, clean scent of him, savoring the security of having his arms around me.

"Your family okay?" he says.

I nod wordlessly. I can't speak. No words can describe how good it feels to be back in Nathan's arms after everything.

"Listen, Meddy, I know something's going on," he says softly.

I squeeze my eyes shut. Of course he does. He's one of the

most intuitive people I've ever met. It's one of the many reasons he's such a successful businessman. Back at Tom and Jacqueline's wedding, he figured out that my family and I were the ones behind Ah Guan's corpse. Of course he senses something is wrong today. I look up at him and blink rapidly to stop the tears from falling.

"What is it?" he says. "You can tell me anything."

"I—uh—" It sounds so ridiculous in my head. My family's being blackmailed by the mafia, and coincidentally we have kidnapped three men and my aunts might be in the process of murdering one of them. "It's nothing," I say finally.

Disappointment washes over Nathan's handsome features.

"Everything's fine," I quickly add, and that sounds like a lie, even to me. But the night's almost over, and Staphanie and Ama have lost three of their main players, so how likely is it that they'd be able to carry out whatever they were plotting? My family and I are winning, dammit. "It will be," I say again, and this time, my voice comes out more confident. "And I'll tell you everything when it's all over." And we're all home free and unlikely to get Nathan in trouble for being an accomplice or an accessory or whatever.

Nathan sighs. "Meddy, I—"

The door to the dining hall cracks open and Ama's head pops out. "You up," she says, shooting me a death glare behind Nathan's back.

Nathan and I straighten up and look at each other. "I love you," I say, finally. It seems the only thing left to say.

Nathan's features soften. "I love you too. Let's go in." He crooks his arm and I slip mine through his.

The doors yawn wide open, and together, we enter the gorgeous reception hall to loud applause.

Christ Church College's dining hall is iconic for a reason. It's the place that the Hogwarts dining hall is modeled after. All the walls are gilded with opulent gold and hung with plenty of paintings. The long tables are set with vases bursting with flowers, and huge chandeliers hang from the vaulted ceiling. Next to the stage, there is a beautiful dessert table with all sorts of sugary treats, and in the center of it is a towering, gargantuan wedding cake with a cascade of delicate sugar flowers wrapped around it that would make any Chinese-Indonesian bride happy.

It's a scene straight out of the most prestigious wedding magazines. The guests clap and cheer and whistle as we walk in. The attention of over two hundred people is so overwhelming that my legs become watery and I would've fallen if I hadn't been holding on to Nathan. I force myself to take a deep breath. We walk past the rows of clapping people and take our place at the front dining table. Annie and Chris are seated there and I give them each a hug and an air kiss.

"Where's your family?" Annie says, her expression clearly puzzled and also disapproving.

It's a good question. Where indeed? *Probably somewhere in the meadow trying to convince a cow to eat someone* is not going to fly as an answer.

"Um, it's a long story," I say with an apologetic smile. "I think they're—uh, a bit indisposed at the moment."

Annie sniffs and exchanges a sneering look with Chris. It hurts. I know it shouldn't, but it does. They're my parents-in-law now, and I wanted so badly for everything to go well, to fit into Nathan's lovely, functional family. I wanted them to embrace me and my family, to tell me I'm the daughter-in-law they've always wished for, and that my family is delightful.

"I suppose it's just as well, isn't it, dear?" Annie says to Chris, who shrugs cautiously.

I bite down on my lip so hard I almost draw blood.

"Mum," Nathan says in a warning tone.

"What? They've been absolutely—"

The doors slam open again and Annie stops talking as my aunts and mother explode into the dining hall. I can't help but smile at the sight of them. It's true that they've been absolutely—whatever Annie was about to say—but they're also my family and I would've been crushed if they missed my wedding reception. I'm about to rush over to give them each a big hug when Ma shifts, revealing something behind her. My blood freezes. My heart stops beating. All noise is suddenly muted.

Because right behind Ma, being pushed along by Second Aunt, is Third Uncle, still wrapped up like a burrito in the wheelchair. My brain implodes. They've brought along the guy they kidnapped to my wedding reception.

27

This can't be real. It just can't. I'm in a nightmare. A really long, really elaborate nightmare, but still a dream nevertheless. Just something my mind cooked up. Maybe I'm drunk. Maybe Ma slipped some of her TCM into my morning coffee and now I'm hallucinating. Yeah, that's it. This entire day has been nothing but a hallucination. The question is: how the hell do I wake up from it?

I can do nothing but stare in absolute horror as my family makes their way down the aisle toward us. As usual, Fourth Aunt relishes the attention. She's waving and blowing kisses as she walks. Big Aunt is striding like a matron off to catch a naughty kid, and Ma and Second Aunt walk along with their heads slightly bowed, obviously uncomfortable with all the attention. Third Uncle is still knocked out.

"Oh, is that your grandmother in the wheelchair?" Annie

says, forcing a smile. "How lovely and unexpected. I don't re-call seeing any grandparents on the guest list."

"That's um—it's—my. Uh. Yeah." I catch the frown on Na-than's face and quickly say, "Yep, that's my grandmother."

Instead of dissipating, the frown grows deeper. "I didn't know your grandma's still around," he says, clearly not buying my lie.

"Yeah, I rarely talk about her because she lives in Indone-sia?" Goddammit, whenever I lie, the lie always comes out as a question. I'm pretty sure Nathan catches on to it too, because his eyes narrow for a second.

"Okay," he says, finally. That look of disappointment weighs down his handsome features, cracking my heart like a chisel, and before I can say anything else, he turns away slightly.

This is the fucking worst. My hands ball up into fists. The last thing I wanted to do is to hurt Nathan, but obviously all the lies have done exactly that. Tears burn the backs of my eyes. I just—god. I just what? I don't know what the hell to do, and anyway, there isn't anything that can be done now. Not in front of our two hundred guests and his parents and Staphanie and Ama. All I can do is greet my family with false warmth when they get to us and say, loudly, "Ah, you've brought Popo! What a wonderful surprise!" before bending over to kiss Third Uncle on the cheek.

Annie approaches, hugging Ma and the aunts stiffly and giv-ing them polite air kisses before stopping in front of Third Uncle. She bends over slightly and calls out, "Hello! Welcome to England!"

Of course, Third Uncle remains absolutely still. Annie glances at us, a hesitant smile on her face. "Er, it's lovely to have you here!" she half-shouts at Third Uncle again.

"I think my grandmother is asleep," I say quickly. "Long flight and all. Isn't that right, Ma? Grandmother is asleep?"

It takes a moment for what I said to click with Ma. She blinks at me, mouthing the word "grandmother" very slowly. Then she brightens up and says, "Oh yes! Yes, grandmother. Yes, this our grandmother."

Annie's eyebrows shoot up into her hairline. "Oh my. So this is your great-grandmother? That's incredible!"

"No, she's my grandmother," I cut in, then wonder why I felt the need to cut in. What does it matter whose grandmother we're pretending Third Uncle is?

"Ah? Right," Annie says. "Well."

There's an awkward silence as we all stand and smile with aching politeness at one another. Nathan gives a small nod to someone in the distance, and with a start, I realize he's nodding to Ama. Right, of course. She's the wedding planner, after all. He's just telling her to get the festivities started.

There's a bit of a rearranging to be done, chairs to be shifted to fit Third Uncle at our table, but it finally gets done and we all take our seats with obvious relief. The doors reopen and waiters stream in, carrying trays of food. My mouth starts to water. When was the last time I ate? Wow. I think it was actually the night before. I've gone nearly twenty-four hours without food. No wonder I feel so jittery and brittle.

But just as the beautiful salad is placed in front of me, I realize with a start that this is it. This must be how Staphanie and her family are planning to kill Lilian! It would be so simple. We all have assigned seating, so they'd know in advance which would be her plate, her glasses, her forks and spoons. Oh god. I look over at the next table, where Lilian is sitting. The food hasn't reached her table yet.

I pat Ma's arm with urgency. "Ma, si itu," I whisper to her.

With Nathan on my other side, I can't say anything more specific than "the thing."

"Apa itu?" What thing?

I grit my teeth. Dammit, Ma. Come on. "Itu," I say meaningfully, widening my eyes.

"Eh? Apa? Kenapa?" Ma's getting louder.

"Everything okay?" Nathan says wearily.

I nod and force a smile before turning back to Ma and whispering, "The pembunuhan." The murder.

Her eyes widen in shock, like the thought of murder has come as a surprise. Oh my god, there are no words for how awful it is that Ma is drunk. Then, fortunately, realization dawns on her face and she nods sagely. "Oh yes. The pembunuhan." She leans across Third Uncle and whispers something to Big Aunt, who's already halfway through her salad.

Big Aunt's head shoots up and they both look over at Lilian. My heart sinks. The waiters have gotten to Lilian's table and are serving everyone their salads. Ma and Big Aunt must have realized this too, because they both shoot up to their feet. In fact, Ma shoots up so fast that her chair clatters to the floor. The deafening thump slices through all the noise in the dining hall, and instantly every voice is silenced. Everyone is looking over at us. Shit, shit.

Ma looks terrified, and who can blame her? *Oh my god, do something!* my mind screams at me. But everything is a blank. All I can see are the stares from everyone, especially from Annie.

Luckily, Big Aunt, who has a lot more forethought than I do, lifts her chin proudly and says, loudly and clearly, "Iello, everyone! My name is Friya, and I am Meddelin's Big Aunt."

A soft murmur goes through the crowd and shoulders visibly relax as everyone thinks, *Ah, speeches. Right.* Speeches are understandable. Thank god for Big Aunt's quick thinking.

But my relief is short-lived. Because after she's done introducing herself, it becomes obvious that Big Aunt has no idea what to say next. She looks at me. She looks back at the crowd.

"Thank you, everyone, for you coming here," she says, faltering. The silence is deafening. I should save her. I'm about to stand up when she forges on. "For you coming to my Meddy's wedding." She looks back at me and her face softens. "You know, I not Meddy's mother. But I always feel like she is my daughter. Ever since she little, I have love her like a daughter. Because daughters are blessing, yes?"

The crowd murmurs its agreement. Most people are smiling genially. Holy shit, this might actually work. But I can't just sit here and relax, because what's going to happen once Big Aunt finishes her speech? People will go back to eating, and we'll be back to square one.

As Big Aunt continues talking, I whisper to Ma, "We need to stop Lilian from eating."

Ma looks at me with wide eyes. "Yes," she says slowly. She takes out her phone and writes a text. A few seats away, Second Aunt and Fourth Aunt take out their phones and glance at them before typing their replies. I can't help noticing that Annie has noticed this exchange and is watching with open disapproval. I guess from her point of view, Ma and the others are being incredibly rude, given that their big sister is giving a speech.

A strange note in Big Aunt's voice makes me look up, and to my horror, I find that she's crying again. ARGH. I'm frozen in horror as Big Aunt sobs, "And now my beautiful daughter leaving me, get married in foreign country, maybe after this live in foreign country, who know? Like my son, you know, Russ, you also leave me, live so far away, never visiting me."

I jump up and hurry to Big Aunt, giving her a hug and loudly thanking her for the wonderful speech. Belatedly, I realize that by doing that, I've signaled the end of the speech. There is a smattering of polite applause, and then the tinkle of cutlery as the guests start digging into their food once more. I look desperately at my family, and Second Aunt jumps up and shouts, "I also have speech!"

"Good grief," Annie mutters, letting her fork drop and dabbing at her mouth with her napkin.

Everybody stares expectantly at Second Aunt, who glances over at me with wide eyes. "I—uh—I am Second Aunt. My name Enjelin. Hello. Yes, hi. Ah, you know what I like to do?"

Oh no. No, no, no.

"Tai Chi!" Second Aunt says proudly, getting into her stride. "Come, we all do Tai Chi!"

Everyone looks around with WTF expressions.

"Yes, this all part of Chinese-Indonesian wedding," Second Aunt says. The few guests from our side of the family frown and shrug. "Is will bring good luck to the newlywed. Otherwise, they be cursed forever. Come, stand up, everybody!" She claps loudly and starts going around the room, urging people to their feet.

Oh god. This is so much worse than I thought it was going to be.

"Is she serious right now?" Annie says.

"Well, it's good to get a bit of exercise in before eating," Nathan says. He turns to me and shoots me a "What the hell is going on?" look.

I shrug helplessly. But then, through my mortification, I realize that Second Aunt has given us the perfect opening. Now, while everyone is distracted by the Tai Chi, is our chance. I go to the other side of the table and whisper to Fourth Aunt, "Can you distract Lilian somehow? Stop her from eating?"

Fourth Aunt nods, squaring her shoulders and cracking her

neck. "Leave it to me, kid." She walks away, each step convey-ing confidence. I walk back to my seat.

"So, not to be judgy or anything," Nathan says, "but I've hosted about half a dozen Chinese-Indonesian weddings at the hotel, and none of them has involved Tai Chi."

"Well, none of them has had Second Aunt in it," I point out weakly.

"True . . ."

"Come on, everyone, stand up!" Second Aunt says again.

Chris stands up, looking like a terrified kid, and who can blame him? Annie's hand shoots out and lands on his arm with unforgiving firmness. She glares at him and says, "Have you forgotten what happened the last time you followed this ma-larkey?"

Part of me bristles at her calling Tai Chi "malarkey." I guess it's the whole "I can call my mom a bitch, but you can't call my mom a bitch" thing. Except I would never, ever think to call Ma a bitch, or even think it in my own head. Even thinking about thinking about calling her a bitch makes me grimace.

Okay, get a grip and focus on the real issue. Which is that Second Aunt is providing us with the perfect opportunity to get Lilian away from her potentially-very-probably-poisoned cut-lery, and we're not exactly doing anything about it. Well, Fourth Aunt is. Though I have no idea what she's planning on doing, exactly.

"Hello, test, test," Second Aunt says, her voice booming across the vast dining hall. Oh god, she's gone up onto the stage and grabbed hold of a mic. "Hello, testing one, two . . ."

"We can hear you!" Big Aunt snaps, her voice coming out almost as loud as Second Aunt's despite the lack of a micro-phone.

"Oh, is working? Okay, good." Second Aunt looks across

the hall and seems to realize that she's the subject of every-body's attention for the first time. "Oh." She falters. My heart thumps so hard in my chest I swear it cracks a rib. She's going to choke. She's going to get stage fright, and oh my god, so much secondhand embarrassment—

But then a smile slowly takes over Second Aunt's face, melt-ing across it like ice cream, and quite suddenly, she's beaming like a little kid. I guess it's the weed in her system, but Second Aunt looks about ready to take over the world.

"Okay!" she says. "Woot!"

Oh my god, she really did just say, "Woot." This is definitely the work of the marijuana. Just how much did Ma put in that dose?

"Tai Chi!" she cries. "We are doing the Tai Chi!" She is practically vibrating with excitement. I guess she's always been dying for people to do Tai Chi with her, and now she has an entire dining hall full of hostages. "Starting position. Hands out like this, and then we parting the wild horse mane. We do slowly, the horse is wild horse, very easy to scare, yes. Oh yes, you in the front row, very good. You, the one in blue dress, you less good."

I am staring with obvious horror at the spectacle before I realize that this is the time to do something, in the likely situa-tion that Fourth Aunt fails to get Lilian to safety. With extreme effort, I manage to tear my gaze from the spectacle that is Sec-ond Aunt and look at Lilian's table. My heart stops.

Her seat is empty. She's nowhere near it. Shit, where has she gone? I scan the room, a lump forming in my throat, and release my breath when I spot Fourth Aunt and Lilian at the side of the stage. What are they doing? I stare hard at Fourth Aunt, willing her to look at me, and somehow, some little miracle happens and she actually does. She grins proudly and wiggles her eyebrows, cocking her head at Lilian as if to say, *See what I did? Look! I got her!*

I try my best to convey, *Yes, great job, Fourth Aunt, but what's the plan?*

It's kind of hard to get that across a room while half-heartedly doing Tai Chi—we're now into White Crane Spreads Its Wings, apparently.

Fourth Aunt nods, then shakes her head and mouths a whole bunch of words I can't make out. I frown at her and she mouths them with more exaggeration. I shake my head. This is hopeless.

A flash of movement catches my eye, and all the blood drains out of my head. It's Staphanie, and she's moving smoothly, silently, like a snake creeping through the grass toward its prey. Shit. What is she about to do? Have they figured out that this whole Tai Chi thing is just a ruse to buy us more time to save Lilian?

"Ma," I whisper. Ma is doing Repulse Monkey with intense concentration, though she's wobbling hard.

She looks up and I cock my head toward Staphanie. Ma's mouth thins into a pinched line and she sidles over to Big Aunt. The two of them whisper to each other before leaving the table quietly.

"Will you please tell me what's going on?" Nathan says in a low voice.

I don't even spare him a glance. "I—please, just let me focus."

Ma and Big Aunt stride over to Staphanie. My heart is beating so fast I think I might pass out. I struggle to keep breathing. I need to do something. I don't know what Ma and Big Aunt have planned, but I can't just leave my family to deal with the actual goddamn mafia on their own. What if Staphanie has a gun? Oh my god. Of course she does. She's mafia! I grip the side of the table hard. What do I do now? Do I scream? Do I bring everything crashing down? Will that just trigger Staphanie into action? What if I get Ma or Big Aunt hurt?

But when Ma and Big Aunt get to her, nothing happens. Words are exchanged, and then the three of them kind of just . . . stand there. Meanwhile, Second Aunt has come to the end of the Tai Chi session. "Very good!" she says, beaming at the crowd. "Maybe we do again—oh—" She's interrupted by Fourth Aunt, who strides onto the stage with Lilian in tow. Fourth Aunt grabs the mic from Second Aunt and grins out at the audience.

"A round of applause for my very masterful sister!" Fourth Aunt calls out. There is a weak ripple of applause. "And now I have a treat for all of you. As you all must know, I am Mimi Chan, a well-known celebrity. I have performed for the likes of Oprah and Ellen DeGeneres."

Even from where I'm standing, I can hear Ma's snort of derision.

Fourth Aunt side-eyes Ma and plasters on an even bigger smile. She gives a little shimmy and says, "And I am about to give you a performance you will never forget! Oh, and Lilian too. Lilian, give everybody a wave." Lilian gives us all a terrified grin. Fourth Aunt nods at the band manager and says, "Hit it, boys!"

The band starts up with a rendition of "I Will Always Love You."

Ma and Big Aunt are looking even more tense than before. Ma says something to Staphanie, and Staphanie gives her a smile so smug it turns my stomach. Ma looks over at me with a frown. I feel it too. Something's about to happen. But what? They've outsmarted us. They haven't poisoned Lilian's food after all. No, it's something else. What could it be? Think, brain!

Okay, let's see. They're mafia. They're mafia—okay, we've been over this. So they're mafia, so what? What do we know about the mafia? They're all about sending out a message. Right, yes! So they'd go for the most dramatic kill, one that will be seared in everybody's mind. Oh my god.

A bomb. Oh god. That's what it—no. That doesn't make sense. If they've planted a bomb, Staphanie wouldn't be here. Not this close to the action, anyway. Ama might be a ruthless mafia boss lady, but I can't imagine her sacrificing her only granddaughter like that.

So, then, what is it? And where the hell is Ama? I look around me and catch a sudden reflection up on the banister on the second floor. A small gasp escapes me. Is that—could that be the scope of a rifle?

When we first met, Staphanie had mentioned how Ama used to hunt when she was younger, and what a sharp shooter she was. How else would she have ascended the ranks to become the matriarch? This is it. She's going to actually snipe Lilian from there, right in front of everyone. She's going to assassinate her. We've been focused on the wrong thing this whole time. It was never going to be poison. Poison would've been too quiet, too subtle. Remember the Chinese-Indonesian adage: the showier, the better.

I struggle to get out of my seat, to navigate around my chair in my huge dress. Ma catches my eye and she must have spotted something in my expression because she grabs Big Aunt, who grabs Second Aunt. Together, the three of them approach the stage slowly, cautiously.

"Where are you going?" Nathan says.

"Bathroom."

He doesn't buy it, but he can see the panic in my eyes. "What's going on—never mind. Just tell me what you need me to do."

"We need to—" From the corner of my eye, I catch sight of something. Someone's moving, and the movement is so weird and awkward and just plain wrong that it robs all thought from my head. I look over and freeze.

It's Third Uncle. He's awake.

Chris notices him at the same time. "Oh, your grandmother's awake," he says.

I understand, now, why people say, "Rooted to the spot." *Move!* my mind screams, but I swear roots have sprouted from the soles of my feet and dug deep into the ground.

Even as I watch, Third Uncle lurches out of the wheelchair, struggling with the blanket that's twined tightly around him. He sways drunkenly to his feet, looking like he's about to topple over, but then he takes a small step, and another. The bindings around his ankles must've gotten loose.

Ma and the aunties have yet to spot him; their eyes are locked on Lilian, singing and swaying meekly next to Fourth Aunt.

My legs unlock and I move toward Third Uncle. What am I about to do? I have no idea. I reach out for him and he lurches away from me in a panic.

"No, wait—"

He takes a wild swing, loses his balance, and stumbles straight into the towering wedding cake behind him. The entire dessert table, along with the eight-tier cake, comes crashing down with a magnificent *bang*, and my family leaps into action. I turn to the stage just in time to see Ma, Second Aunt, and Big Aunt tackle Lilian to the ground.

28

Chaos. Someone has shouted "Gun!" and now there are shouts and screams and everybody is running everywhere, and for the longest second in the history of seconds, I stand there, mouth agape, staring at the crazy shambles that is my wedding reception. Then something grabs me—Nathan, taking my arm and urging me to get out of the dining hall. I pull my arm out of his grasp and register, dimly, the look of confusion on his face.

"I need to—my family—"

"Get out of here," he says. "I'll come back for them."

This snaps me out of my shock. "No! You take your parents out of here. I'll get my family."

For a moment, he looks like he might argue, but I say, "Lilian," and he nods grimly before rushing over to the stage. We had all seen my aunts and mother bodychecking poor Lilian, and I have no idea how she's faring. Probably not great.

At the stage, Lilian is miraculously sitting up, looking dazed. Ma reaches out to help her up, but Lilian gives a terrified little shriek and shrinks away. Who can blame her? Nathan catches Lilian gently, and together they stagger off the stage and limp toward the nearest exit.

Where has Staphanie gone? I look around but don't see her or Ama anywhere. But there's no time to search for them. I need to do something about Third Uncle.

I rush to the remnants of the dessert table and find Third Uncle trapped under the smashed giant wedding cake. With his wrists and ankles still tied up, he's finding it near impossible to get up. It doesn't help that he's now covered in a thick, greasy layer of coconut cake with slick, rich lime cream.

I bend over to help pull him up, but he shies away from me just as Lilian had with Ma. I consider grabbing his arm anyway but decide against it. Despite the direness of the situation, I still can't bear to get my dress covered in cake. Which is crazy, I know. He opens his mouth. I steel myself for the scream that's about to come out, but instead, he coughs and then turns his head and vomits a little. Shit, I wonder if he has a concussion. I stand and wave frantically at the stage, catching Ma's eye. "Help," I mouth.

Ma helps Big Aunt up, Fourth Aunt helps Second Aunt to her feet, and together, they all come hurrying down the stage. To my surprise, they're all smiling proudly.

"We do it!" Ma says.

"What?"

"We save Lilian!" Second Aunt crows. "You see how fast I move? Like striking predator. Ooh, that should be Tai Chi move, ya? Striking Predator. Maybe I can submit move to Tai Chi organization."

"You didn't save her."

"What you mean?" Big Aunt says, frowning. "We all hear gun shoot, so we all shield her, wah, so brave." Tears shine in her eyes. "We all almost die, lho, Meddy."

"Er, yeah, about that . . ." I cock my head toward the floor, at the struggling form of Third Uncle. "That wasn't a gunshot; it was Third Uncle crashing into the dessert table." A noise that is completely unlike a gunshot, I want to add, but I decide not to push them. "Speaking of Third Uncle, we need to get him out of here, fast."

They seem to notice him for the first time.

"Aduh," Ma says. "Why he lying there like that?"

"I think he has a concussion? I don't know. Doesn't matter, let's get him out of here."

"Ih, he get our dress dirty, then how?" Second Aunt says.

I want to snap something mean at her but realize I'm being a hypocrite because, well, wasn't that the whole reason why I didn't grab him in the first place? *Snap out of it, Meddy,* I scold myself. Moving Third Uncle > clean dress. Yes. Okay. I reach down and flip over the blanket that's around him so the clean side is facing up. "Okay, now we can move him without getting our clothes dirty."

"Wah, very good idea, Meddy," Ma says, smiling proudly. Again, the things she's proud of me for really need work.

Lifting Third Uncle requires a bit of coordination, but by now, my family and I are disturbingly adept at carrying unconscious men. We each automatically get to our stations—Fourth Aunt taking the left armpit, Second Aunt taking the right, Big Aunt at the head, and me and Ma each taking a leg. We heave, he comes up off the floor, and we slowly move him onto the wheelchair.

Thank god we're so efficient about moving bodies now, because just as we finish tucking in the blankets, the doors to the dining room burst open and a pair of security guards come striding in. Oh my god. They're here to detain us, they'll take us away and then call the cops and—

"Ma'am, you need to vacate the premises now," one of them says.

"Yeah, yeah, we're just about to leave; don't get your knickers in a twist," Fourth Aunt mutters, winking at us as she pushes the wheelchair toward the exit.

My heart whines a supersonic beat as we hurry out. Unbelievable. We're walking past security guards with a kidnapped man. As we go past them, one of the guards gives me a small nod and says, "I'm sorry about your wedding day." Emotions bubble up in my chest and I have to swallow a lump in my throat. I nod back at him and then rush through the doors.

Outside, I close my eyes and release my breath. That was way too fucking close. "Let's get him back to the, uh—" I falter. Where should we put him? We can't take him back to the Randolph, not after all the commotion and fuss with Dan from the reception desk. It'll attract way too much attention. "The bedroom here," I say finally. We've already got two kidnapped men in there. What's one more?

And oh god, what are we going to do with them? The pit in my stomach widens. I feel sick at the realization. We can't just let them go, because who knows what they'll do? Report us to the police for kidnapping, probably. Or put out a hit on us. But if we don't let them go, well . . . what the hell are we going to do with them? We can't keep them with us forever. Can't do this, can't do that. Maybe Second Aunt is right, maybe we should chop them all up into little bits and—

Okay, clearly all neurons in my brain are misfiring. We turn to go down the hallway toward the antechamber when someone shouts, "Stop!"

I freeze, then turn. What I see is worse than guards—it's Nathan and his parents.

Annie looks furious. Even Chris looks stern. And Nathan looks disappointed, which is somehow worse.

"What is going on?" Annie cries. "What the hell was that? You all almost killed poor Lilian."

"Go to the bedroom first," I whisper to Fourth Aunt, who nods and pushes the wheelchair along as Nathan's parents descend upon us.

"No, no," Ma says patiently, "we save Lilian."

"I told you, Ma, it wasn't a gunshot," I mutter.

Annie shakes her head. "You have all been quite—quite—" She struggles for the right word, her eyes flashing as she gestures at my family. "I mean, these outfits, those hats—"

"What wrong with hat?" Big Aunt says, and suddenly she's back in full Big Aunt mode, exuding towering authority and intimidation.

Annie sputters. "Oh for goodness' sake, look at them! They are ridiculous! You're a laughingstock!"

The word slices through my chest like a knife.

"Mum, you're out of line," Nathan hisses at Annie.

A laughingstock. It's true that my family talks differently, and does a ton of ridiculous things, but I've always understood why they say and do the things that they do. *Laughingstock*. It twists, burning with white-hot guilt. I guess part of me has always tried to hide my family because I know they can seem strange to outsiders. So maybe I'm a hypocrite for feeling this rage, especially since I'm complicit in trying to make my family conform. Haven't I been trying to tone them down all my life?

But the look on their faces is too much to bear. I can't stand it. I won't ever be able to erase that look of hurt on Ma's face from my memories. I glare at Annie. "Maybe they don't fit into your anal view of what the world should look like, but they are not the laughingstock here."

Annie narrows her eyes at me. Chris sighs and clears his throat. Hope rises for a second. Maybe he'll tell Annie she's out of line.

"I'm very sorry, Meddy, but I have to agree with Annie. Your family's behavior is very strange, and I'm not saying that to mock them," he quickly adds. "But it's honestly quite unacceptable."

"It's ridiculous!" Annie says.

"That's enough, Mum, Dad."

I'm burning up with so many emotions. Anger at Nathan's parents, mostly, for daring to speak about my family like that. But deep down inside, there's also shame. Because I know they're right. An outsider, looking at my family objectively, would think they are truly a ridiculous bunch. And we've spent the entire day running around doing utterly ridiculous things. Things that, under the circumstances, are understandable—to those in the know, at least—but are inexplicable to an outside observer who isn't aware of what's going on. And even without the whole mafia threat, my family is a lot to take in. I know this, I know, but still. To have Nathan's parents point them out with such awful ferocity is too much.

"Look, can we please just talk?" Nathan says, lowering his voice.

"Ah, yes, you kids talk, okay?" Ma says before I can answer. "We get out of way. Okay, toodles, cheerio!"

"And stop talking like that!" Annie snaps.

"Don't tell them how to talk," I snap back. As soon as the words are out, I clamp my mouth shut. Holy shit. What have I just done?

"Meddy, you cannot talk to elders like that," Ma gasps, a look of absolute horror on her face. "You say sorry now."

"I'm sorry," I say immediately. The words just flop out automatically. I couldn't have stopped them if I tried.

"You don't need to apologize," Nathan sighs. "Mum, you're being quite horrible."

"Nathan!" Ma cries. "You cannot talk to your mama like that, no!"

Nathan and Annie stare at Ma with confusion.

"But I'm defending you," Nathan says slowly.

"No matter, you cannot say such thing to parent," Big Aunt says, sternly.

Second Aunt nods with her mouth pressed into a thin line. "Meddy, you embarrass us, talking to mother-in-law like that."

I throw up my hands. Of course this is what unites them. Annie can be as horrible as she wants toward them and they'll take it in stride, but woe befall anyone in the younger generation who dares to talk back to Annie. I take in a breath through gritted teeth. "You're right, of course. I'm sorry, Annie."

Ma's eyes go so wide they look like they're about to fall out.

"I mean, I'm sorry, uh—Mom," I bite out.

Ma relaxes, smiling proudly at me.

"Oh, that's alright, you can keep calling me Annie," she says, obviously uncomfortable.

"No!" Big Aunt barks. "Impossible. No, cannot."

Second Aunt shakes her head in agreement. "Cannot, no. Tidak boleh."

"Not respect," Ma explains to them. "How can younger generation call us by name? Impossible. No, I cannot allow."

Annie grimace-smiles. She's thrown off-balance, and I can't blame her. Just minutes ago she was geared for a fight with my family, and now they're defending her right to be horrible toward them.

"I think maybe it's best if we all retire for the night," I cut in. "We can all sit down and talk tomorrow?" Plus, it's just hit me that I don't know where Staphanie and Ama are. I need to get rid of my family and Nathan's and somehow find Staphanie.

Annie and Chris nod slowly.

"Can we talk now?" Nathan says. "Just you and me."

"Oh, I was going to—" Excuses fire through my mind. All of them fall flat. "Yeah, okay."

Nathan leads me away from the group and we walk in silence toward the meadows. Night has fallen, and the place is deserted. The song of crickets fills the air, and the loveliness of our surroundings just highlights what a terrible catastrophe I've turned everything into. Tears sting my eyes. I'm glad that it's dark so Nathan can't see them.

"So," he says, after a while.

"So."

"You ready to tell me what's really going on?"

"I—uh." By now, Fourth Aunt must be back in the antechamber. There will now be not one, not two, but three tied-up men in there.

"Why did your family tackle Lilian?"

"Because, um—they were trying to protect her?" Technically not a lie, but it comes out sounding shady as fuck.

Nathan sighs, his shoulders sagging. "Please, Meddy, tell me the truth."

There are no words for how badly I wish I could tell him everything. But what about Staphanie and Ama? For all I know, they could be lurking in the shadows, listening to us. What would they do if they catch me telling Nathan? Come to think of it, what are they plotting now, after we've so clearly gone against their warnings and ruined their plans to kill Lilian? What would their revenge be?

It's all too much to figure out. "We were trying to protect her," I insist. The words fall out of my mouth heavy with untruth.

Disappointment washes over Nathan's face, weighing down his handsome features. "Are you seriously still lying to me after what just happened?" The hurt in his eyes is almost a physical blow to my gut. "I can't do this." And then, just like that, he turns and walks away, leaving me alone with the chirp of the crickets as company.

29

It's a weird thing, heartbreak. What a strange word, but it is the most apt description of what it feels like—my entire being cracking, first the heart, then the cracks going out farther until each finger shatters and I crumble into a pile of rubble.

Okay, that sounds melodramatic, but try being abandoned on your wedding day in a meadow with cows and then tell me you don't feel as if you've just shattered into dust. Maybe the cows will put me out of my misery and eat me.

I'm losing him. Maybe I've already lost him.

He's leaving me because I've pushed him away, and if I've pushed him away, then it's down to me to pull him back.

"No!" I scream.

In the distance, the retreating figure stops. I start running, nearly tripping over the dusty, pebbly ground.

"Don't you fucking walk away!" I cry, not at all sounding like an unhinged bride.

"Meddy, I just need a—"

I tackle him. A full-on body slam straight into the middle of his chest. I suppose I am my mother's daughter after all.

Nathan staggers back but holds on to me tightly. His arms encircle me and don't let go, and because they don't let go, I allow myself to cry.

The tears flow out of me uncontrollably, an entire river of everything—fear, panic, anxiety. I shouldn't tell him, I shouldn't put this burden on him, I shouldn't—

Why shouldn't I? Because I wanted to keep this day perfect and worry-free for him? Well, that's definitely ruined now. Because I wanted to protect him? This is definitely not an ignorance-is-bliss situation. Or is it because of pure selfishness? Because I feel guilty for dragging him into this mess in the first place? Ah Guan was all my fault, and it very nearly cost Nathan his entire career. I guess part of me has never gotten over that, even after everything worked out fine. Except it turns out that everything hasn't worked out fine. Oh my god, my thoughts are not making any sense whatsoever.

"Staphanie is mafia!" I blurt out.

Nathan's arms go rigid. He looks down at me. "Come again?"

"Staph and her family, they're *the family*. Like the Godfather, or the Sopranos, or—"

"I know what mafia is," Nathan says gently. "I'm just—hang on, I need a second." He cocks his head and stands there looking stunned, and who can blame him? "Did you—wait, when did you find out?"

"I only found out yesterday. After my bachelorette night, I overheard Staphanie talking to someone and it sounded suspicious as hell." God, that felt like it happened a lifetime ago. Could that only be last night? "I confronted her about it and she came clean and told me she and her family are mafia and they're here to kill off somebody."

"Jesus," Nathan mutters.

"Yeah, I know! And she told me I can't call off the wedding because then she'd report me and you and my family for killing Ah Guan."

"What?" Nathan's mouth drops open.

I shake my head. "That was my reaction too. I don't know how they found out about Ah Guan . . . they have enough information to get us all in serious trouble. So we had to go along with it. But obviously we couldn't just let them kill someone, so . . ."

"That's why you and your family have been acting so weird the whole day? Because you were running around trying to outwit the mafia?"

I can't decipher the expression on Nathan's face. He looks equal parts horrified and awestruck. I guess I don't blame him either way.

When I nod, Nathan's breath comes out in a long *whoosh*. "But why didn't you tell me?"

"Staphanie said if I told you, she'd call the cops on us. I'm so sorry; you have no idea how much I've been dying to tell you. We figured out who their target is and we've been trying to protect Lilian ever since."

"Wait, why Lilian?" Nathan frowns.

"We found these messages on Second Uncle's phone about 'the queen' and stuff, and we figured that they were talking about Lilian because she's your biggest investor."

Nathan blinks, looking like he just got hit by something large and heavy. Like a truck. "Lilian is my biggest investor?" He looks up at the ceiling and mutters something.

"Yes, she is, isn't she? She's on the board of . . . something?"

Even I can hear the desperation in my own voice now. "You always treat her like royalty."

"Because she's my godmother!"

His. Godmother.

His godmother?

What. The. Fuck.

"And she was on the board of a large company, but she sold her stake a long time ago. She's retired, Meddy."

"But." But what? I can't think of how to finish that sentence, because WHAT? I don't understand what's happening. "But she's not—wait." I struggle to wrap my head around it. "She's not the target? She's not the queen?"

"I don't see how she can be. I mean, unless she's secretly an arms dealer on the side or something, but I really don't think so. She's my godmother. I think I'd know if she's doing something big enough to warrant an actual hit on her."

"But what does that mean? Someone else is the target? We've been protecting the wrong person this entire time?" I feel sick. When was the last time we even saw Staphanie and Ama? They were at the reception. And then they left before all of the commotion started, and I'd thought we'd won, we'd successfully protected Lilian, but now—

"Who the hell can 'the queen' be?" My mind is screaming: OH GOD OH GOD. "Who, Nathan?"

"I don't know, I don't—I don't know of anyone on my guest list who's powerful enough to piss off the mafia." Nathan shakes his head, looking lost.

I'm suddenly filled with a burning need to locate Ma and my aunts, to see them with my own two eyes and make sure they're okay. The fear is choking. "I need to find my family." I take Nathan's hand and turn in the direction of the dormitory. "Come with me?"

"Of course."

Then I pause. Shit. I'd better tell him everything. "Um."

"What is it?" Nathan says.

"Before we go inside the room, I need to tell you something else . . ."

We knock on the door to the bedroom. Ma's voice comes from the other side. "Who there?"

I breathe a sigh of relief. She's okay. "It's me, Meddy."

"Oh, Meddy!" There's a flurry of excited chatter from inside the room, and then the door swings open and Ma comes out and gives me a great big hug. "Aduh, so happy you okay, wah, why you take so long to come—oh, Nathan!" Ma looks at me with panicky eyes, probably wondering why I've brought Nathan here when I know damn well there are three kidnapped men tied up in the room.

"He knows."

"I know," Nathan says. He pops his head inside, sees the scene before him, steps back outside, and closes the door behind him. There is a beat of silence. Ma and I stare at him, too terrified to say a word. Finally, he says, "When you said, 'We might have kidnapped three people,' I didn't think you meant it quite so literally."

I throw up my hands. "How else can that be interpreted?"

"I don't know, Meddy, I've never had to think about how to properly tell someone that you've kidnapped three people!" Nathan cries.

I blanch at his words and he softens.

"I'm sorry. I'm freaking out a little because it seems you do actually have three men trussed up like turkeys in here."

"Oh yes," Ma says proudly. "Very good, ya? We do ourselves, you know."

I shake my head at her. Nathan gives her a weak smile.

"We should probably have this conversation inside," I say.

Nathan takes a deep breath before nodding, and we open the door and file in.

It looks bad. I mean, I know it technically *is* bad, but it looks even worse than expected. My family has lined up the three men side by side. Big Uncle is still passed out. Second Uncle is awake and struggling against his bonds, and Third Uncle is blinking and looking around all confused, still covered in the remnants of the wedding cake.

"Nathan!" Big Aunt says. "So good you come here!" She is, of course, sipping tea with the other aunts. "Come, you have tea with us. Si Mei, give him tea."

"That's okay, I don't really—"

"One tea coming up," Fourth Aunt cuts in, getting up and pouring him a cup.

Nathan accepts the tea with a stunned expression. He thanks her and takes a sip before putting the cup down. "We need to let these men go."

The room explodes in a rush of arguments.

Big Aunt: "Impossible."

Second Aunt: "We let them go, they kill everyone!"

Ma: "Aduh, how can? They very naughty boys, very bad!"

Fourth Aunt: "You mean after we kill them?"

Second Uncle: "Mmmf mm mfmmf!"

I can't take this anymore. "Shut up!" I shout. "SHUT UP."

Miraculously, they all stop and look at me. Now what? "We need to—well, we do need to figure out what to do with them," I say finally.

"Isn't it obvious?" Fourth Aunt says. "We hold them hostage until their psycho mafia family promises not to kill us."

"Oh, so easy, ya?" Ma snorts. "You think so easy? We just

tell them, 'Eh, you promise don't kill us, ya?' and they will say, 'Okay, we promise.' Then we let these men go, and then the mafia will say, 'Oh ho ho, good, you let them go, now we kill you!'"

Everyone starts speaking and arguing again until I clap and say, "One at a time!"

Second Aunt raises her hand and waves it at me. "Me, I have idea!" she says. I nod at her. "Okay, easy, we kill one of them to send message: you dare come after us, we kill you all," she says, nodding and smiling eagerly.

We all stare at her, the woman who thinks Tai Chi is the solution to all of life's problems and couldn't even bear the thought of touching Ah Guan's body a year ago. "Um," I say finally. "We'll, uh, we'll take that idea into account. Anyone have any other suggestions?"

"Maybe we kill him more slower? You know, send very clear message, very clear," Second Aunt says.

"So not just death, but horrific death," Nathan mutters. He glances over at me, wide-eyed, and I wonder if he's thinking of running off into the dark of night and never coming back. Can't blame him.

"Stop that," Big Aunt snaps to Second Aunt. "Why everything must be kill-here-kill-there with you? So unlucky."

"Yeah, Big Aunt's right, it's very unlucky," I quickly say. I frown at Big Aunt, noticing that she's taken the time to put her fascinator, dragon and all, back on her head. Of course my family would prioritize making sure their outfits are complete even though the wedding festivities are over. But whatever, her dragon, her choice.

"Yes, you murder someone, you will bring bad luck to family," Ma says, because of course.

"Not true," Second Aunt says. "We kill Ah Guan, it actually

bring good luck to us. You see, business go so well, Meddy finally get married. Maybe if we kill one of them now, Meddy get pregnant, give you grandbaby."

Ma's face brightens. "Oooh, grandbaby! Yes, good point. Okay, done, we kill him."

"NOT good point!" What is wrong with my family? "This is not how any of this stuff works."

Ma and Second Aunt glare at me.

"Meddy, I tell you, I not getting any younger," Ma says sadly. "I might die before I see my grandbaby."

"I can't believe you're using this as an opportunity to guilt-trip me into conceiving," I moan. "Look, I'm going to pretend that you didn't just say any of that stuff and go back to the original question, which is: what do we do with them? And for the record, no, we are *not* killing them or cutting them up into little pieces or skinning them or anything like that."

"Aduh, Meddy, choy, touch wood, who say anything like skinning them?" Second Aunt says, flapping her hand at me and looking horrified. "Aduh, that one very cruel, you know."

"So that's where you draw the line? Chopping them up, A-okay. But skinning is going a step too far?"

Ma and Second Aunt nod.

"Good to know. Anyway, any other ideas that don't involve hurting anyone?"

"How about we just go to the police and tell them everything?" Nathan says. Then he sees all of our faces and he quickly says, "Okay, bad suggestion, never mind."

"I think maybe we tie up Nathan also. He talking about going to police," Second Aunt mutters.

"Enak aja!" Ma snaps. "No one tie up my son-in-law, okay?"

Nathan, looking terrified, says, "Um. Thanks, Ma?"

"Just don't say anything stupid like 'going to the cops' again," Fourth Aunt says.

"Right." Nathan nods quickly. "I mean, it's just that since these guys are mafia, we could just tell the cops that they were endangering everyone and . . ."

"But then they'd tell the cops about our involvement in Ah Guan's death," I say.

Nathan's mouth presses into a thin line. "Yeah," he says quietly. "But I think maybe that's the price we have to pay. I have contacts at the DA's office, they'll help us—"

"Eh, ngga ya!" Ma cries. "No, no, no. Later go on our record, who want to hire criminal for wedding?"

"And your hotel, nobody will want to stay there, lho," Big Aunt says.

Nathan sighs and they plunge into yet another heated discussion, going in an endless nightmarish circle about what to do.

I am tired. The last twenty-four hours have been a whirlwind of intense emotions, and I don't know what to do. Thing is, there isn't anything good we *can* do. Every option comes with its own punishment. And the act of coming clean to Nathan, though it feels good and right, has been utterly exhausting. I feel as though everything inside me has been carved out, leaving me an empty husk.

Slowly, my muscles turn to water and I droop onto a nearby chair. Nobody else notices; they're too busy arguing, which is just fine. I rest my cheek on my hands and survey the scene absentmindedly. It's as though I've walked out of my body and am watching things unfold from a distance, like a ghost. There's Big Aunt, crossing her arms and shaking her head imperiously. There's Second Aunt, arguing about the merits of chopping people up into little cubes while Nathan gapes at her in shock.

Ma is flitting back and forth between appeasing her older sisters and her son-in-law, and Fourth Aunt is studying her nails and sipping tea. This is my family. It's a funny thing, family.

Speaking of family, those three men we've got tied up are family too. My gaze flicks toward them. It's weird how alike they look. How much like my aunts they behave. Big Uncle is now awake too, blinking slowly. Second Uncle looks terrified, which—you know—I can hardly blame the guy. Third Uncle is grimacing as if he's got the world's biggest headache, which he probably does. Three mafia men, all of them somehow captured and tied up by my crazy family. We're not even mafia, and somehow we've managed to overpower these actual professional killers and tie them up with zip ties, and—

Wait a second. Zip ties. I frown and sit up, looking closely at the three men. Big Uncle and Second Uncle are both tied up with Fourth Aunt's black zip ties, but Third Uncle . . .

I jump up, hurry over, and fling the blanket off him. And gasp.

"Oh, shit!"

30

"Apa?" Ma says. "Kenapa, Meddy?"

"What is it?" Nathan says, rushing over. "Did he hurt you? Are you okay?"

"Yes, I'm okay, just shut up a second." I pause. "Sorry. Love you."

"It's okay."

"Okay, um," I take a deep breath and turn to face my family. "So, who tied up Third Uncle?"

Fingers shoot out and I get a tangle of finger-pointing. Big Aunt, Second Aunt, Ma, and Fourth Aunt are all pointing at each other and glaring.

"Okay . . . clearly this isn't going to work," I mutter. "Who noticed him first?"

"Aduh, by the time I see him, your Fourth Aunt already tie him up!" Ma says.

"I never touched the guy. It was probably you in your weird

drunk state," Fourth Aunt snorts. "Who can't handle a single glass of champagne, seriously?"

I close my eyes and take a deep breath. But hey, at least it seems like the effects of the drugs and alcohol have worn off. They're acting more or less normal. Well, normal for them, anyway.

"Ngga, not Natasya, I think Natasya too drunk to power over man," Big Aunt says.

"Yes, Natasya not big enough to do it," Second Aunt says, side-eyeing Big Aunt so hard I half-wonder if her eyes are going to roll all the way around. "But ada orang, who is." She side-eyes Big Aunt even harder. "You know, orang yang all day carry big, heavy cake, probably can carry big, heavy man, no problem."

Big Aunt's gaze snaps toward her, and it's a testament to Second Aunt's courage, or maybe her lack of survival instincts, that she doesn't flinch. I mean, I'm not even the subject of the Big Aunt glare and I flinch. Big Aunt narrows her eyes and the temperature in the room drops a couple of degrees. "What you saying? You saying I do?"

We all shrink away as Big Aunt takes a step toward Second Aunt. In that moment, Big Aunt is so terrifying that I can totally picture her overpowering anybody. I can easily imagine her advancing on Third Uncle like Annie Wilkes in *Misery*, except worse because not even Annie Wilkes has the wrath of a slighted Chinese-Indonesian auntie.

I need to cut this exchange short now. "Zip ties!"

Big Aunt frowns at me. "Apa?"

"Zip ties."

She looks at me blankly.

"Cable ties," Fourth Aunt says. The other aunties look at her blankly. She says it again but pronounces it "kah-bell-tiss."

"Oh, cable ties, yes, kenapa?" Second Aunt says.

"You packed cable ties, didn't you, Fourth Aunt? Black ones. We used them to tie up Big Uncle and Second Uncle." I gesture to the two men, whose wrists and ankles are indeed tied up with black cable ties.

"Right . . ." Fourth Aunt says.

"So who brought white cable ties?" I say.

"Huh?"

They all look confused.

"Look at Third Uncle's wrists."

As one, we turn to look at Third Uncle, and sure enough, the cable tie around his wrists is white, not black. "Apa arti-nya?" Ma says.

"It means . . ." It's impossible to sort through the thoughts chasing one another like weasels in my head. But a thought bubbles up, rising through the murk ever so slowly. "Um, hang on."

As Nathan and my family watch, I pick up my phone and make a call.

The call is picked up and a polite voice says, "You've reached the Randolph Hotel, Oxford. This is Daniel speaking. How may I assist you today?"

"Hi, Dan, it's Meddy. The bride from earlier today, re-member?"

"Miss Meddelin, always a pleasure," he says in the tone of voice that clearly states that it is anything but. "What can I do for you?"

"I think my friend's upstairs in my room, or maybe my mother's room. Could you check both rooms, just to make sure? And pass her a message for me?"

"Certainly. What is the message?"

"Tell her that what she's looking for is at the Christ Church room. And that I know everything."

It's as cryptic and weird as messages get, but Dan, first-rate receptionist that he is, doesn't even skip a beat. "Perfect. I shall relay the message to your friend right away."

I hang up and turn to find everyone gaping at me.

"Care to explain what just happened?" Nathan says.

"You may as well sit down. I think we have about ten minutes before Staphanie and Ama get here."

The room explodes in a chorus of "WHAT?"

With a sigh, I gesture at them to take a seat, and then I compose myself and tell them my ridiculously far-fetched theory, hoping against everything that I've got it right.

Even though we're expecting it, we all jump when there's a knock at the door. Well, more like a pounding.

"Open the fuck up!" Staphanie shouts from the other side.

Right. I take a deep breath and look at my family. They all nod. When I open the door, Staphanie barges past me. Or tries to, anyway. My humongous dress gets in the way and she ends up squeezing past me.

"Eh! Hati-hati!" Ma cries.

I want to laugh. Why's she telling Staphanie to be careful, as though it weren't painfully obvious that Staphanie meant to shove me out of the way?

Ama comes in behind Staphanie, not sparing me a glance. I close the door and remind myself to inhale again. They're not looking at me. They're distracted by the sight of Big Uncle, Second Uncle, and Third Uncle, all tied up in their various chairs.

"Big Uncle, Second Uncle!" Staphanie rushes over to them and gives Second Uncle a tight hug. "Oh, thank god you're all okay. We thought—" Her voice ends in a small sob and she clears her throat before straightening up. "What's going on? Why are they all here?"

"Jems, Hendry! Aduh, kok bisa begini? You let them go now!" Ama cries.

Staphanie glares at me. "You won't get away with this. We're going to report you to the police for kidnapping."

Somehow, through the sea of terror and panic, I find my voice. I hear myself say, "No, you're not. Because we didn't kidnap Third Uncle. He kidnapped himself."

31

Staphanie's eyes widen and she barks with laughter, but not before I catch it—a split-second glimpse of the truth. My cheeks flush hot. I was right. *I was right*. My crazy theory was right. Third Uncle did plant himself in my room, and Staphanie knew about it.

"He didn't—"

"Yes, he did, he already confirmed it," I say.

Staphanie closes her mouth abruptly and glares at Third Uncle. "You told them? You had one job, Third Uncle. One!"

"He didn't, but you just did. None of us has white cable ties, so the only explanation is that Third Uncle brought them himself. And I've been wondering why Dan kept coming to the room about the noise in the middle of the day, when most hotel guests would be out of the hotel. It's because you were the one calling to complain about noise coming from my mom's room. Because you wanted him to go in and find Third Uncle."

Staphanie grits her teeth.

"Looks like I was right." I shouldn't gloat. It's not nice to gloat. But damn, look at me go, outsmarting Staphanie!

Ma must agree as well, because she claps and says, "Wah, Meddy, very good." She looks around at everyone, smiling and nodding, and says, "Very good, ya? Pinter, ya?"

Big Aunt nods with a small smile. "Yes, pinter sekali."

Again, that little part of me that has the maturity of a five-year-old beams and skips while crowing, *Big Aunt says I'm very clever!* I smash it down and force myself to focus.

"Okay, but what about Big Uncle and Second Uncle?" Staphanie snaps.

Ah. "Yeah . . . those ones we kidnapped," I mumble, deflating a little. "But it doesn't matter, because we'll let all of them go."

Everyone stares at me with wide eyes. "Meddy, I think you say wrong thing, deh," Second Aunt whispers.

"I said what I said. We're going to let all of them go."

The corners of Nathan's mouth curl up ever so slightly, and I take some comfort from that.

"But before we do, I want to know the truth. Why did you make it look like Third Uncle was kidnapped by us?"

"Because—I just—everything was a mess, and we couldn't get a hold of Second Uncle, and then Big Uncle went MIA and, I don't know, we had to come up with a plan at the last possible second to get you in trouble with the authorities, okay?" Staphanie says. "Can we all go now and forget all this ever happened?"

"No!" Several people shout it at the same time, and we all look at one another, taken aback.

"I need to know why you did any of this in the first place," I say. "I know you weren't actually after Lilian. What were you truly after?"

Now all eyes turn to Staphanie. For the first time, I see her falter. She takes a small step back, her gaze flitting nervously from Ama to each of her uncles. "None of your business. Just let them go."

"You tell us now or you all die!" Second Aunt barks.

"Whoa, Second Aunt, I didn't—"

"Yes, if you not tell us, I kill this one," Big Aunt says, striding forward and standing ominously behind Third Uncle. "We mafia, you not messing with us."

Third Uncle whimpers.

Big Aunt raises her arm, looking menacing as hell.

"Stop!" Ama cries. "It's because—because—you kill my only grandson!" she cries, before bursting into tears. Deep, gut-wrenching sobs that shake her entire body, a sorrow so deep my eyes tear up in response.

"What? Where got kill your grandson?" Big Aunt says. She looks at us as if to say, *What the hell is going on?* The other aunties shake their heads and shrug. Big Aunt shuffles forward and pats Ama's shoulder gingerly. "I think you make mistake, deh."

That's when the awful, horrible, earth-shattering realization sinks in. It's so enormously bad it almost brings me to my knees. The dead cousin that Staphanie had mentioned back at LAX. The one she had been close to.

My voice comes out in a hoarse whisper. "It's Ah Guan, isn't it? Your grandson is Ah Guan."

32

"Hanh?" Ma says. "Meddy, you say what?"

Nathan, who's a bit faster on the uptake, looks at Staphanie with a new light of understanding. "He was your cousin?"

Staphanie nods, her face a warring combination of resentment and exhaustion.

"Eh? Who is your cousin?" Ma says.

"Tch, how slow can you be?" Fourth Aunt snaps. "It's Ah Guan, innit?"

"I think you can drop the British accent now," I plead. Though why the hell I care about the British accents now, I can't say.

"Ah Guan your grandson?!" Second Aunt says. "Waduh. This too much." She plunges into a Tai Chi position, muttering quietly to herself and shaking her head.

I take a deep breath, but I swear no air comes in. Because, oh god, the family of the man I killed is right in front of me, and

Second Aunt's right. It *is* too much. Ever since the incident, I've largely managed to move on by reminding myself that he was a "bad guy." I'd mused to Ma once about his family, on a horrible occasion when I suddenly wondered if perhaps he might have kids or something, but Ma had just waved me away and said, "No, such bad boy like that, how can have family?" And I'd wanted to believe her so badly I quickly accepted it, no questions asked.

But how wrong we were. Because, well, here they are. His family. And they're so much like ours it's not even funny.

"Ama—" Staphanie says, reaching out to her, but Ama pushes her hand away and continues weeping. "Look what you've done," Staphanie hisses at us. "This is going to kill her. The only thing that's kept her going ever since Ah Guan's death was the thought of taking you down."

My head swims. "Why didn't you just report us to the police? And how did you know we were involved in the first place?" There are so many questions I can barely get them straight in my mind.

"We always knew Ah Guan had loose mafia ties, and when he ended up dead, we went to the island and asked around. We talked to the sheriff, to the staff at the hotel—"

"You talked to my staff?" Nathan asks. "But we have a policy to not discuss the incident with outsiders—"

"I got myself hired as a dishwasher," Staphanie says flatly. "I made friends with the other staff members and gossiped a *lot* during our breaks."

"You were employed at my hotel?" Nathan says, his mouth dropping open. I can't blame him; we're all gaping at Staphanie by then.

"Yes. I thought that was the best way to gain information. And I did. I gathered a lot of intel. Like how there was a group of really suspicious Asian women who were carting around a huge cooler the day that Ah Guan was found dead."

I swear my entire face is on fire. Even Big Aunt is wringing her hands guiltily.

"Did they mention how hot one of the suspicious Asian women was?" Fourth Aunt says.

"No."

Ma snorts. Fourth Aunt purses her lips, shrugs, and continues studying her nails.

"And a couple of them told me how there was a theft that same day. The tea ceremony gifts had been stolen. The moment I found out about that, I knew Ah Guan had something to do with it."

"Ah Guan was good boy; he never have something to do with that!" Ama snaps.

Staphanie sighs. "Ama, I think we both know he probably had something to do with it, and that was why he was killed." She turns to look me straight in the eye. "Because he stole from the mafia."

Time stops. Planets stop revolving, just for a second.

There's a bark of laughter from Fourth Aunt, and Ma goes, "Eh? Apa?" Even Second Aunt pauses in the middle of her Tai Chi stance.

"Ah Guan has always had a—a rebellious streak," Staphanie says. "He was always on one get-rich-quick scheme or another. I figured he stole from the mafia and was killed because of it. I mean, even the way you killed him—stuffing him in a cooler, literally fridging him, is—" Her voice wobbles as her eyes fill with tears. "It's classic mafia execution."

It takes a moment to find my voice. "We're not—"

"Yes, classic mafia execution. It's what we'll do to you next, if you don't play by our rules," Fourth Aunt says, running a sharp fingernail across her neck.

"Stop that, Fourth Aunt." I glare at Fourth Aunt until she rolls her eyes and shrugs, then I turn back to Staphanie, trying to sort out my confused thoughts. "Wait, but if you're so sure we had him murdered, why didn't you just report us to the police?"

"We tried!" Staphanie cries, and now the tears finally come, making her blink rapidly. "Of course we tried. We went to the sheriff—um, McConnaughey?"

"Sheriff McConnell," I mutter, thinking of the inept man in charge of the whole island.

"Right. We went to him with all of the evidence I'd managed to gather, and he laughed us out of the office. He told me I had to stop digging, otherwise he'd make life a living hell for me. He was going to report me for all sorts of made-up shit like, uh, snooping? I don't even know. Basically, he shut us down. He's deep in your pockets, isn't he?" she says bitterly.

I frown at Nathan. I can tell we're both wondering the same thing. Why would Sheriff McConnell be on our side? Then it hits me: he's not. He's on his own side, and he's filed the report that solved the case of Ah Guan's death. If new evidence surfaces that refutes his report, he'll lose his job and cushy pension.

"Um, it's not what you think," I say, or try to say, anyway, because just then, Ama gives a blood-curdling yell and lunges at Big Aunt.

33

"Holy shit!" I don't know what I was expecting. Well, I know at least what I *never* expected, and that is a seventy-something-year-old woman with gray permed hair lunging at another sixty-something-year-old woman with gray permed hair. Another thing I never once expected? For the two of them to actually kick ass.

Ama sinks her claws into Big Aunt's huge hair, and Big Aunt yelps and slaps everywhere like a whirling slapping machine. Staphanie jumps in, shoving Big Aunt back, and Second Aunt cries a war shriek and rushes in as well, followed quickly by Ma and Fourth Aunt.

Nathan, frozen with shock thus far, finally snaps back to his senses. He jumps into the fray and pulls Ama off Big Aunt. But as he holds Ama back, he gets pummeled by the others, who are still flapping at Ama. One manicured hand smacks him in the face. "Ow!" he cries. He stumbles, and Ama breaks free and lunges once more at Big Aunt. The two of them topple to the floor with a loud thump, and suddenly, the room is covered in a cloud of—

"Tea leaves?" I mutter, blinking hard. In my panicked, exhausted, practically delirious state, my first thought is: *Did Big Aunt just metamorphose into a bed of leaves?* Wouldn't have been the craziest thing to have happened today.

"That ain't tea leaves," Fourth Aunt mutters. She turns and glares at Ma.

"Apa? Why you look at me?"

"I'm looking at the resident drug dealer," Fourth Aunt says. "Good grief, Nat, I didn't think you'd bring a whole cargo of weed with you to England."

Ma's eyes widen. "Eh? Apa? I not do that."

Nathan coughs, waving his hand before his face, and crouches down to help Big Aunt up. "Is everyone okay?" Once Big Aunt is on her feet, he reaches down and helps Ama up. She must have been too dazed to swat his hand away, because she accepts his help and soon they're all back on their feet, looking markedly winded.

The Komodo dragon atop Big Aunt's head has snapped clean in two, and I can see now that the inside had been filled with the small, dried leaves. I quickly pick up the piece that has broken off and examine it. "Big Aunt, I think—I think your fascinator was filled with marijuana."

"What?" Big Aunt booms. She slaps at her hair as if there's a bee buzzing in it. The other half of her hat falls off and she kicks it across the room as if it's a cockroach. "Nat!" she yells.

Everyone stares at Ma, who stares back with terrified eyes. "Apa? Why you all look at me?"

"Ma," I say, struggling to keep my voice gentle. "All this time, I've just dismissed your whole TCM thing as, you know,

Chinese medicine, but I think it's time we all have an intervention about your drug problem."

"What drug problem?" Ma cries. "Is not me!"

"Okay, Pablo Escobar," Fourth Aunt snorts.

"Who Pablo Escrow?" Ma snaps. "I tell you, is not me!"

"It's okay, Ma," Nathan says, "there's no shame in it. We'll get you the best care . . ."

As everyone crowds around my poor mother, I bite back the tears. I've failed her. I've been so focused on my own shit that I completely missed the fact that my mom has a drug problem. And it's so bad that she's even willing to put her own sisters at risk by smuggling the drugs in their hats! That's terrible! What happened to putting family first? What happened to the woman who cares so much about saving face that she insisted on having me cut up fruit for my aunts when they came over to help me get rid of Ah Guan's body? This is so completely unlike Ma.

It's SO unlike her, in fact, that maybe it wasn't her—

No. I refuse to hope. I can't afford to be disappointed again, not today.

And yet. I look around me at the huge fuss going on and the shambles the bedroom is in. I reach out and tap Second Aunt on the shoulder. She turns around, and I ask, softly, "Second Aunt, can I see your Komodo dragon, please?"

Her eyes widen. "You think she hide inside mine also?"

I shrug. "Do you mind?" She lowers her head so I can get at it, and I see a mess of hair clips and pins securing the Komodo dragon in place so tightly that it'll probably take me half an hour to get it off her head. I recall, then, how Second Uncle had asked to see the fascinators months before the wedding, and his insistence early this morning on making sure the hats stay secure on their heads. I hadn't spared it a second thought then, since I'd been distracted by other things, but now, his attention to detail seems suspicious as hell.

"It's not Ma," I gasp. "It was her." I point straight at Staphanie, who glares back wordlessly. "Or them. I don't know, it's part of their whole scheme. You guys planted the weed in the fascinators. Before we left, you kept checking to make sure they'd brought the hats. It was part of your revenge process, wasn't it? Along with making it look like we kidnapped Third Uncle."

Staphanie looks like she's about to fight, but Ama says one simple word: "Yes." And it's enough to slice through all of the noise in the room.

Silence.

"It was the only thing I could think of," Staphanie adds quietly. "I mean, I wanted to plant cocaine, but I don't know where to get coke. So I thought maybe weed would be bad enough."

"What kind of lame-ass mafioso can't get their hands on coke?" Fourth Aunt mutters.

"Hang on, so that was your whole plan for revenge?" I say. "To smuggle weed in Big Aunt's hat?"

"Kind of a pathetic plan," Fourth Aunt says smugly. God, the woman can be obnoxious. But she's right. As far as revenge goes, it is pretty tame.

Ama glares at her. "Of course not just that! You—" she snaps at Big Uncle, who flinches. "You suppose to die!"

Whoa. We all stare at them in horror. Okay, this is a lot more hard-core than I was expecting.

"Wah, you going to kill own son to frame us?" Second Aunt says, her expression a mixture of horror and awe.

"No," Staphanie groans. "Of course not. Ama watched

Gone Girl and was very inspired by it, and we thought maybe we could do something like that. Big Uncle was supposed to go missing in the middle of your wedding and we were going to pin it on you and get the cops to investigate you and your family. We figured you're such ruthless killers the cops were bound to find something on you."

"Operation Gone Uncle," Fourth Aunt says, and laughs. Nobody else laughs along with her. "Come on, that was a good one."

My head is spinning. "So Big Uncle was going to fake his own death? How does that even work? That's such a long-term plan. Was he ever going to come back to life?"

"He suppose to hide with our family here," Ama grumbles.

"You have family here?" Big Aunt says.

"Of course. My sister husband nephew cousin punya cousin," Ama says.

Big Aunt nods. "Ah, close family."

"So he was supposed to hide with your relatives and then what? Just live out the rest of his life here?" I say, aghast.

Staphanie frowns at me. "Of course not. We were going to make it look like he was kidnapped by you and your family and then afterward, when you're all in prison, he was going to be 'found' all tied up in an abandoned house or something. That was why we decided to do it during your wedding. Well, that, and also when we found out you were getting married, we sort of—uh—booked the wedding before having a plan. We knew we'd be able to come up with something if we were able to control the day. Anyway, Big Uncle was going to pick a fight with one of you during cocktail hour and we were going to steal into your hotel room and make it look like there had been a struggle before Big Uncle disappeared."

"Jesus," Nathan says.

"But then Second Uncle went missing—"

"You suppose to find him!" Ama barks at Big Uncle, who flinches. "Such small thing also you cannot do."

Big Uncle moans into his gag and looks so contrite that, despite myself, I feel bad for the guy.

"It's not his fault we kicked his ass," Fourth Aunt says.

Staphanie takes a deep breath. "Anyway, Second Uncle and Big Uncle went missing, and then the fascinator went missing too . . . I don't know. We panicked. So at the last minute we got Third Uncle to pretend that he was kidnapped by you so we'd get your rooms searched. We didn't think—"

"No offense, but your plan has some pretty glaring holes," Fourth Aunt says.

"I know, okay?" Staphanie snaps. "It wasn't easy to come up with a plan to take you people down, and this was the best we could come up with. We were hurting and desperate and we just wanted to—I don't know—make you all pay for what you did to Ah Guan."

"I can't believe you went to all that length to frame us." Honestly, I don't know if I'm amazed or horrified.

"Ah Guan my only grandson," Ama says suddenly, starting to cry again. Despite everything that's happened, it's torture seeing this powerful, haughty old woman being reduced to nothing but sorrow. "We do anything for him."

At this, all of the fight leaks out of me. I can sense the same happening to Ma and the aunties. Because of course they would do anything for him, exactly the same way that Ma and my aunts would do—and have done—for me. No crime is too big to commit if it means saving us. Any plan, even a terrible, flimsy one, is enough for them to act upon.

"You all kill him, why? Just because he steal some jewelry from you? Jewelry worth kill him for?"

"That wasn't why," I whisper.

"He such a good boy—"

"That wasn't why!" This time, my voice comes out so loud it booms like thunder. I force myself to keep going, even though it means I'll be shattering the broken remains of Ama's heart. "Ah Guan died because he was trying to assault me. He was driving and didn't stop when I asked him to, then he took me to an abandoned area, and—god, I was so scared. I Tased him and we crashed and—" My voice cracks then. Nathan's arm tightens reassuringly around my shoulders.

"You Tased him?" Staphanie says. Realization dawns on her face. "When we were at the airport, you said your Taser had once saved your life. Were you referring to him?" I nod, and she looks up at the ceiling, blinking back tears. "He was going to—um, he was gonna—"

"Yeah," I say softly. "I told him to stop, but he wouldn't."

"Fuck," Staph mutters under her breath. She turns away so I can't see her face, but she's shaking her head.

"No, all this is lie," Ama snaps. "My Ah Guan is good boy, he is best boy. He will never do something like that!"

"No, Ama," Staphanie says. "No. I'm sorry, but he would. Ah Guan was a sweetheart toward you, but he wasn't a 'good boy.' I'm sorry, Ama."

"No! What you know?" Ama cries. "You not know anything! Ah Guan always such good boy, always bringing me my favorite food, every Monday he grocery shopping for me from Ranch 99 market, always buy me good sausage and—"

"Bok choy, char siu bao, kangkung, soya milk," Staphanie lists out.

Ama's mouth stops moving, then closes as Staphanie continues rattling off a long list of grocery items.

"—Fuji apples," Staphanie finishes. "Right?"

Ama just stares at her without answering.

"I know, Ama," Staphanie says gently. "Because it was never Ah Guan doing it. It was me. It was always me. Ah Guan loved you in his own way, but he wasn't reliable or caring or any of the things that you thought made him a 'good boy.'" She looks over at me and gestures at her uncles. "Can I?"

I nod, and she goes over and pulls out the sock from Second Uncle's mouth. "Tell her, Second Uncle."

Second Uncle licks his lips and says in a hoarse voice, "Staph is right. Sorry, Ma. Ah Guan not good boy. We always cover up this and that mess for him."

"Is our fault," Big Uncle says as soon as Staph pulls out the sock gagging him. "Is just, we know he your favorite, so we want make you happy, not see how he is such bad kid."

"We enabled him," Third Uncle says.

"Yeah, you did, you dirty enablers," Fourth Aunt mutters. Ma shushes her.

"But Ah Guan, he always looking after me," Ama says in a small voice. "He buy me phone—"

"That was me," Third Uncle says. "We told you it was from Ah Guan to make you learn how to use it."

"Ah Guan was very good at appearing good," Staphanie says gently. "And yeah, we enabled him."

"We not think he so bad as to attack woman," Big Uncle rumbles. His gaze flicks toward me and then goes back to the floor.

"I'm sorry, Meddy," Staph says, taking a deep breath. "We didn't think—"

"It's okay. How could you have known?" I say.

We all look at Ama, who seems to have shrunk to half her size in the last few minutes. Staphanie goes to her and puts her arm around her shoulders. "Ama—"

Ama's voice comes out in a broken whisper. "Is my fault."

"No, Ama—"

"Because his parents no more, so I raise him, I spoil him, is why he become like that," Ama says.

"Yes, a bit your fault," Big Aunt says.

I grimace, trying to signal to Big Aunt to stay out of this.

"But mostly his own fault," Big Aunt continues. "Maybe yes, you spoil him, but he also need to have, you know, sadar diri."

Self-awareness.

The two women stare at each other for a tense second before Ama nods, and something in the atmosphere lifts. It's like coming up for air after being underwater.

"Can we untie my uncles now?" Staph says.

"Oh, yeah, of course," I say. "Wait, I mean, assuming we're all okay here and you guys aren't trying to frame us as drug-dealers-slash-kidnappers?"

Staph sighs and shakes her head. "We're done."

"Wait, we cannot trust them!" Ma says. "They mafia!"

Staph frowns at her. "Wow, you really bought into that, huh?"

"What?" We all stop and stare. I feel like we've been doing that a lot the past hour or so. "You're *not* mafia?"

Staph grunts and looks over at her family. "See? I told you guys she believed me." She rolls her eyes. "I only told you that to scare you into not calling off the wedding. I panicked when you overheard my phone call. I had to stop you from calling everything off somehow."

"WHAT?" I didn't think I had any breath left inside me after all the surprise reveals, but now I feel winded again. I'd spent so long thinking of Staph as a friend, and then suddenly I had to think of her as a mafia gangster and somehow I'd managed to buy into that so completely that readjusting to seeing her as a normal person once more is . . . really freaking weird. My mind grapples with it, stumbling over every memory of today.

When Second Uncle had arrived to do our hair and makeup and we'd been so scared of having him touch our hair because "MAFIA!" And then we'd gone ahead and kidnapped him because, of course, what else do you do with the mafia? And then—god—going through his phone to find the target they wanted to assassinate—

"The assassination?" I whisper.

Staph shrugs. "I told you, I had to think of something on the spot. That was the best I could come up with. I know it's a bit far-fetched . . ."

Now that I'm seeing the truth for what it is, I'm like, *Yes, of course it's far-fetched!* Why would the mafia try to take out a target at a wedding? It makes zero sense! There are so many witnesses, so many ways that it could go wrong. The very thought is laughable.

And the rest of my brain agrees because, suddenly, a laugh bubbles out of me. Everyone looks at me as if I've finally cracked, and I can't stop laughing. I bend over with the force of it, clutching at my stomach.

"Are you okay?" Nathan says, and I try to tell him yes, but I'm laughing too hard to say anything coherent.

"—we thought—kill Lilian!" I gasp in between laughter.

Big Aunt snorts. "We kidnap Big Uncle and Second Uncle because we think they so dangerous!"

"And we spike champagne with Mary-Joanna," Second Aunt joins in.

"And then we end up drug ourselves!" Ma cries.

"At least it felt good," Fourth Aunt says. They all look at her and then, as one, they all lose it, doubling over with laughter.

I join them, putting my arm around Ma's shaking shoulders and the other around Fourth Aunt and laughing until we're all half-crying. I pull Nathan into the hug and he laughs and joins us, wrapping his arms around us all. Everyone else looks confused, but I don't even care anymore. In this moment, I've found sharp-edged clarity that has cut away all of the strings of reservations, and it is this: I am exactly like my family.

I suppose a small part of me has always thought I was somehow better—more modern, more educated, more sensible. I'm not as flappy or showy or loud. In many ways, I *am* different. I speak flawless English. I don't stew Chinese herbs into drinks that I force on others. I don't guilt-trip my loved ones into doing things I want. I don't shout unnecessarily. I speak in a normal tone of voice, and I strive to blend in instead of stand out.

But now I realize these are all just surface differences. Deep down in my core, I am precisely the product of my family. When skin and flesh are ripped away, I am an exact replica of them. Case in point: look how easily we all bought into the mafia story. Anyone else, anyone normal, would have poked so many holes into Staphanie's cover that it wouldn't have held up. Nathan would've figured it out, probably. Maybe. I'd have to ask him later. At the very least, he would've probably revealed the truth to me instead of hiding it this whole time and then he would've sacrificed himself and gone to the police. There are so many alternatives to how all of this could've worked out, but every one of my actions has shown me that I am my mother's daughter. Minus the penchant she and her sisters have for playing down the seriousness of murder and chopping up bodies, that is.

And I love it. Some—okay, most—of our choices have been suspect, yet here we are, having worked everything out somehow. We've managed to survive. And that's what my family has always taught me. Over the years, when the men in the family left, one by one, my mother and aunts have shown me what it means to pick up the broken pieces of your life and keep plodding along until everything's okay again. Through everything, I've never once questioned whether or not they'll be here for me. I just assumed they would be. Because of course they will. Even Fourth Aunt, despite her lifelong rivalry with Ma, has always been there when I needed her.

I hug them all tightly and tell them I love and adore them, and from the corner of my eye, I see that Staph and her uncles are holding Ama tight as she gently breaks in their arms, mourning the loss of her grandson once more. I look away to give them some privacy and meet Ma's eye. She nods and gives me a smile, one that goes back in time and shows me her face from thirty years ago.

It looks exactly like mine.

"So," Nathan says, handing me a cold drink.

I take a sip and sigh happily. "This is delicious."

"Elderflower and gin," he says. "And it's not delicious, it's scrumptious."

"My bad. It is very scrumptious."

"No, you don't say 'very scrumptious'; it's just scrumptious."

I laugh and take another sip. "Thank you, I needed a strong drink after today."

"Yeah." He sits down on the bed next to me and undoes his bow tie, which is inexplicably sexy.

"So I owe you an apology," I say.

Nathan cocks his head at me and frowns.

"For not being upfront from the start. The moment Staph told me she was mafia, I should've just come clean."

"Yeah, you should've." He says this simply, without any

malice in his voice. "But it worked out, and I'm glad. Sort of. Well, I'm relieved. Please promise you'll tell me the truth next time something like this happens?"

I have to laugh at that. "Next time someone tells me they're the mafia and they're planning to assassinate someone at our wedding?"

Nathan's face is completely serious as he answers, "Well, not exactly that situation. Look, there will always be shit coming up. And I'm in it as deep as you are. I'm as complicit as you are with the whole Ah Guan incident—"

"That's not true."

He shrugs. "Well, if you go down, I go down with you. We're in it together. Forever, Meddy." He takes my hand. "I'm your husband."

Goose bumps prickle up my arms and warmth expands out from my belly to the tips of my fingers. "Yeah, you are." I can't stop the smile from taking over my face.

"So please tell me the truth next time you get in trouble?" he murmurs.

"I promise. I am so sorry, Nathan."

"Don't be sorry. I know you were trying to protect me. I'm just trying to make you see that I can totally handle all of this criminal activity you and your family are always up to."

"Criminal activity?" I laugh. But then I realize he's right— we're hardly upstanding citizens.

"In it together?" Nathan says.

"Together." I lean over and kiss him. He leans into me, his mouth soft against mine, and I hardly notice when the glass slips out of my hand and falls with a soft thud on the thick carpet.

Epilogue

Nathan's hand is warm and firm around mine as we walk down the stairs. I feel as though I'm living the song "Walking on Sunshine." Every step I take, I'm pretty sure my feet don't touch the ground. There's hardly any weight on me; gravity has stopped working, I'm sure of it.

I'm married. Never mind the fact that our wedding was basically a disaster that everyone will probably use as an example of what not to do. None of it matters. All that matters is that we woke up this morning as a married couple. As we brushed our teeth at the his-and-hers sinks, he called me "Mrs. Nathan Chan" and I called him "Mr. Meddelin Chan" and we grinned foamy grins at each other.

"You ready?" I say to him as we walk into the restaurant.

He nods and stifles a yawn.

"Gotta get some coffee in you," I say.

"Yeah, I didn't get much sleep last night." He squeezes my hand with a smile.

We're still beaming idiotically when his mother spots us and waves with a panicky grin. It's clear why she's so eager to have us there—Ma and the aunts have arrived before us and they're all wearing matching ridiculous outfits with, of course, equally ridiculous hats. These ones have little orangutans on them in various poses, but that's not even the worst of it. No, the worst part is that the orangutans, like my mother and aunts, are all decked out in the iconic Burberry check. I'm talking tan tartan from head to toe, along with Burberry logos everywhere— chest, back, arms, thighs, even shoes.

Normally, the sight of this would have made me cringe and wish for a hole to fall into, but now I merely bite back a smile. Because now I see that they're not trying to embarrass me. This has nothing to do with me. My family has never played by the rules. They don't care how others might perceive them. They're just making the best of their trip to England, embracing everything about the place and having the time of their lives, and how can I not love that?

"Hi, Ma," I say, planting a kiss on her cheek. I greet everyone at the table, pointedly ignoring Annie's panicked staring. What does she expect me to do, anyway, tell my family to leave the table and change?

Ma grins cunningly as Nathan greets her. "Nathan, you good boy," she says, patting his bicep appreciatively. "You two make good grandbabies for me already?"

Annie chokes on her Earl Grey. Chris takes a big swig of his mimosa. Nathan, who's had more practice dealing with my mother, merely laughs and tells her he loves her outfit. I glance over to see if he's being ironic or mean about it, but he's smiling genuinely at her and my aunties, and my heart swells because I know he's come to the same conclusion as I have. He loves the fact that my family charges headlong into things, and we love how fiercely they embrace everything.

We settle into our seats, but before we're able to take a sip of our coffee, Ma nudges me. I look up to see Staph walking toward us. My chest tightens.

"Hey, everyone," she says, smiling hesitantly.

For Annie and Chris's sakes, we all return the greeting.

"Just wanted to say bye. We're headed to Heathrow," Staph says.

"Well, thank you for all the hard work," Annie says. She looks around the table, probably puzzled at why none of us is more forthcoming with the praise. "It's been wonderful having you and your family at the wedding. Isn't that right?"

"Mm-hmm," Fourth Aunt says, studying her nails and pursing her lips.

A painfully awkward silence follows.

"Anyway. See you guys," Staph says, and walks off.

The weird sensation in my chest builds until I can't stand it anymore and run after her.

"Staph, wait up." I catch up with her at the door. "I do have one last question."

Staph looks at me expectantly.

"For fake wedding vendors, you guys actually managed to pull off a pretty amazing wedding. I mean, aside from all the kidnapping and stuff . . ."

"Oh, yeah," Staph says with a wry smile. "We did as much research as we could before meeting up with you, but Second Uncle really got into the whole hair and makeup thing because of Second Aunt. Big Uncle didn't really give a crap about flowers, so we ordered them from a local wedding vendor. And Ama is just a natural at ordering people around. I think she's missed her calling as a wedding organizer. I don't know how well Third Uncle would've pulled off being an MC; he's actually a dentist."

I gape at her. "A dentist?"

"Yep, has a practice in Arcadia."

"Wow, okay."

"So what did you want to ask me?"

I hesitate, then plunge ahead. "Well, it would've been so easy to let the entire day be a disaster from start to finish. I mean, yes, you did ruin all our photos, not that I'm bitter or anything—"

"I'm sorry about that," she says with a grimace.

"—but everything else was gorgeous. The decorations, the food, the cake, the music. Why didn't you tank the entire wedding?"

"Oh, that. You know Ama, she's got too much pride to do something badly."

I stare at her. "Seriously?"

"Well, partly that, but also partly because we wanted to make sure that the event was believable and natural for the guests. We didn't want anyone getting suspicious about us."

"I see." I guess that makes sense. And in a strange way, I can totally see Big Aunt taking pride in pulling off a fake wedding, even if it is a fake wedding where she's plotting to take down the bride and groom.

"Anyway . . ."

"Yeah." We look at each other for one beat. "Um. I just wanted to say—" What do I want to say? There are simultaneously too many things and not enough things I want to say. "I—um. I'm sorry." And I am, for so much of it.

Staph's eyes are bright with tears, and I realize mine are as well. Over the past few months, she's become more than just my wedding vendor. She's become my friend. A confidante and a source of emotional support. Someone who totally gets where

I'm coming from, because her family is exactly like mine. And now I realize that even though we've resolved the insane secret conflict between us, we'll never go back to that again. Our friendship is well and truly dead, and I would be lying if I said I wasn't a bit broken because of it.

"I know," she says. She holds out her hand. "Truce?"

"Truce." We shake hands.

"If you happen to know anyone who needs a wedding photographer . . ." she says.

My smile disappears.

"Too soon to joke about it?"

"Way too soon." Nevertheless, something close to a smile passes between us, and when she leaves, she takes a piece of my heart with her. Just a small piece, though.

When I get back to the table, Big Aunt is grilling Nathan about what he thinks of their outfits.

"You really like or not?" she says, her mouth half full of bacon. What is it with Chinese-Indos and our inability to refrain from talking while we chew our food?

"Yeah, it's very . . . authentic."

Big Aunt nods primly at Second Aunt, who bends over and picks up a package from under her chair. She stands and presents it to Nathan as solemnly as the queen bestowing a Fabergé egg on one of her subjects. "Present for honeymoon."

"You didn't have to," Nathan says.

Big Aunt waves him off. "You say no tea ceremony, so we not get to give you red packet. Ya sudah, we do like white people, give you present, not money, okay?"

"Here one for you also," Ma says, giving me an identical package. "You open."

"Now?" I say. Foolish. Of course now. With some trepidation, I take off the wrapper carefully. Nathan just rips his apart.

I didn't think our eyes could go any wider, but when we finally open our boxes, they turn into perfect circles.

Because inside is—

"Wow," Nathan says, holding up a traditional Indonesian-style shirt. But instead of the typical batik cloth, it's been made out of Burberry check print. Or rather, the front sports the trademark Burberry tan check, while the back is made of an elaborate batik cloth. I swear it practically blinds me. I hold mine up. "This is very . . . interesting," he ventures in a tone of mild horror.

"Wow, a Burberry qipao," I add, holding mine a safe distance away from me and reminding myself to keep the grin on my face.

"They look—uh, they look very, uh . . ." Nathan says, "traditional?"

"Yes, exactly!" Big Aunt says happily. "You see, is symbolize marriage between English and Chinese-Indonesian."

Annie and Chris, along with the rest of the restaurant, are openly gaping at the awful creations.

"This must've cost you so much money," Nathan says.

"Aduh, Meddy, you forget something inside box!" Ma cries.

"I did?" I pick up the box and, sure enough, there's something else inside. I pull it out and immediately all of the tension leaves my body. Next to me, I sense Nathan relaxing too. There's no question that we'll not only keep the hideous outfits, but also wear them and have a ton of photos taken in them.

Because in my hands is a tiny, identical tunic. One that would fit a baby.

"Oh, Ma," I whisper, and give Ma a tight hug. "You nutty, lovable woman," I mutter into her hair.

"Thank you," Nathan says, giving my mother and aunts a hug. "We love the gifts. But *please* don't get us anything else."

"Hang on, you said these are gifts for our honeymoon?" I say.

My mother and aunts exchange sly glances with each other.

"I don't . . . understand. Nathan and I are going to Europe for our honeymoon next month, remember?" A sense of trepidation is rising inside me.

"Oh yes, of course, and then . . ." Ma says, reaching inside her bag and whipping out a piece of paper. "Then you coming to Jakarta! Just in time for Chinese New Year!"

"Yes, and all your cousins will be there!" Second Aunt says. "We tell them they were such awful boys to miss your wedding, they better come to Jakarta for Chinese New Year, or else." She narrows her eyes menacingly, and I cringe inwardly at the trouble I've landed my poor cousins in. I'd thought that giving them a pass on this wedding was a favor, but it looks like it ended up being a double-edged sword.

"Look, we got tickets for you two already!"

Our mouths fall open and I blink at the itinerary in Ma's outstretched hand. It says:

First passenger: Meddelin Chan
Second passenger: Nathan Chan
Route: LAX (Los Angeles) outbound to CGK (Jakarta)

"Ahem," Big Aunt says, not bothering to conceal it as a cough. "You got notice that it is business class ticket or not?"

It is indeed a business class ticket. I shake my head slowly, not knowing what to say.

"This is amazing!" Nathan cries, his grin eating up half his face.

"It is?" I say.

"Not the word I'd go for," Annie mutters.

"I've always wanted to see the place your family came from," Nathan says. "Of course it is. What better time to go than for our honeymoon? I could figure out a way to work remotely while we travel. We could go to Bali, and maybe the Komodo Islands, and maybe the Thousand Islands—I can't wait. Oh my god, this is the best gift. Thank you so much."

He goes around the table, hugging Ma and each of my aunts again. As I stand there, taking in the scene, it hits me that my husband (husband!) is so delighted at being able to see my ancestral roots that it's weird that we never brought up the possibility of visiting Indonesia. I guess part of me has always wanted to but assumed that nobody would ever want to go to that part of the world, because why would they? Most Californians don't even know where Indonesia is. They think it's part of Vietnam or Cambodia or something, not that they'd ever be able to find either of those countries on a map. It's taken Ma and the aunts to make this happen. It's as if they've taken a peep into the deepest recesses of my heart and figured out what I want before I even realize it myself. Story of my life.

I smile at my family. "Indonesia it is."

Ma squeals with joy. "Aduh, Mama so happy. Everyone will also so happy, we have Chinese New Year celebration, you will meet everyone. Maybe have second wedding celebrate there, so everyone can come?"

"Er—" I say.

She waves me off. "Okay, we discuss later. Indonesia! You will love."

Nathan grins down at me. "I can't wait." Then he bends down to kiss me, and everything melts away and I know that whatever the future holds in store for me, I'll be fine because I'll have my crazy family and this perfect boy by my side.

ACKNOWLEDGMENTS

As with *Dial A for Aunties*, I have so many people to thank, people without whom this book wouldn't exist. I wrote *Four Aunties and a Wedding* as soon as *Dial A for Aunties* sold to my dream publisher. I knew they wanted a sequel, and I wanted to write the story down while *Dial A for Aunties* was still fresh in my mind. What I didn't foresee was how tough sequels are to write. I'm so grateful to my magical agent, Katelyn Detweiler, for being so supportive while I whined to her nonstop about how awful the process was. Whenever I think of Katelyn, I see her with a rainbow around her head, plus sparkles and glitter and everything that's good in the world.

I described Cindy Hwang as my dream editor before, and I stand by that description. She is truly a dream come true. Her feedback has not only sharpened both Aunties books, but also ensured that I approach the cultural aspect with as much respect as possible. Cindy understood everything I was trying to do with both books, and working with her has been so effortless and joyful.

Berkley has some of the most brilliant people in the industry, and I have been so fortunate to be able to work with them. Erin Galloway, Dache Rogers, and Danielle Keir have managed some truly astonishing publicity. Jin Yu and the marketing team are always coming up with the catchiest content! And Angela Kim has worked so hard on coordinating everything.

Thank you also to the rest of the Jill Grinberg Literary Management team—Sophia Seidner, Denise Page, and Sam Farkas, for handling everything mind-boggling on my behalf. And there have been so many mind-boggling things, I would be truly lost without you.

As always, my writing friends are my lifeline, my chosen family. My menagerie-fam: Toria Hegedus, who is always gentle and loving and wonderful; SL Huang, who is brilliant and kind; Elaine Aliment, who is the wisest leader; Tilly Latimer, who is raising the future president of the entire world; Lani Frank, who is the fastest, most attentive reader; Rob Livermore, who never fails to make us all laugh; Mel Melcer, who remains an inspiration; and Emma Maree, who is the sweetest soul.

A big thank-you to Laurie Elizabeth Flynn, who I'm convinced is the next Gillian Flynn and keeps me sane by listening to me moan and whine about everything every single day. My Untitled Authors' group: Nicole Lesperance, who writes the most gorgeous stories; Margot Harrison, who writes the creepiest, most harrowing stories; Marley Teeter, who is about to blow us all away with her story; and Grace Shim, whose YA is going to be a highlight in 2022. Thank you also to Kate Dylan, who manages to give insightful feedback despite describing herself as three raccoons in a trench coat pretending to be an author.

My husband, Mike, has put up with a lot over the years, but

he's especially put up with an incredible amount of heightened emotions (Excitement! Anxiety! Joy! Stress!) last year, during the roller coaster of *Dial A for Aunties* publication. Through it all, he has remained patient and unwavering and so massively supportive. I'm not sure how he did it, but I am grateful for it.

To my Mama and Papa, who have also been so supportive in every way possible. My mom rounded up her friends for a photo shoot for *Dial A for Aunties*'s release and has started planning a photo shoot for *Four Aunties and a Wedding*'s release. We shall see if I am able to scrounge up a wedding dress for the shoot, but if it doesn't happen, know that it wasn't for lack of trying on my mom's part! To the rest of my family, the Sutantos and the Wijayas, for reading my books and giving me so much love and encouragement. Thank you so much for always being there for me.

Last but not least, thank you to my readers. So many of you read *Dial A for Aunties* and reached out to tell me how much you loved it. How it reminded you of your own aunties, regardless of cultural background. I have read and loved every single note I received, and I will cherish them forever.